Copyright © 2024

All rights reserved

The characters and events portrayed in this book are
fictitious. Any similarity to real persons, living or dead, is
coincidental and not intended by the author.

No part of this book may be reproduced, or stored in a
retrieval system, or transmitted in any form or by any
means, electronic, mechanical, photocopying, recording,
or otherwise, without express written permission of the
publisher.

ISBN-13: 9798320041865
ISBN-10: 1477123456

Cover design by: Art Painter
Library of Congress Control Number: 2018675309
Printed in the United States of America

To my daughter Laura, my son Mike and all those delicious grandchildren you've given me.

The Exquisiteness of Death

Introduction

My name is Emily England. I was born in 1999 in Leigh, Lancashire, England. I'm still alive and well. My name before this was Dorothy Hatt. Dorothy was also born in Leigh, in 1929. She died when she was 59 years old, eleven years before my birth.

I know that I have lived many lives before Dorothy's, (and I know that I'll have the option to live many more), but I haven't any real recollections about any of them other than hers. Just wispy snippets, silky threads, almost like the edge of a lovely dream that you try to snatch and hang on to as you wake but can't.

When I was a little kid, I remembered lots of them and in great detail, but their memories started to fade when I'd be around six or seven. I don't claim to be psychic, I'm not a medium or a fortune teller. In fact, I have no supernatural gifts at all. I'm not even intuitive.

Whilst I was being Dorothy, I'd thought that I was only ever Dorothy, that I was born once and would live and die once. Dust to dust and all that. Sounds absolutely crazy doesn't it my story?

We all know that the world is full of people with

weird claims. Strange characters on television with their deadpan faces telling us that they've been abducted and are frequented by aliens. Then there are the folk who say they're psychic or can bring messages back from the dead for a piece of your silver. I know. And now I'm one of them.

From being a tiny girl, I have despaired about actually having to write all of this down though I have always known that it was what I had to do. Honestly, it's caused me to have so very many sleepless, restless and anxiety ridden nights. I've literally been putting it off for years and years.

It was never because of the ridicule and disbelief you understand? Nah, I don't care about that, no one has to read it, or believe it for that matter.

It's just that the vocabulary required to give you a real description, a true picture, a real sense of what I know, doesn't exist. The words don't exist in any language. The sensations don't have a description. I'm neither clever nor articulate enough to be able to narrate the story in its rich depth and with the intricacies of detail that it so deserves. But I feel the truth so very deep inside of me and it's absolutely bursting to get on the outside of me and onto paper.

But I'm just Emily England, a Lancashire lass, educated at the local comprehensive, who barely managed to scrape a reasonable grade for my English GCSE, trying to give you the heads up about what will happen when you die. Even attempting to explain the glorious, heavenly colours, will be like describing the spectrums of red on a dewy, softly blooming rose to a blind man, describing the harmonious celestial sounds and how each note has its own personality, will be like describing an emotive, soulful symphony to a deaf man. And describing telepathy will be like describing it to...well, to you actually. Do you see why I've kept putting it off, kept burying my head? It feels to be verging on the impossible and it's the reason I have procrastinated for years. Simply attempting to put the words into the chronology of events that lasted last hundreds of years on the other side is enough to dissuade my head on a daily basis and have me reaching for my wine. How on earth has this little foggy brain managed to hold on to all this knowledge?

Anyway, I'm going to try. I don't feel that I have an option really. Because you see, from the moment I was born, I've been compelled to tell it. Obligated even. But I've just been too scared to start. And yet, strangely, just a month or so ago, following years of inward turmoil, I woke one morning, dusted off my laptop and simply began. From the second I made the decision to put down the first line, I've found a weird compulsion to continue, an unwavering drive and fixed focus, an irresistible urge. I'm unable to relax and concentrate on anything else without thinking of how to order my story, which words

I'll use, which scenes I'll tell, which scenes I won't.

I have never been interested or intrigued enough to search my deeper memories for recollections of Dorothy's life or to look for her family, her home or her kids. I'm actually completely disinterested. I recall snippets of information or conversations or happenings from her life, though I never probe even the edges of the memory to explore it, or I might see a familiar face in a crowd that I know that she knew but I don't. It doesn't interest me at all. I know all that I need to know about Dorothy's life, from her death. I know the lessons she learned because they were my lessons too. So, you see, it's not her life that compels me to write, but her death. Ah, the exquisiteness of death.

So, there she was, living my last life as Dorothy Hatt (nee Gough). Dorothy, 59 years of age, seemingly fit and healthy, sporadically loving wife of Harold, mother to 26 year old Caroline and 24 year old Pamela, driving her Ford Cortina into town, singing Boney M's Rivers of Babylon on top note, with no clue whatsoever, that she was about to die, no idea that she would be choosing me to live the next life to come back and tell our tale.

CHAPTER ONE

The Death

'I fancy a nice piece of Hake for tea love if you happen to be going into town today?' Harold's tone was pleasant despite the fact that she had fallen out with him again last night over his loud snoring. Dorothy couldn't understand how he never held a grudge or got annoyed with her. She had bawled and shouted at him saying she'd be shattered all day, and all that he had replied in an agreeable tone, was that she could be nicer about things and that she needed to file down her abrasive corners a bit. It had made her chuckle, but she didn't let him hear and anyway, she would make it up to him now by calling at the fish stall and offering a hake tea as her apology.

She was singing heartily, her mood was buoyant despite her broken sleep, and she felt healthy and well. Life's normal worries, though nothing too taxing or needing attention floated about in her head. Then, with no warning whatsoever, she felt what can only be described as the onset of a feeling of sheer terror.

Her heart began to bound and race. An impending sense of dread and doom. An unexpected panic that washed over her completely and utterly. Her hands were suddenly wet with sweat, slippy on the wheel. She could hear her heartbeat pounding in her head and neck, pulsing hard through her veins. Breathing rapid, short and panicky breaths, she instinctively took her foot from the accelerator and quickly scanned the roadside for a safe place to pull over.

As she looked left, she felt an excruciating, all-consuming crushing, stabbing and burning pain in her chest and neck. It instantly began to radiate down her left arm and into her hand. It took away her breath and her ability to do anything other than to wildly panic. The agony was so severe that, without consideration or thought of anyone being in danger from her car, she let go of the steering wheel and clutched instinctively at her chest. She clawed at the neck of her jumper to give her some freedom to catch her breath. Then, inexplicably, just as suddenly as it had begun, she was free of the pain. Still fully conscious, she closed her eyes with blessed relief and began to relax and compose herself.

She became aware of what can only be described as a beautiful deep, rhythmic, pulsing, humming, penetrating vibration which was filling her body from head to toe. Every cell, the very essence of her, was a relaxed and harmonious vibration.

She imagined this to be her body's relief from that horrendous, crippling pain and the fear that had had her thinking she was going to die with a heart attack. So beautiful was this sensation that she could have stayed here forever when suddenly, what sounded like a whooshing, sucking noise, lifted her like a vacuum, clean into the air.

There, to her absolute amazement she found herself hovering above her body and looking down onto herself. 'What the hell?' she thought. Though she didn't have any sensation of panic or distress. The vibrations had stopped. She was fully conscious and could see the scene below in its entirety. She could see what was her body clearly slumped over the steering wheel.

'How can this be?' she wondered. The car roof didn't seem to impede the vision of her. She could see that the car had come to a standstill into the side of another car. There were shop assistants stood at the front of their shops and passers-by staring and wondering why the woman in the car hadn't got out to look at the damage she'd caused. A tall, thin, older, grey-haired man with a wizened and whiskered grumpy face and a woodbine hanging from his lips, passed by muttering, 'Bloody women drivers,' whilst slowing his pace so that he could crane his neck for a better look. His rotund wife shoved him along with her hand in the small of his back saying 'Oh shut up Gerald, you can't even drive.' Dorothy absorbed all of it.

There was a man shouting, he was yelling for someone to find a telephone, then he was opening the car door and Dorothy watched him pulling on her shoulders to help to sit her back in the seat.

She looked down at her face. Mottled red and puffy, swollen and bloated looking and she could already make out subtle shades of blue under her pink lipstick and at the tip of her nose and earlobes. She hadn't looked like that this morning, she'd looked quite pretty for a fifty-nine-year-old, kept her figure too.

She saw her permed, curly dyed brown hair and could smell the pungent, chemical scent that lingered with a new perm as it mingled with her cheap perfume.

The sudden recognition that the actual being that she was now, she had never not been. She realised with a bit of a shock, that she actually wasn't Dorothy after all. Dorothy was dead and she wasn't. She'd never been Dorothy. In fact, now, at this moment, she felt more alive than ever. That bag of meat slumped lifelessly back on the car seat, with half open sightless eyes and jaw hanging slackly, was simply her mode of transport. And that's just how it looked to her now. A heavy, cumbersome, shackled, lump of a body.

The panicking man continued to shout out. 'Help

me someone, help me get her out, I think she's dead.' And Dorothy watched as another man got into the passenger side to help. Yet for her, looking down on the scene, there was no sense of urgency whatsoever. Dorothy was hoping that they didn't do too much to help since she had absolutely no desire whatsoever to get back into that heavy thing, that unwieldy, awkward body. She continued to observe, almost as a disinterested bystander.

Then. Blackness.

A blackness so loving and embracing, so absolute, so vast, so very tender. So infinite and welcoming. So quiet, so relaxing, so calm, so serene, so utterly peaceful, so velvety, so cushioned and softly comforting, completely enveloped her. She was aware, conscious, she was still her with her same thoughts and feelings, unscathed, separate from the Dorothy that she had actually thought was her.

Her whole being was relaxed. She might have been here for hours, or months, or maybe years in this state of complete bliss. There wasn't a thought to be anywhere else. Nothing to hurry for. Not a care nor a worry, no concerns about anyone or anything. She was unaware of any real idea of time because there simply wasn't a form of time. Certainly, no measure of time like the earthly clock and its measure of the nights and days, the years and decades. This was a place where she could rest for all eternity, and she would feel completely marvellous. There was just here and now, this soft, safe, all encompassing, welcoming and comforting blackness. Then, as she began the first thought of idly wondering where it was that she could be, just a mere whisper of a passing thought, she instantaneously found herself hovering above the scene again.

EMILY

Letting Go

I only started to write a week or so ago and it's been, without doubt, the strangest time of my life. I'm no stranger to feeling like the weird one, but this is off the scale even for me. I've been deliberately allowing all the suppressed visions to completely unfold in my head so that I could write them down. You just can't live properly if you let yourself ruminate on them and I'd been deliberately smothering them since I was a little kid.

One of my constant frets before I began, was that I wouldn't be able to describe stuff, or put any of it into any kind of order. You see, in my head, it's always been a big pot of mishmashes, a confused jumbled mess with everything seeming to happen all at once, together, with no beginning, middle or end. Over in an instant, yet exceeding thousands of years in the same instance. I imagined it to be impossible to unravel and untangle enough to make any sense, and yet, once I began to write, the memories were forming themselves crystal clear, setting themselves not in a vague semblance of order, but a completely legible and readable prose. See, little things like writing prose, who'd have thunk it? I didn't even know it was a word.

Now I know that that bit doesn't sound too weird, does it? But here is what's happening. I try to write around five hundred words a day, it takes me a couple of hours to do that, and it absolutely exhausts me. Anyway, like I've said, the words and the structure flow, but when I reread what I've written so that I know where to begin the next bit, it all reads like someone else wrote it. I know they're my words and I know that I wrote them, but all the memories that were bursting out of my head, that have always burst out of my head and that I've already written down, have completely disappeared. Gone. Not there at all. I can neither add to it nor edit it. If I try to alter a paragraph because it isn't flowing right, then it just begins to feel like I'm making the whole thing up, like I've imagined it all and I'm completely unable to conjure up any real true detail. It's as though once it's on paper, I'm free of it, memory wiped, erased, cleansed.

It's completely liberating for me. I can feel the tension that I've known for my entire life, ebbing away with each word.

The first time it happened, I'd just opened the laptop, read the last hundred words or so I knew where I'd left off and where to start my writing, when I realised that the story seemed alien to me, as if it were belonging to someone else, a fictional tale, and I'd presumed I was either just too tired, or maybe hungry. So, me being me, I'd plumped for hunger and just nipped out and cycled to the bakery for a pie and a custard. Back home, pie, custard and a brew demolished, and I was facing the same issue. After that, and the further along with my story I got, I became aware that it happened every time.

As I wrote each page, my inner turmoil was being quelled, I was sleeping better and feeling better. When some clever sod once said that writing something down could be cathartic, they really didn't understand the depth of cathartic-ness. I am finally setting myself free.

DOROTHY

Calla

Dorothy calmly took in the scene of the accident, hovering above it and soaking in all of the detail, still lazily trying to make sense of all that was happening to her. Some innate sense told her of another being within her vicinity and her interest suddenly piqued, she took her concentration from the scene and closely surveyed all around her. She looked and looked, this way and that, up and down.

Then, she saw a tiny speck of light, the warm embrace of love emanating from it. As it began to move towards her, growing and becoming brighter, Dorothy heard a tinkling of laughter, a sweet angelic sound and she saw what was an outline of pure light emerging right in front of her, beckoning her, calling her. Dorothy recognised her instantly. Her heart soared as she rushed to her. 'Calla, oh my word, it's you. How could I have been so blinkered and muted that I'd forgotten you so utterly and completely? I should have been missing you so very badly.'

Dorothy reached out to touch and embrace her and found herself both inside and outside of her at the same moment, they absorbed into each other, their joined lights shining and glowing fluidly.

The depths of her very being was overjoyed to be back with Calla, back in the love that she had forgotten existed. Her Calla, her beloved guide. She had guided Dorothy through all of her lifetimes. They were very deeply entwined and connected.

'I've forgotten absolutely everything Calla, I know I'm not Dorothy, but I don't know who I am or where I am, only that I feel complete, I feel loved and happier than I've ever been.'

'You're home Dorothy, you've completed another life, it'll take a while for you to settle and understand. You've been through this hundreds of times and it'll all make complete sense shortly. Just relish every moment, enjoy yourself.'

Dorothy realised that Calla must be communicating this with her thoughts because she couldn't see her mouth moving and she knew she wasn't moving hers. Calla chuckled daintily at Dorothy's confusion. 'I've been with you forever Dorothy, through all your lives and I'll be with you for any future lives you decide to take. I'll take you through all the reintroductions, everything. I'm always with you, every step of the way, guiding you, helping you to grow. You'll remember it all soon.'

Dorothy looked at Calla's glow. Lighter and brighter than her own, she was made of what seemed to be billions of shards of different coloured jewels of light. She basked in her welcoming warmth.

Then, without thought, she was back, looking down again on the scene of her death, Dorothy could see that her body was now out of the car and on a stretcher in the back of the ambulance. She was covered from head to toe in a crisp, white cotton sheet. There was medical paraphernalia scattered haphazardly here and there from the crew's resuscitation attempts. There was still a bag of saline attached to a drip leading to her covered right arm, though any attempt to save her had by now been abandoned. The two ambulance crew had closed the doors and were chatting between themselves, one writing notes on his papered clipboard while the other was picking up and tidying away the detritus. Dorothy was fascinated to observe the lights and different auras that emanated from these men. She looked at her own lights, then at Calla's luminescent ones and she reached out to both men in turn, to gently touch and feel these living lights. She found that she had a full picture of their entire lives, all their hopes and dreams and worries and she realised for the first time, that everyone and everything had a connection.

Outside the ambulance, were three policemen. One was sat in the passenger seat of her car emptying out her old brown leather handbag contents onto the driver's seat. He pushed her embassy regal cigarettes and Bryant and May matches to one side and located her purse. A couple of the new pound coins, some loose change and a small photograph of two young women were shaken onto the driver's seat. A stick of blusher and a frosted, pink lipstick rolled off the seat and into the drivers footwell.

No form of identification. He'd have to get the woman's details from her car registration. As he bent forward, stretching himself over the gear stick to reach down and retrieve the fallen items, Dorothy very gently touched the lights around his shoulders after wondering why his lights weren't as bright and colourful as others were and she instantly felt herself recoiling. She looked to Calla in astonishment and was instantly given an awareness from her, that the man hadn't lived a good life this time, but Dorothy now knew that it would only ever cause him any pain in the bigger scheme of things. She watched as he pocketed the cigarettes and climbed out of the car.

Another policeman, was requesting that the crowd disperse, waving them away with his important arm and dulled aura, which Dorothy chose not to touch. The third who positively glowed with pinks and yellows and wisps of gold, was stood in front of the fruit shop with its trays of apples, bananas and pears (priced and boxed on sturdily built tables carried outside each morning). He was taking notes from the two men who had tried to help Dorothy and an elderly lady who had seen the whole incident unfold. She gently caressed his glow and was instantly rewarded with a vision of his selflessness, his kind and forgiving nature and she felt love for him emanating from herself causing her lights and aura to sparkle. It utterly delighted her, and she laughed with pleasure.

Dorothy intently watched the whole scene, watching the whole crowd with fascination for their lights and auras, she allowed herself to slip in and out of each glow and felt herself captivated with the sensation of connection between them all. She grieved with them for their losses and pains in life and felt herself cheering for them when they experienced love and joy, fun and laughter. Again, she was reminded that time didn't exist, nothing took any time, time was here and now, there and then, all mixed up together, present, future and past, all happening now.

Dorothy became aware that she was being guided by Calla, to retreat from her focus on the scene. She allowed her gaze to fall on a light in the distance. 'Go towards the light Dorothy, I'm with you, just call me if you need me,' Dorothy smiled and headed towards the light.

It seemed to be welcoming her, beckoning almost, warm. She began to go towards it, and it appeared to be coming towards her too. Then, immediately, she became bathed in it. This wondrous, beautiful, living, loving light. Unlike any earthly light and yet brighter, it seemed to be alive and filled with joy and love and recognition. Dorothy looked around her. An explosion of fertile lushness lay all about. She was on a woodland pathway, a gurgling stream to her left with the clearest, bluest water she had ever seen. All the background was of gently sloping, rolling hills which stretched on infinitely and unbounded.

She could feel a warm breeze on her face carrying the sweetest, most delightful perfume and she could hear birds singing and tweeting in the sky. The ground was a thick carpet of grass, green and lush with every blade almost glowing and pulsing with the same light which engulfed absolutely everything around her. The many trees, in shades of the most beautiful pale green to the richest, darkest burgundy that ran alongside her and on the other side of the river, swayed ever so gently in the breeze.

Although she was a good few hundred yards away, she could make out each and every branch of each tree, the shape, textures and sometimes furred surface of each leaf and the feathered veins which pulsed with the same light that everything else was enveloped in. She could see the vibrant rich bark of each tree and somehow, she knew that they had been there for thousands and thousands of years.

There was an abundance of blooms of flowers clustered all along the pathway. No shade to stem their growth and no heat to shrivel and dry them. Huge, gloriously coloured, silky flower heads tumbled voluminously towards the ground and beautiful. She took in their heady aroma. Plentiful clusters of the tiniest most delicate flowers rose up from the ground with their jewelled shining, tiny heads in a kaleidoscope of the brightest colours, each one magnificent and rich, many of them with unknown and indescribable colours and scents which Dorothy hadn't encountered in the earthly realm. Their individual, sweet and fragrant perfumes rose on the breeze, blended in perfection and Dorothy absorbed all of it, every sensation, every colour, every scent, every sound deeply and with joy.

She moved with a lightness, a freedom. She knew that she was now made of molecules of energy and lights and though she didn't feel that there was form to her body, she still felt that she had arms and legs, ears and eyes, fingers and toes.

She could see the grass beneath where her feet would be, softly compressing where she trod, as though there were some weight to her, yet her entire being seemed to be a mass of light energy, an outline almost. The flowers and the grasses moved with a rhythm and a will of their own. She'd never felt more content or more alive and that amused her, because she'd just seen who she'd thought she was, dead, in the back of an ambulance.

In the distance, Dorothy was aware of a huge wooden gate entirely spanning the end of the pathway, an old, gnarly, shiny and knotted wood with extraordinary age. All around it glowed with a brighter light, welcoming and beckoning and she was aware that on the other side of it, she would encounter the truth. As she headed towards it, she wished that she could tell Harold and the girls about the bliss and wonder that she had found.

EMILY

The Lights

A couple of weeks after I'd started to write, I'd risen early and was off work for the day, so I'd decided to take Hettie out for a decent walk. We'd normally walk all the fields down by the back of my flat, you can make it a one mile walk or a twenty-mile walk depending on how the mood took you once you'd set off. But today I'd fancied a different route and a mooch round the cemetery.

I rang mum to tell her to leave the key under the mat before she left for work as I would come and get Henry then he'd get a walk too. So, we set off, Hettie, still only a puppy at eleven months old, all bounce, wayward limbs and with a permanent wag and a scruffy, mixed brown coat, the runt from my friend Jess's unexpected litter of five and therefore a freebie and of course, mum and dad couldn't refuse Henry, her fat brother. Horace had long since died and they'd always said they'd get another but never got around to it. He was certainly bigger than Hettie, but otherwise they looked just the same. And yes, they were named after the vacuum cleaners that hoovered up everything, since that was what they both did with. Socks, shoes, paper, you name it, these two ate it or chewed it.

I donned my walking boots, fleece, (preloaded with treats, poo bags and a rogue disintegrating tissue) and my woolly hat. I clipped on Hettie's blue starry, spangled lead (blue was cheaper than pink), and off we went. We set off down the stairs and bumped straight into Barry, my rarely sober but pleasant enough downstairs sixty-odd year-old neighbour, just returning from the shop at the top with his carrier bag full of breakfast beers. 'Out for a walk then, are we?' he asked, 'Who's a good boy then?' as he bent down and gave Hettie a vigorous neck rub with his free hand. 'Yep, wanna come?' I asked, knowing he'd decline and say he might tomorrow because he was too busy today. 'Nah, not today, I've too much on, maybe tomorrow.' I chuckled as I walked on, pulled now by an excited Hettie eager to be on her way.

As we got to the communal door, she pulled right to head our usual route towards the fields and I walked left towards the top of the street and the main road leading to Leigh, pulling her gently to heel. At the top of the street, we turned right and waited to cross at the pedestrian lights. Inwardly I beamed with pride at Hettie, who immediately sat down on my command as we waited for the green man, her cute head cocked towards me as she waited for her treat. 'Good boy,' said the elderly lady waiting alongside me.

Once over the road, we turned right and began the mile or so walk to mums. In front of us, a small group of schoolgirls from the local high school dressed in black knee length socks, short navy skirts, navy blazers and huge black rucksacks, left me smiling and feeling cheered as they all screamed with laughter after leaning into one blonde girl who must have had something funny on her mobile. I could hear their shouts of 'Send it to me, and play it again,' and more giggling.

The day was beautiful, still a cool breeze gently blowing but it was bright and sunny and perfect walking weather. Twenty minutes later, a left turn and we were at mum and dads. I walked around the back of the house and located the key in its usual place under the doormat. I could hear Henry barking as I turned the key, and he came bounding out excitedly as we entered. I unclipped Hettie and let them get on with their diving all over each other with their overzealous hello's. I could see henry's lead on the kitchen table, a couple of poo bags and a note.

'Hi Emily, thanks for thinking about Henry, here are some poo bags just in case you've forgotten yours, please wash his paws if he is muddy when you return and then leave him in the kitchen. If he's dry and not muddy, he can go in the front room. There's some homemade pea soup and crusty bread if you're hungry when you get back. Grace and dad say hi, be safe on your walk, love you, speak later, mum. xxx'

I looked in the fridge, spotted the huge Pyrex bowl of soup covered with a now misted, wet, cling film, briefly considered eating a bowlful now and only resisted when I thought it might make me feel too sluggish to walk far. I left the poo bags where they were, picked up both leads, clipped in Hettie and Harry and then headed out the back door, locking it and putting the key in my back jeans pocket.

We headed to the top of the street, waited for a lull in the busy traffic and crossed straight over and took a right along the ornate green and cream, ivy trailed railings, towards the cemetery gates. The plan was, as I regularly do, was to walk haphazardly here and there throughout the pathways, stopping now and then to read a headstone then spend some time near the older graves which I absolutely love. Then, nip through a gap in the railings at the back and continue our walk for a few miles. The dogs trotted along either side of me, sniffing here and there, glad to be out.

It's a vast cemetery, with older style weather worn headstones, some with ornate carvings dating from the 1800's and newer modern types now with attached ceramic photographs and beautiful etchings. I love to look at the older ones, often precariously still standing, and I can easily well up when I think of the grief of the parents who buried child after child after child. One says William, who drowned aged seven, it gets me every time.

Then you get the ones with an inscription at the top with a big space underneath clearly waiting for their husband or wife that never came to fruition. Mary, loving wife of Albert, but even 80 years later, Albert hasn't arrived. Grace says there's something wrong with me enjoying mooching around the cemetery, but it's not macabre I don't think. It's really quiet and peaceful and I regularly start or finish my walks here.

Anyway, this day, as I took a left on the pathway towards the newer graves, something caught my eye and caused me to look towards the middle sections on the 1980s to 90s plots. I only ever stick to the paths really unless I'm at the older end so it wouldn't be somewhere I would usually go. I could see some sort of lights, I was thinking maybe it could be the sun glancing off a glass vase or something. I stopped and furrowed my brow to stare and to try to work out what they were.

There were two older women, perhaps mid 60's obscuring my view as they tended their grave, chattering away between themselves. Intrigued, made my way over. As I approached, they glanced toward me mid conversation, nodded a brief hello, then turned away and carried on chattering. I think I may have had my mouth wide open at this point. I told you I have no psychic abilities whatsoever, didn't I? Well, I kid you not, these two women had light filled auras around their heads and shoulders, streams of pinks and golds dancing all around them.

I was completely mesmerised, it was beautiful, utterly entrancing. I glanced down at the dogs to see if they were acting peculiar at all, but no, they didn't seem to think anything unusual was happening. I just had to get closer, I've never seen anything like it and they both seemed oblivious. I wondered if their dead relative was trying to send them love as I trampled the ground between the rows of graves, dogs still either side of me.

I got to within a couple of graves and pretended to be mourning one Martha Lewis who'd died aged 81 in 1988, whilst furtively snatching long glances at the backs of the glowing women. One of them looked around, 'Do we know you from somewhere? We've just been saying as you walked down that you look really familiar.' I looked at her face and that of her friend, 'I don't think so,' I said, still distracted and in awe of their glowing lights. 'Well, we both said the same thing,' said the one with the bobbed grey hair, 'Maybe it's from here?' 'You visiting your nan love?' the other one asked. 'Hmm, yes,' I replied, glancing down at Martha's headstone. 'Anyway, nice to see you love,' said bobbed woman, and her friend nodded in agreement and off they went, glowing away obliviously down the row of graves.

I waited until they were a good distance away and stepped towards the grave they'd been visiting. I swear I've not had a normal life like everyone else, but by God, this shook me up. The stone read, In Loving Memory of Dorothy Hatt, Loving Wife of Harold. Born 1929 Died 1988. Loving Mother of Caroline and Pamela. Harold Hatt Reunited with Dorothy. Born 1927 Died 2009. Those women were Dorothy's daughters. No wonder I am shook. I didn't recognise them, but my soul certainly did. I headed back to mums. Walk abandoned.

DOROTHY

Beyond the gate

As Dorothy made her way along the bright and glorious living pathway, she felt enveloped in its warmth and love which seemed to be its every emanating from every single thing around. She felt connected, as though she were a part of all the things she could see, as though a strand of infinite, ethereal thread was woven into her every fibre and moving fluidly in and out and through everything around her, connecting them, giving her a sense of oneness with everything, a completion of self.

Consciously, moving slowly now so as to absorb every delightful detail, she continued toward the warmth of the lights and the wooden gate, she knew instinctively that she was on her way home, truly home, the most emotional experience of coming home that she'd ever felt.

As she approached, the lights around the gates danced and shimmered as though they were excited to see her. The huge, heavy looking and mighty gates, began to pull backwards, heaving and creaking with age and weight as they began to open from their centre.

Dorothy became aware that there were clusters of lights behind them, all seeming to push and shove forward excitedly even before the gates had opened fully. With a growing sense of amazement, she suddenly realised that these lights were all beings, souls, her friends, not only from her life as Dorothy, but from all her lives lived. Hundreds and hundreds of excited, laughing souls, all wanting to hug her and welcome her home. She greeted each of them individually with delight, no sense of time or waiting for anyone meant that she could embrace each and every person and reminisce with them, enjoy and appreciate them all within the same moment. She paraded proudly through her homecoming. 'Dad, dad, oh dad, I thought you were gone forever,' she joined him and held him, their lights entwining with love and joy. 'I know sweetheart, it really hurt me when I had to say goodbye, but you're here now. I helped Calla guide you on many occasions.' Calla nodded her agreement. 'Granny Annie,' she squealed and rushed over to embrace her grandma. 'Oh Gran, I was destroyed when you died, I missed you endlessly.' Their lights migrated in and out of each other in bliss. 'I know kiddo, I watched you grieve, and I held you so close every night. But here we are now, truly home at last, congratulations on your life, you must be so very proud of yourself and I'm so proud of you I could just burst.'

She could see that each person was made of a pure light and energy and yet she could clearly see their faces. Sometimes the face would shimmer and alter to become a different face of a different life once lived but Dorothy, although she knew she still had a lot to learn as though she were wakening after a deep sleep, didn't need a face to recognise the souls. 'Aunty Bessie, come here,' she said as she warmly pulled in Bessie, 'You made mine and Helen's life so much easier. I love you for it.' Some she knew, had lived their mortal lives frequently with her as her mother or her friend, her father, wife, husband, cousin, grandma, grandad, daughter, son, teacher, neighbour, every possible human connection, every possible colour. 'Tom,' she squealed, as she spotted her old neighbour who'd been so lovely to her and Harold. 'You look absolutely wonderful, so vibrant. And so very bloody young!' Tom roared with laughter, 'Well done Dorothy, we're so proud of you.' She saw dogs and cats frolicking and romping around, she hadn't had any pets in this life, but she instantly recognised a beloved past life dog as he bounded up to her with his lights flashing maniacally. As he jumped up to welcome her, she felt a waterfall of his devotion splatter unheeded into her core and it caused everyone to laugh. 'Pluto, come here big guy,' she nuzzled and hugged him as he danced excitedly from paw to paw, thrilled to be back with his mistress. Her cat Cleopatra, from a life lived in the Victorian period, sidled up to purr and rub against her. 'Come here Cleo my precious little rat catcher,' she scooped her up tenderly and watched her mesmerised with the way her lights tracked throughout her fur.

Other's souls she could see, had a higher vibration and had been life guides like Calla, or her teachers in this realm. Some souls that she could see, had denser, heavier lights and she knew that these were the younger souls who still had lessons to learn on earth. She loved each and every one of them.

'How could I have forgotten? How could I not have known?' she exclaimed. Then in an instant she found herself hovering over a sleeping Harold on the day of her funeral.

EMILY

Hushed Child

I can't help but notice, while I'm writing or I'm thinking about writing, that I'm wrestling with my own life's memories and recollections of stuff. It's been a strange existence for me. I've always known about Dorothy and the afterlife, always, from before I could even make sense of this world. It's just been just there, a fact, a part of my life, a knowing. I've always known that Calla is with me, guiding me, though I've never actually seen her or sensed her, and I often wonder if she's forgotten to attend this life with me.

When I was a small girl, I used to threaten to throw myself off the top bunk and kill myself if she didn't help me with one thing or another. 'Please Calla guide, tell mum and dad to buy me that pink bike with the basket on the front.' I'd clasp my hands in prayer. 'I'm absolutely begging you.' That usually sent Grace off to tell mum that I was scaring her again and mum would come to tell me I'd have to go to the funny farm if I carried on being silly. And still Calla didn't make herself known.

I'm beginning to wonder recently just how much my knowing about all this has impacted on my decisions and my life. I've always known that everyone else is in exactly the same boat as me, they just don't remember it. I also know that it wasn't an accident, a blip of nature that I was able to retain it all. I was supposed to tell people. But no one would listen, not ever and not to this day. Not my parents, my sister or my friends. 'All your imagination Emily,' mum would say, 'and stop talking about it because it scares Grace.'

Even then, as a snippet of a kid, I knew deep inside that I'd have to write it all down when I was a grown up. Maybe that's a part of the bigger plan, it's been allowed to fester inside me for all these years with no outlet, so the only way for it to be released from me is to write it down and hopefully that way, at least one person will read it. An audience of one is better than no audience at all.

I can recall what I think was my first foray into disclosing what I thought everyone already knew. I was four years old, a skinny, good kid with boundless energy and a real zest for life and mud, Barbie dolls and Nemo, with long, straight blonde hair which rarely stayed in its ponytail. I had a cute, upturned nose, deep brown eyes, a liberal smattering of the tiniest freckles, a bizarre dress sense, a new sister and a hairy, white, lurcher dog named Horace.

We lived on an estate just off the main road which runs from Astley to Leigh (mum and dad still live there now), in a two up, two down council house.

From my bedroom window, I could see the canal and would regularly watch as pushbikes, prams, barges, groups of school kids and hand holding couples would pass by. I'd watch as fishermen threw in their boilies, tinned sweetcorn and mulched up bread, then triumphantly catch a large pike, look around for any admirers, hold it up, admire its size and gauge its weight, only to disgorge their hooks from their poor scarred mouths and throw them back in the murky depths to await their next catch.

I'd stand at my bedroom window, only my head and shoulders above the windowsill, lifting and scrunching up the net curtains and pressing my nose against the window, pushing aside the pink shiny curtains with their unmatched Nemo tie backs that I'd insisted on as my gift for being a good girl and sister when Grace was born, so that I could press my nose against the window and look for ducks and the two swans that were frequent visitors.

I loved my life, my pink bedroom, my mum and dad, my dog, my home and I suppose Grace was slowly growing on me. I hadn't yet started school, mum was a housewife and stay at home mum and dad was a mechanic at the garage down the road.

This particular morning, dad had just left for work, mum was downstairs with the baby, and I'd just woken up. I lay and stretched a while, smoothing my Barbie quilt cover with both my hands so that I could see her pretty face, idly listening to the baby crying loudly downstairs while mum busied herself in the kitchen below calling out soothing words to her while she hurriedly prepared her bottle.

I could feel a breeze wafting gently through the curtains which were softly billowing, and I was enjoying its sweet coolness against my cheek, and it promised the start of a beautiful spring day. I pushed back Barbie and climbed out of bed, pushed my feet into pink, fluffy slippers, straightened Barbie out again so she wouldn't be squished and headed downstairs.

Mum was sitting on the chair under the window with the baby nestled close and wrapped in a pink crocheted shawl, smiling at me as I walked in sleepy eyed. Grace was suckling heartily and noisily on her bottle, a trail of milk dribbling down the side of her mouth and settling in a wet soggy mess on her bib. 'Mummy, can we go for a walk down the canal today with Grace and Horace? I can wear my Nemo wellies. You said we could if it was a nice day and it's nice.' 'Good morning my special girl,' mum nodded her tousled bedhead motioning down toward the baby, 'Say good morning to your sister.' 'Good morning Grace, can we go for a walk mummy?'

But I already knew, just from her fleeting expression, that it was a no. I'm four, I don't understand rationales and reasoning, I didn't even wait for her response. 'You promised, you promised,' I angrily accused and immediately began to wail, hot tears bouncing freely down my face.

'It's not fair, you said we could, and you lied. I wish I still had my other mummy, you're not as kind as she was, she didn't tell lies, I wish I'd never have picked you.' I carried on wailing, upset that I wouldn't be spending my morning doing what I loved. I watched her face through my tears, part nonplussed, part amused, and part hacked off because all the commotion had stopped Grace from her suckling.

'Well then young lady,' you'd better jolly well pack your bags and go back to that other mummy then since she is so much better than I am, perhaps she wasn't awake all night with toothache and a new baby.' I stopped the crying instantly as only a kid can do and looked at her quite incredulously. What could she mean? 'But how can I mummy? I died didn't I, 'member? I got trapped under that horse and cart and those men pulled me out, but it was too late, and I got dead. My mummy cried for lots and lots but then I came back here to be Dorothy and now I'm being Emily with you instead.'

I can laugh now when I think back on it, mums

poor face, ashen.

Hands shaking, she immediately put a now wailing Grace into her Moses basket, walked over to the sideboard, picked up the handset on the red house phone, dialled the garage and asked Frank if he could put John on the line as a matter of urgency. Lauren heard Frank trying to shout over the racket of a revving car engine and various bits of machinery 'John, it's Lauren on the phone, she says its urgent.' She heard him pick up the receiver and hurriedly began talking. 'Emily is saying strange things again John and it's freaking me out.' She regurgitated the conversation in a high-pitched shaky voice, mimicking my childish tones.

I could hear daddy laughing through the earpiece as he repeatedly tried to calm her down.

I couldn't understand how she had possibly forgotten. It was like forgetting your own name. I set about reminding her while she was still on the phone. 'Don't you 'member mummy? Your name was called Alf then and you were my brother that time, then you were Annie, Dorothy's Grandma.' I carried on quickly chattering away trying to remind her.

She replaced the receiver with a bang, probably annoyed at dad for not taking her worried conversation too seriously and looked at me, 'Daddy says you've got a wild imagination and I think he's right. But I still have toothache and we still can't go for a walk because I need to go to the dentist. We can go tomorrow though, but only if you stop telling silly stories.' No amount of protesting now would get her to change her mind. She picked up Grace to carry on with her bottle and I turned the television on completely deflated.

I suppose I just got used over time to people not liking, or not comprehending what I spoke about. I recall so many instances over the years of being shut down. It's not like I was a naughty kid, or an attention seeking one. I would just say what I was thinking or tell of an experience. All kids do exactly that, it's how they learn the art of socialisation, a part of play. I wasn't to know that my experiences scared other kids or freaked out adults. As good as mum was, she used to permanently fret about my mental health. I'd hear her repeating to dad or grandma some of the stuff I'd said. Dad was completely unfazed, 'She'll grow out of it Lauren, she's just an imaginative kid,' he'd say soothingly. Grandma would gently chide me, 'You'll upset mummy if you keep saying silly things like that Emily, you'll get taken off in a yellow van.'

Once, I think it was for my sixth birthday, I'd been allowed a small party at home, the kids parents had attended too. One of the girls was throwing a hissy fit, (as you do when you're six) because it wasn't her birthday party and so therefore it wasn't fair. She screamed and wailed and was ruining my party. So, face like thunder, hands on hips, I stood right in front of her and yelled, 'You need to shut up right now because when you're dead you'll be very, very sorry. You'll go for your life review and the spirits will hate you for doing this. You'll make all their lights turn out!' Some parents laughed, some looked perturbed, and some were already muttering that I was a strange one. Anyway, the kid carried on screaming regardless of how the spirits lights would dim and I learned that it was probably better not to make statements like that. Mum said that there were better and more sensible things to say to an already upset child. So that was the end of parties for me, even though mum always maintained that that wasn't the reason.

I played with all kids up until high school. They were by and large the same to me, all growing up and learning. I counted them all as friends. Now that I'm grown, I have a smaller group of pals, you know the ones, you text them, have a laugh with them and meet up at the pub and stuff, but my only real close friend is Jess. Beth is getting there slowly. I met Jess on the first day of high school in registration and we've never had one fall out.

It's like she understands my weirdness, she's always understood me and doesn't judge me for it. She's a genuinely sweet and kind person and not just to me, she's lovely to everyone, even those who are mean to her. As we grew and matured together, word got around (as it does at high school and especially these days with social media), that I used to tell people I'd died and gone to heaven and that I'd lived previous lives. Other kids would either taunt me and do walking dead impressions, or maybe snigger about me as I passed. Some kids asked why I told lies, others had been told by parents from primary school to give me a wide berth. Not one kid asked me if it were true. Not ever, not even Jess.

Jess always tried to protect me, once shoving over a boy in our art class who had painted blood around his mouth and was walking zombie like towards me for the amusement of his pals who were clearly enjoying the show. It was kind of her, but I never needed her protection. I was never bullied or picked on, in fact I got along (and still get along) with almost everyone I meet. I'd certainly said some weird stuff during my younger years but by eight or nine, I'd begun to realise that it was better to keep my mouth shut about some things. Jess was a natural choice for me, we sort of gravitated together. She has this fascinating capacity to be able to walk into a room, interact with someone, and immediately know them, what they're about, where they stand, who they are. She has this higher sense of intuitive knowledge about others. She has this genuineness about her. Like everything she does comes from a place of love. After I'd got to know her quite well, I told her I thought our souls must know each other from a past life. I thought she might say I was weird or odd, but she didn't, she said maybe that was true. I took that as my cue to gently broach other afterlife area's, but she simply closed my talk down and changed the subject.

I had already learned, even at that young age, that people were just constructs of their conditioning and the identity of the physical body that they possessed this time around. You're a boy, a girl, pretty, slim, ugly, kind, mean, stupid, tall, short, fat, thin, handsome, weak, strong, rich, poor, popular, unpopular. Far too much emphasis is put on what we can achieve, what we own, what our careers are, it's seen as a way to define someone, and it shouldn't be. I'm completely unselfconscious about who I am and what I want from life. It makes me feel both lucky and emboldened. So, I had learned to dismantle all their traits and look for the real them underneath it all and try to find the subdued spirit, the muted soul. I chose my friends accordingly. Jess, a startlingly pretty, blue-eyed, dark-haired girl who was oblivious to these gifts, seemed a natural fit.

As we both matured and started to visit each other's houses, I learned that her parents were the same, warm and welcoming. She was having a lucky life this time around. Perhaps her soul was already bright, and she wasn't in need of many lessons, or maybe these were on the way, who knew?

I once heard her mum whisper to her friend that I was a lovely girl though a troubled soul. It actually made me laugh. In every way possible I was untroubled. I had a wonderful family, I had friends, I was settled in school. In retrospect, I think it must have just been things that I'd said that were odd. I'll have said things out loud that probably had no place coming out of a kid's mouth.

One day, when I was perhaps fifteen or sixteen, I recall being sat at the dining room table at Jess's house discussing which tattoo's we should get when we were older. We had sheets of paper nicked from her mum's printer and were using felt tips to draw our designs and scrolling through our phones for inspiration. Jess's mum walked in and asked what we were designing. 'Our tattoos,' we chorused together. 'Oooh, don't do that,' she said, her face scrunched up with distaste, 'once you get a tattoo, you're stuck with it forever.' 'Nah,' I replied, 'just while you're in this life, it'll be gone the next.' I felt Jess boot my shin under the table and we both dissolved into fits of laughter as her mum stood with her mouth opening and closing but not a word coming out. 'She's joking mum,' Jess said laughing and I went along with Jess as I had learned to do over the years after I had come out with some obscure afterlife fact.

To date, I have six tattoos and Jess is still trying to pluck up the courage for her first. And Beth?

Well, Beth is the polar opposite of Jess, and yet somehow, we all meet in the middle.

DOROTHY

The funera

1

Dorothy looked down on Harold. He was fast asleep on their couch as she'd known he would be. He hadn't slept in their bed since the day the police had been to tell him Dorothy had died. Tragic, the copper had said and put a sad expression on his face that didn't reach his eyes or light up his aura.

She looked closely. Poor Harold looked cold. He had attempted a half-hearted, sleepy, effort to form some semblance of warmth and had pulled a cushion from behind his head and covered his chest with it. 'He looks dreadful Calla, doesn't he?' His skin was grey, and the weight had dropped off him. There was an untouched casserole in the fridge that Caroline had brought round yesterday and a large egg custard tart which Pamela had bought to try to tempt his appetite. 'Dad, you need to eat,' they'd both implored, looking at him with worried eyes. 'I'll just have a cup of tea for now thanks all the same,' he'd answer, 'I'll have that later though because it looks delicious.' But the food lay untouched day after day.

Her mam had visited him every day and accompanied him to the funeral directors and the town hall for the death certificate. She hadn't been able to persuade him to eat more than a morsel either. 'I don't feel like eating either Harold,' she'd chided, 'but you'll cope better with everything if you do. You're going to make yourself ill and then what will the girls do then?'

Dorothy could see a vibrating, swaying illumination of lights above Harold's sleeping form and she'd known that this was Kaeral, Harold's guide. Calla had already explained that they weren't able to communicate with him while he was guiding the living Harold. 'He won't even be aware that we are here Dorothy, his entire focus is executed onto Harold and his well-being.'

Dorothy allowed her lights to settle on and around Harold. He was sleeping just deeply enough for his spirit to dislodge slightly, which gave her enough scope to begin to merge with him. She climbed into the corner of his dream, nudging her way in slowly so as not to startle him awake. She very gently gathered him up and pulled him upwards with her. Out he came, glorious flames of shimmering lights. My word, this is a good soul, she thought, as she watched the glory of lights and colours that flowed from him. She'd always known that he was a good man, but my word, his soul was divine. She watched the pulsating, ethereal cord that bound and anchored Harold to his earthly body, it flashed and sparked with the energy required to keep his soul stable and tethered to his human form. 'Harold, I'm here,' she spoke gently and watched as he sleepily focused on her. 'Oh Dorothy, my love, I thought I'd lost you. Look at you, you're so young, I love you.' Dorothy laughed out loud. 'You won't remember any of this Harold I'm afraid, but you will remember that I've been with you. You'll take comfort from it, but you'll put it down to a dream in the end, so let's enjoy this wonderful moment together.' She whirled her lights in and out of him and he laughed and laughed heartily. 'I've come to offer you a little peace.'

They chatted and danced and whirled in and out of each other with utter delight. 'You have to feed him Harold, you're starving him to death,' laughed Dorothy as they both looked down at Harold's scrawny frame. 'I can't help it Dorothy, I've been beyond heartbroken since you died, my stomach feels as though there's a brick in it. Please let me remember this experience Dorothy, please, I'm begging you. It'll be so much easier to cope with if I know you're okay. I can't help but keep picturing you in your coffin and it doesn't even look like you.' Dorothy smiled in sympathy and gently caressed his glows, 'It's impossible I'm afraid Harold. But you will remember that you dreamt of me and that we chatted and danced. It'll give you a lot of comfort, I promise.' Then she tenderly rotated him back into his sleeping form and crept out of his dream.

'Grief is a lousy lesson to take Calla,' she said, feeling immense compassion for him as his soul slipped back into its place.

They watched as he awoke with a start, his loss momentarily forgotten and then the dawning as it crept up and attacked him right in the gut.

What time was it? Why was he on the couch? Where was Dorothy? Within seconds his belly had dropped with the memory of her death. A crippling sensation of grief and anguish hit his heart. His throat constricted. It was an all-consuming, physical pain, the worst pain he'd ever experienced in his life. He was certain it would never go away, and he wasn't sure he could live like this. He could barely muster up enough energy to accomplish even the most basic task. He swung his legs off the couch, put his elbows on his knees, his face in his hands and howled. How on earth would he get through today? 'Dorothy please,' he said aloud, wiping tears and snot from his face with his sleeve, 'Please give me a sign that you're okay. I'm begging you.' He looked around the living room in hope. Nothing. Not a stray feather, nor a robin or a butterfly at the window. He sobbed some more.

He pottered off wearily into the kitchen

completely fatigued after another restless night on the couch. He'd been dreaming, hadn't he? Hadn't he seen her in his dream? He furrowed his brow and whipped through what details he could recall before they were lost with the morning sunrise. 'That was it,' he shouted out loud. 'I remember.' He sat down and closed his eyes, trying to filter through the scraps of hazy images. They'd been dancing, Dorothy was in her late twenties again. She'd definitely visited him. He felt his heart lift a little. He supped his cup of tea and slowly allowed the dream to unfold in detail. It was the best he'd felt since the day she'd died.

'Dad, we'll be with you at one and our Caroline and Rob just after,' Pamela was checking that he would be ready on time, 'try to have a bit of toast or something dad.' He put the phone down, went into the kitchen and turned on the grill. Dorothy watched as Kaeral tenderly soothed his wretched body with its jaded aura. 'Poor Harold,' she said aloud.

The shiny black hearse pulled up at the front of the house followed immediately by a black limousine. The undertaker strode respectfully up the front path, hat off and secured under his arm and gently tapped on the door. Pamela opened it. 'You may come to view mums coffin and flowers if you wish,' he said solemnly, nodding towards the cars. 'Dad,' she gently called out, 'Mums here, would you like to come and look at the flowers?'

Caroline and Geoff walked either side of Harold as he walked around the hearse. Pamela, with Rob and her grandma just behind. 'They're beautiful,' Harold remarked, looking at the largely, white display that bedecked the coffin. 'She'd have absolutely loved them.'

Dorothy observed as the loaded cars were led by a walking undertaker down the street. She watched as neighbours came out to make the sign of the cross or bow their heads in respect as they passed. At the church, Dorothy breathed in the scent of age and wax and incense, their smoky, spicy and musty aroma's proffering perfect companions to prayer and peace. She watched as the rows and rows of dark oak pews, lovingly waxed and polished by the church custodians, began to fill. She observed the red leather hassocks cracked and hued with the hundreds of knees knelt upon them in worship.

She flitted in and out of the pews looking at all the people who had taken time out of their day to attend. 'How absolutely lovely of them,' she said to Calla, 'I never expected that all these people would turn up.' She skittered in and out of their auras and glows, feeling how her death had affected them, how they were sympathising with Harold and her mam and the girls. She laughed when she entwined with an unkempt man wondering how she had known him in life, only to discover that she was unknown to him, and he was chancing his luck for a couple of butties at a free wake.

She stopped in front of every single soul in the church and asked, 'Can you see me? Can you feel me here?' but no one did, not even her mam or Harold or the priest.

She lingered in front of the marble altar and exclaimed to Calla how there were similarities between the earthly structures and the heavenly ones. 'It's beautiful isn't it and just look at that magnificent crucifix.' She joined in with the priest swaying and swirling herself around as he sang with a tenor gusto the post communion hymn 'I watch the sunrise.' She loved that hymn, so uplifting and beautiful words too. How thoughtful that they had remembered that she enjoyed it.

Pamela, dressed in an ankle length black dress and pointed toed stiletto's, nervously made her way up to the pulpit to read the eulogy that Caroline and Harold had prepared. Dorothy saw her cheeks and neck were stained with a deep red blush and her hands were shaking with anxiety. 'Oh sweetheart, come here.' She grazed Pamela's glow and entwined lovingly with her. She watched Harold and her mam as they tenderly supported each other in their grief, her mam rooting through her handbag to supply him with another clean and pressed handkerchief and retrieving the sodden one from him to push back into her bag.

Dorothy followed her coffin down the aisle and out of the church and into the sunshine and watched as friends and family offered their sympathies to each other. As they all began to exit the church car park, Dorothy placed herself at Leigh Cemetery above her own dug out grave. She was having a conversation with Calla.

'A eulogy that lasted exactly six minutes. That was a quick run-down for fifty-nine-years of life.' Calla laughed with her, 'Beautifully read though didn't you think?' Dorothy nodded along, 'Yes, I'm so proud of her. Proud of them all actually.'

They both watched as the priest said his final words and blessings and the coffin was lowered slowly into the ground. Harold, Pamela and Caroline gently tossed a pink rose on top. 'Bye mum, I'll miss you,' said Pamela as she tightly clutched Caroline's hand. 'Bye mum, love you.' Harold couldn't speak at all.

They surveyed the sad scene, 'It's the strangest thing, they think that's me in that box and that I'm gone forever. It's a bloody cruel lesson, isn't it? When I go back, I'm going to make sure that people know that it isn't final. I'm going to try to help people deal with their grief.' Calla nodded in agreement, 'It would be lovely Dorothy, but good luck with that.'

EMILY

About Me

I can't seem to concentrate and write at all today. I'm a carer at the local residential home 'The Sages.' I love it but it's been a tough shift today. Marnie rang in sick which left us short staffed and there's loads of folk who need two staff to assist them with their care. I've tried my best, but I hated it today when I couldn't give folk that extra special bit of care. You know, like finding time to put a bit of lippy on Doreen or trimming Bernards fingernails. 'Aw, it doesn't matter cock,' said Bernard when I asked if I could do them in the morning instead. The residents all know that I'll normally find time for the little bits and bobs that make life nicer for them. That it's the little things that you do which make someone feel special and cared for. It was just go, go, go from the moment I set my bike down in the foyer at 7am, to finishing my shift at 3pm and then cycling home through the school traffic, getting home and taking Hettie for her walk.

When I finally settled down on my bed to write,

I realised that I'd been preoccupied throughout the day with the fact that you don't know much about me so far. That's what was eating away at my concentration, I think. So today, on our walk, I was thinking about how I could tell you more about me.

It's so easy to write about Dorothy because it's almost as if the words are coming out pre-written, but me, well, that's another matter entirely. And I think you need to know about me you see, because I'm all mixed up with Dorothy, aren't I? Well, I am Dorothy, aren't I? It's the strangest thing how I have to keep referring to her as Dorothy, because that isn't her name just as Emily isn't mine. I can't even begin to think how to spell our other name, our real name, our only name. I've thought and thought about it, but it isn't really a name, or a word for that matter. I can see it and hear it in my head, and I can actually feel it too, but it's more of a light, a musical note, a vibration. Imagine if you whistled out loud, then tried to write down and spell that whistle. She'll just have to stay as Dorothy.

So, about me then. I left home much to mum and dad's chagrin, when I was eighteen. I desperately craved some freedom. I'd behaved for a lot of years like I was on camera, due to my knowledge of the afterlife, but as I was maturing I'd found it to be fake and too sickly sweet to live that way and I wanted to be a more authentic me.

I understood more than anyone else, that life experience equals soul experience. I vowed to try to always be honest and truthful with myself and to seek out things and experiences that I really wanted to do. So, having literally just left school, I determined that I needed my freedom from my parents. I was also absolutely desperate to set up a little home with Jake. Jake, the love of my life, (at least up until this far), wholly unsuited to me and who promptly abandoned me in under a year. Handsome Jake. All six feet two inches of him, towering over me by a massive nine inches. Resplendent in his joinery clothes and rigger boots. Masculine with his beard stubble, circular saw, nail gun and hammer drill. He made my heart soar. 'Emily, I love you, you're so different from all the other girls, with their trout pouts and spider lashes,' he told me after three and a half weeks. 'I love your crazy clothes and the way you are just you. No airs and graces, no pretence, no games.'

I'd had other boyfriends and they lasted perhaps a month or two maybe, but Jake I was absolutely wild about. He was made more than welcome at home, and I was welcome at his. Both sets of parents were at a loss when we decided to rent our own place because they just couldn't see what we'd gain from it other than bills and debt. Mum and dad had wanted me to go to university, but I had zero interest. Why would I go to university when I didn't even know what I wanted to do with my life? I simply wanted to go to sleep with Jake, to wake up with Jake, to come home to Jake and eat with Jake and he was exactly the same. So, that's when I got my job as a care assistant at The Sages, and we started to look for a rental property. Jake at twenty years old, me at eighteen when you think you're grown and know everything. We figured that our joint wages would be ample to support us and indeed they should have been.

I suppose if Jake hadn't wanted all the latest gaming gear, the designer trainers, the mates round every weekend, the multiple takeaways, the expensive TV packages, the latest mobile phone and all the other trappings of luxury, then it might have worked. But after a wonderful, heady six months, we became jaded. I didn't want to stop him getting all the things that he desired, but it was untenable financially. 'Emily, stop trying to tell me what I can and can't do with my own money,' he'd say. And I didn't want to spend my days pushing our bank statement and bills under his nose when he was ordering some new thing or something to eat or organising a night out. A fundamental breakdown I suppose you'd call it in the end. So, one day I arrived home from work to a Dear John letter. He'd chose to let go. He said he was sorry to leave me and that I could keep all the stuff we'd bought together and that he'd gone back home. Back home he'd written. That hurt my heart.

This was his home. Our home.

So, I stayed, lonely and bruised, begging the never listening Calla to send him back home to me but she wasn't listening. Time passed and my heartache healed, it's been a few years now and I'm perfectly happy. Our flat became my flat. It's a poky little thing and I love it. I wonder how we could have fitted two people in here in the first place.

It's filled with mismatched furnishings, everything perfectly practical and mostly purchased from the local charity shops or car boot sales. I have a multi coloured, crocheted bed spread which clashes with absolutely everything, but when I look at the detail of it, the work that went into making it, it makes me love it. Someone sat for hours and hours carefully crafting it, and so I appreciate it accordingly.

None of my crockery matches because it doesn't need to does it? And I remember exactly where and when I bought each piece, I'd bought them because they were lovely or characterful and I knew I'd enjoy eating or drinking from them. That gave me so much more enjoyment than if I'd just purchased a matching set from a supermarket. All my glassware is courtesy of the local pub.

The mirror over the fire is so old and heavy that it looks like it would take the wall with it should it fall down, but I love that too with its old, tarnished reflection and I wonder how many other people have stared into its depths.

My hair is kept short and scruffy, so I have no need for a hairdryer or any of the trappings required to keep luscious hair and my only makeup is a slash of red lipstick that I reserve for a night out. I have an old chest of drawers in the living room filled with tee-shirts, socks and underwear, because it won't fit in this room. There's no room for a wardrobe for stuff that needs hanging up, so all my clothes are hung on a rail. Jess says they're not clothes anyway, they're jumble, someone else's cast offs, crap. I like it this way. Why would I need to buy new stuff when other people's old stuff is still like new. As long as I'm clean and warm who cares? The only clothes I ever iron are my work uniforms, so they're ironed on the kitchen worktop because there's nowhere to store an ironing board. What more could a girl want? Seriously? I really don't need stuff to make my life unnecessarily complicated. I have everything I need.

Mum and dad still ask me to come home every day. 'Your room is still yours Emily, it doesn't make sense that you're throwing good money away on rent when you could still be here with us. You could be saving for a deposit and buy your own place. Grace is at university more than home now, so you'd have your own space.' 'No thanks,' I always reply. 'But it's not safe where you are Emily, you've got a drunk living underneath you,' mum sometimes wails with exasperation, 'And there's probably druggies in the same block.' 'Mum I'm absolutely fine, I promise I'll come home if I'm ever worried about anything, but you know I love my flat.' I'd certainly never mention to her that 'the drunk,' has a key to my flat because he kindly lets Hettie out for a toilet break when I'm at work. He's the gentlest, kindest, sweetest man and I trust him implicitly. He's more likely to leave me something than take anything.

So here I am, still single, sat on my made for two bed with my pillows fluffed up behind me, with my laptop on a cushion and Hettie upside down, legs akimbo, tongue lolling and eyes closed. I'm increasingly relieved to be getting Dorothy's life out on paper and I can hear the words thundering around inside my head waiting to be heard. So, I'll start the next chapter now while I wait for Jess who has just text to say she's on her way with pizza and wine.

DOROTHY

The Library

Calla watched over Dorothy with a huge sense of pride and love, like a mother hen watching her excited chick as Dorothy's spirit began to open and unfold before her. She knew that it all felt like a new experience for Dorothy even though she'd been through it hundreds of times already. This was her true home and she just needed to disconnect totally from what she'd she thought she was. Calla simply observed her enjoyment and quietly supported her in the background. She'd guide her into the library for her reorientation when Dorothy felt ready, when she'd started to question a little more about where and what she was.

With all time constructs dissipated, Dorothy felt that she must be in a dozen places all at once, though it wasn't confusing at all. It all made perfect sense. She could constantly and completely be around Harold or the girls, or her friends, or Calla, her relatives from her earthly life or her spirit life, or maybe even following her body over the travelling ambulance. As instantaneously a thought appeared and she could be back on the heavenly pathway headed toward the gate, sinking into the exquisite blackness, or at the scene of her death. All of that at the same time and yet all the while, absorbing every detail in its minutia, whilst in this harmonious, pure state and yet still be aware that there was far, far more to come. She relished every detail, every encounter, every glorious feeling that flooded through her.

'Calla, how am I here? What am I? What are we?' Calla chuckled softly, 'Come on, let's get you reorientated.' In an instant, both were stood on the outside of the most magnificent, towering building that Dorothy had ever seen.

The floor beneath them was made of lustrous, compressed shingles which shone and glistened and tinkled lightly with a harmony of angelic sounds. They moved over and across it, making their way forward toward the building. Dorothy looked at its height. It absolutely dominated the skyline above with its sheer vastness. She noted that it was not unlike the earthly structures she had seen in books and magazines and on the television in life. 'Bloody Hell,' she uttered in sheer awe, then shyly glanced at Calla to see if she'd been heard. 'Calla, if I could turn beetroot red now, I would, fancy cursing in heaven.' Calla laughed loudly, 'Dorothy, you've definitely come out with worse before now.'

There were magnificent, lead edged stained-glass windows. Some were huge expanses which reflected the most stunning, elaborate designs of heavenly bodies. Others were tiny mosaics, all glittering and joined together to form a singular masterpiece.

A gigantic, heavy looking old wooden sign, floated impossibly at the front and centre of it. 'The Library.'

'The library?' she asked Calla, 'You've brought me to a library to reorientate myself?' Calla tinkled with laughter. 'It's the only building here Dorothy. It's infinite, it contains everything ever. It's a library of knowledge and teaching, it's a restaurant, a dance hall, a beach, it's where you learn to be a guide, an ocean, a galaxy, it's simply everything, you'll see.' They moved forward and stepped through its monolithic, exquisitely decorated archway and went inside.

All her life when she'd imagined heaven, it had been a fluffy place. All pretty pastel colours and singing birds flying over white, squishy, perfectly shaped clouds which would be gently scudding by. It would be filled with the sounds of children's laughter and angels with feathered wings wearing haloes would be in a choir singing in perfect harmony. Puppies and kittens would be playing on lush green grass. A chocolate box heaven.

Not for one second had she ever expected grand, solid structures. This was a massive, commanding building from the outside and the inside was no different. Dorothy looked around. She found herself in a vast room. She could see many marble columns supporting its structure. Huge, wide things with exquisite, intricate detail of angels perfectly crafted into the marble. Interlocking grains of pure white stone, mottled with flecks of gold and smooth and cool to touch, the brilliant lights reflecting from its every surface. The expert craftsmanship must have taken thousands and thousands of years noted Dorothy as she saw that every piece of marble was covered with these carvings of absolute, sculpted, perfection. Tiny cherubs, flowers, leaves, trees and vines all with striking detail and perfectly interwoven between the angels. The whole thing was of breathtaking beauty.

Calla watched as Dorothy slowly began to recognise the place. 'I know this, I know this, I know this,' she yelled excitedly and whirled herself around and around with joy and Calla whirled with her in delight.

The room was a light filled, majestic space which somehow still felt cosy and homely, as though she were in her own front room. It seemed full of nothingness and yet this nothingness felt like fullness, like it completed her. She was constantly filled to the brim with a sense of love and well-being. The huge room seemed to be completely empty of any furnishings at all other than these strangely enticing, glowing door like apparatus, which hung and hovered everywhere in their thousands or maybe millions. She couldn't see an end to them. And souls, so many souls, all whizzing around, flitting in and out of them, laughing and twirling and singing.

She looked into one and saw another infinite room beyond, it was welcoming her, excited for her to enter. She peeped in further. There were walls and walls of books. Leather bound volumes of books from floor to ceiling. A central living book which held records of everyone's human incarnations, it was actually alive, precious beyond imagination, a web of vibrant energy woven within its volumes. Gilded books with their waxed pages lay waiting on vast shelves, and scrolls bursting with knowledge and age written at the very beginning of time awaited a reader. Dorothy was desperate to enter.

There were many other spirits gliding in, lights fizzing and popping. Loud squeals of laughter could be heard. 'Calla, can I go in?' she asked in awe. 'Of course you can Dorothy,' replied Calla, 'The choice is always yours, but your usual preference is to complete your review first.' Dorothy looked into a couple of the rooms, each looked absolutely fantastical, and she was bursting to investigate each one. They were all entirely different and she could see the other spirits coming and going filled with laughter and delight. Homeliness, warmth, love, complete acceptance and joy. She whirled herself around in the wonderment of it all. She was properly home.

Dorothy knew what she needed to do next. The life review. She had no particular feelings around it as yet, but she knew it was the hardest task that she would have to bear. She was somehow aware that she had dreaded going into the life review room for every life that she had lived and yet, she knew also that at the end, once it had been relived, it would result in the most joyous outcomes for lots of spirits. And for her own soul, a majestic growth of lights and lightness of being would be bestowed on her. It was beyond exciting.

EMILY

Beth

One evening, a couple of weeks back, I was sat in front of the television, flicking idly through the channels, knowing that I wasn't in the mood for anything that it could offer. I was sipping slowly on my second glass of wine trying to eke it out, knowing I was on the late shift the day after and didn't want to feel hungover. Hettie was beside me sat on a cushion with one paw cutely placed on my knee. I was completely and utterly miserable. I began to absent-mindedly stroke her head and neck. She stood herself up, stretched interminably, yawned in my face and then promptly jumped down from the settee and wandered off to her mat in the corner of the room. Good God, even she didn't want me near her.

I checked my phone to see if Jake had decided that even after all these year's he was still in love with me and had rung, or sent a message perhaps, or put a coded 'I still love you' message on Facebook, but no, nothing. I decided there and then, that if I was that desperately lonely that I was looking for love messages from a man who had left me years earlier, that I would have to move back in with mum and dad again. This was just too lonely. Jess was having an early night because she had lectures in the morning and I knew Grace was out in Leigh with her friends and anyway, that was too far away, and I couldn't really afford a taxi. Then, my phone started to ring. I jumped out of my skin. It was Beth, Bitchy Beth! Beth belonged to my group of loose friends, you know, not the ones you'd ring if you were in trouble or needed a heart to heart, but great to have a night out with or a few drinks down at the pub. I can't even remember how she got to know us all. Perhaps she'd just waded in one night at a rowdy night out and got a few numbers. Anyway, she'd been part of us for around twelve months I suppose and we'd all got to know her quite well.

'Hi Emily,' she slurred, already half cut, 'I was wondering if you fancied coming down the club for a couple?' I looked at my almost drained wine glass, decided I hadn't had nearly enough and stood up as I answered her, 'I'm on my way.'

I stroked Hettie and told her I wouldn't be long. I locked the front door and headed down the stairwell. I could see the flickering lights from Barry's television, so I knocked on. Barry appeared at his window, 'Alright cock?' he mouthed questioningly. 'I'm just going down to the club for a few drinks Barry, would you listen out for Hettie in case she needs to go outside please?' He nodded, 'Course I will cock, don't worry about him one bit.'

As I walked, I found my head conversing with itself. 'I bet no one else wanted to go out with her. I bet she's rang everyone and I'm her last call. I bet she has no money and she'll need a loan for beers.' I'm not really the type to think so badly of anyone, but Beth seemed to just bring it out in me. She is forever criticising someone. 'Look at the state of her hair, or fancy coming out wearing that.' If there is ever a fall out between people, she's in the midst of it all, passing comment and having her say. 'I'm entitled to my opinion,' she'll say indignant that I've told her to keep out of it and mind her own business. 'Beth, we all have our own opinions, but sometimes we need to keep them to ourselves unless we're asked for them,' I'd say, annoyed that she'd hurt someone again. She's always the one who has to join in a debate and present the negatives of any given situation. The one who always posts pictures of badly parked cars on the local Facebook group or put comments on how poorly the government are performing, or how the NHS is rubbish on Instagram. She's a negative Nellie.

I arrived at the club and sent her a quick text to ask if she was there yet. 'I'm two minutes away, get the beers in,' came the text back. 'Hmm, that's handy,' I typed back but deleted it.

I scanned for seats the moment I got in. Phew,

loads of them. 'Two halves of lager please,' I called out to Jim behind the bar as I walked over. 'Coming up. Jess not with you tonight?' 'Nope, she has lectures tomorrow so I'm meeting up with Beth for a few,' I answered. 'Can't think which one's Beth,' he replied, then as he glanced her entering the club, 'Ahhh, bitchy Beth. Why didn't you say?'

'Oye you, I heard that,' Beth laughed good naturedly. She was well aware of her nickname and seemingly cared not one jot. 'Bloody hell, on halves, are we?' she moaned when she saw our glasses. 'I can't get drunk Beth, I'm working the late shift tomorrow and I've already had half a bottle of wine. Go and get yourself another if you want a pint.' Instead, she pulled a purple vape from her pocket and puffed deeply on it, before blowing a cloud of sweet-smelling vapour into the air and already walking away. She could be a prickly one when she wanted to be. 'We sitting here then?' she motioned to a table under a window with a comfy back bench. 'Yep, that's fine,' I replied picking up our drinks and following on behind her.

I set the drinks on top of the cardboard coasters. 'Look at the state of her,' she nodded towards a woman at the bar, 'I swear she's put two stone on since last week and why on earth would you wear those tight jeans with all that muffin top hanging out? It's going to put me off my beer.' She was off already and we'd barely sat down. I glanced over to where she'd seen the offending woman. 'Beth, she looks nice,' I retorted, 'she's just come out for a drink with her mates, she really won't give a damn what you think about her. 'No harm done then eh?' she took a glug of her lager. 'I'm already pissed myself, I'm working tomorrow too, so just two or three for me too.' She picked up a coaster absent mindedly and began shredding it into tiny pieces. 'Josh dumped me,' she announced. 'Oh no I'm so sorry Beth,' I began to console her. 'I'm absolutely fine with it,' she interjected before I got the chance to even raise my arm to cuddle her, 'I was going to end it anyway. He's so boring and he can be nasty too you know?' She glanced sideways at me awaiting my response. 'Well, you look upset nonetheless. And it's as well it's all over if he was nasty to you Beth. Better off without him in that case.' She burst into tears. 'To be fair Emily, I'm gutted. I love the bones of him. And he isn't nasty, not really. He says he can't cope with me being such a bitch about everyone, he said I'm the only one who's a bitch.' She wiped her eyes with the sleeve of her jumper just as a new wave of tears began. 'He says he's sick and tired of always having to defend me when I've behaved indefensibly. He knows I've had a tough upbringing, always having to look out for myself and never being able to trust anyone, but he says it's no excuse and I always go too far.' She looked at me for confirmation that he was wrong, and I had to look down, I couldn't lie to her. It wouldn't help her, would it? 'He's right Emily, I know he is,' she offered before I got a chance to speak. She began dabbing under her eyes to prevent any further mascara run, 'but I can't change. I don't know how to. I'm not sure I want to because I make people laugh, don't I?' I smiled at her, 'You certainly do Beth, you're a real quick wit, but it can hurt when your jokes are a bit cruel.'

'I suppose I pretend that I don't care what people think of me, that I don't care if they hate me, because they can't possibly hate me as much as I hate myself.' She rubbed her eyes with her sleeves again, sniffed loudly and stood up. 'But it's the opposite really, I flinch inside when I have to face people after I've been taking the piss out of them.'

'Anyway, my round,' she offered to my surprise as she began rummaging around in her back pocket for her card. She plonked her phone down on the table and as the screen lit up, I couldn't help but cringe inwardly. She's the only person I know who has a picture of herself on her home screen. Not her with a dog, or a cute baby. No. Just her, pouting into the camera and filtered so much that it barely resembled her at all. I really do try my hardest not to think critically of folk, but sometimes the thoughts just invade and dwell before I can usher them out, like nasty little demons flitting in at any possible opportunity and wreaking havoc with my mental health.

I had seen a new vulnerability in her this evening though. A sharp contrast to the persona she had accidentally created, the inflammatory bitch. I had probably never cared enough to look too closely before. I tended to keep my distance from people like Beth. Even Jess tended not to seek her out, but she is good fun, and she can be hilarious. She can have you doubled over with belly laughs repeatedly, all night long with witty observations and tales. But if she decides to turn her focus onto someone. Well, it's just no longer funny.

I watched as she made her way back from the bar. So very attractive to look at, all tumbling blonde curls and tiny waist, but her personality was so vain, and she was so critical of everyone, it made her appear unattractive. I felt sorry for her and wondered more about the details of what could had happened in her life to make her this way. I wouldn't probe though, but I would try to help. If she was being disingenuous, then I'd cut my cloth. But something told me she'd really like to change.

'Emily, I know I act mean. I know it,' she continued in the same vein as she plonked our two pints on the table. 'I don't always know why though. At night I can't sleep because I'm running through a constant commentary on everything nasty that I did and said since I was a kid. I think I'm just naturally mean. I watch you and Jess all the time and you never bitch about folk.' I laughed out loud, 'We do actually Beth, we bitch about you being a bitch.' We both laughed loudly, alcohol masking my usual reserved demeanour, and we both completely missed the craning necks looking over at us to see what the racket was. 'Well why do you do it then if it keeps you up at night? Why punish yourself? What on earth do you get out of it?' I asked puzzled. 'Laughs mainly,' she said, honestly, 'but then I feel bad. And sometimes, I'll admit, it's to get back at someone who's slighted me in some way. But then, once I've said it, or done it, a great sort of emptiness sets itself in and I'm miserable.' I took a sidelong look at her, 'Well just stop being mean then. Everyone will benefit and you'll sleep, job done.'

'Well, I'll try then but I'm not holding out much hope,' she ventured, in the manner of one who has already decided that the earth is flat.

We whiled away a couple of hours and another couple of pints putting the world to rights. I glanced at my phone, 22:45pm and started to head to the bar to get a last round in before they called last orders. I looked down at her, 'Beth, if you really want to stop all this internal, emotional, churn that's actually wrecking your life, then you just need to be kinder to people.' Somehow inside, I reasoned she was reaching out for help. 'I'm trying Emily,' she said, definitely the worse for wear now, 'I'm actually trying now, at this very moment,' she sighed heavily, 'I know you've not been yourself recently, everyone is saying as much.'

I sat back down again, 'Really? What exactly have people been saying? I'm fine, just busy with a little project that's keeping me in at the moment.' 'No one is saying anything bad Emily, just that you look a bit fed up, or deep in thought when they see you, so I thought, well I thought I'd see if you were okay.' She flipped her palms upwards as if questioning. 'I knew that Jess had lectures tomorrow. And I knew you'd be sitting all alone in that dingy flat. So, I meant to ring you all evening, but I couldn't pluck up the courage until I'd had a couple of drinks because I thought you'd say no. And anyway, I try to keep my mean bitch persona alive for you because I'm a bit jealous about how you're always happy, despite the fact that you live in a God forsaken flat and you dress like shit.' She laughed good naturedly.

'Beth, I'm not going to trade my identity and live somewhere else just because other people don't like it. Neither am I going to dress the way other people want me to dress. It's just not important to me. It wouldn't be authentic,' I defended myself though I'm not sure why, she was right of course, I am the epitome of dorkiness, 'I have no intention of trying to keep up with the Joneses. I wouldn't be me being me. And unlike you, I actually quite like myself and I manage to sleep soundly too. Maybe you could take a leaf from my book?' It was all true, I've never cared about being cool or chic. 'But Beth, thank you, you did do a really kind thing tonight. I was stuck at home feeling miserable, so I'm grateful to you.'

Beth looked pensive, or drunk, I couldn't determine which. 'Okay, I'm going to start properly tomorrow, today was just the start. I'm going to be nice Beth. Tell me what to do please.'

I laughed. 'Okay, we'll start you off with just a couple of things to set you off into being nice Beth. When you feel that you are just about to quip out a mean comment, no matter how funny it may seem, change it into a complement. Don't give out fake complements though, that would be nauseating. Just try it.' I really didn't want to be preachy, but alcohol was oiling my brakes. 'You reap what you sow Beth, karma is very real. If you want to be miserable all your life, then just carry on the way you were doing. If you fancy being happier, then be kinder. Simple really. And on Facebook and X and the like, only say good stuff. If you feel like bitching, scroll past. You'll have less to stress about at night, I promise.'

'I really did want to help you tonight, Emily,' she slurred at me 'But typical of you, you've helped me. I'm grateful, really. I can't remember anyone really listening before.' I hugged her, 'Don't be daft Beth, you were right, I was lonely and miserable until you rang. So thanks, truly, even though I might not thank you tomorrow when I'm hungover.'

I stood up and held out my hand for her to grab

on to, 'Come on, let's get going, we've missed last orders now anyway.' As we made our way out, we passed the woman who Beth had been criticising earlier. Beth stopped right in front of her. My eyes grew wide with trepidation, and I tried to pull her along with me towards the door. Then she opened her mouth and slurred, 'Your hair looks lovely.' The woman's hands shot to her head, touching her hair. 'Really?' she said, smiling all over her face. Then slurred back, 'Thank you so much for saying that, you've really made my day. I was so unsure about coming out tonight, I'm not the most confident person.' She leant in for a quick hug and I watched Beth as she grinned from ear to ear. 'I'm sure that felt better than giving a snarky comment eh Beth? Think about that tonight when your brain is on fire.' Then we staggered off home, holding each other up for support before hugging and parting ways on Astley Street. Right there in the centre of that hug, was where our friendship began.

I climbed up the stairwell, hanging on to the rails for balance, located my key from my back pocket and let myself in. Hettie didn't come to greet me as she usually did. She wouldn't though, I realised once I'd set foot in the living room, because she was fast asleep on top of a sleeping Barry on my couch. I burst out laughing at the sight of them and they shot up as one. Hettie started to dive her welcome all over me, and Barry, startled by my unexpected appearance started apologising, 'I'm sorry cock, I didn't mean to fall asleep, he was lonely you see, so I let him out for a wee and then I stayed a little while just to keep him company.' I quickly put him at ease, 'Barry it's absolutely fine, really, I'm glad you stayed to keep her company, I'm really grateful.' And I was. He started to pick up his empty cans, hurriedly shoving them into his carrier bag as he began to make his way to the door. 'I forget he's a she because you have him, I mean her, in a blue collar,' he said. 'Anyway, I'm really sorry I fell asleep, I'm awful embarrassed.' He was rubbing his head sleepily. 'Aw Barry, honestly it's fine,' I slurred, 'I'm just really glad you stayed with her, please don't fret about it.' I leaned in tipsily and gave him a big tight hug. 'Thanks for that cock. No one's hugged me for years, I'm glad I fell asleep on your couch now,' he laughed and made his way down the stairwell shouting up, 'First time I've seen you drunker than me Emily.' Bless him. A good heart in a life gone wrong.

I brushed my teeth, filled a pint glass with water, launched all my clothes on the floor and fell into an immediate drink induced sleep.

When I arrived home from work the following evening after my late shift, there was a note on my kitchen table. Emily, I let HER out for a wee and bought her a present. There, in a brown paper bag, was a lovely, sparkly pink collar. Salt of the earth that man.

DOROTHY

Life Review

Dorothy looked around the vastness of the library and found her focus was falling onto a shimmer of light that was beckoning her. It was completely different than the other glowing doors and yet she hadn't noticed it previously. As immediately as she'd thought it, it seemed to Dorothy, that she was stood at the front of it. A huge old wooden door, completely incongruous with the rest of its surroundings, it's old and gnarled and similar to the huge gates along the pathway. It was adorned with heavy old metalwork and had beautiful thick green vines trailing from it. It pulsed with a warm glow that welcomed her.

She knew that this was the life review room, she hesitated slightly and looked to Calla for support. 'Only when you're ready' she could sense Dorothy's uncertainty.' They entered together.

There were many other spirits and lights around and Dorothy recognised lots of them. All had chosen to attend to witness her life review. Some were here to learn, some were much higher entities wanting to experience the intricacies of another life lived, many were just wanting to experience the depths of Dorothy's life for themselves. They were all welcome. She knew they were not here to judge, they were not able to judge, that was not their intention. They were there to see, to feel, to absorb each moment of her life and grow from the experience. They were there to feel as Dorothy had felt in every moment, to know the entire truth around her choices and pathways. To know her every emotion and response, to truly feel her.

She knew that her experience in here would observe each and every moment of her life as Dorothy, each nuance, every single iota of all of it would be exposed. She would be naked, laid bare, no place to hide and she knew that she would be her own judge. The only judge. The harshest judge. She knew that she would desperately wish she could halt the whole proceeding many times and go back to her life just to change things. Radically change things.

The room was unlike any that she had ever encountered in life. Infinite it seemed, but Dorothy had the feeling that this one did seem to have walls and ceilings. There was a vast, plain white marble table running straight down what Dorothy perceived was its centre and all the hundreds of spirits were gathered excitedly around it, eager to live her experience. Calla explained to Dorothy, that a life review would take every soul a differing amount of time. 'If you were to look on it in earthly times,' 'she advised, 'it will take your whole lifetime, plus any impact you have had on any other person and then a review of the changes you caused, reflected in that life.' Dorothy listened carefully.

'So, every misdeed and every kind deed I ever did and the feelings that they caused, then the impact on others around them will all be examined?' asked an incredulous Dorothy. 'Bloody hell I'll be in there forever.'

Calla giggled and Dorothy watched her lights sparkle. 'Well in earth years you are probably looking at around five hundred give or take a decade. But it's over in the blink of an eye here.'

Dorothy found herself thinking about those who had murdered people. People doing their misdeeds in secret, thinking no one was watching. No one watching! The whole universe is watching! She let herself run away with her thoughts. 'So, if I had deliberately killed someone, then I'd see the suffering that I'd put them through?' Calla's lights muted somewhat, and Dorothy realised that this was Calla experiencing empathy. 'Yes, and you'd feel it too, as would all the watchers. Plus, the pain of grief for anyone who had known the victim, and anyone who read or heard about it, any of the ripples of pain, upset and distress that it caused. Any children that their victim might have had due in their future, then their children and their children not having a life chance,' she watched Dorothy's aura dulling slightly as she continued. 'If anyone were to see it on television and felt impacted by it, in fact absolutely anyone feeling anything about it at all would be examined in the life review.' Dorothy had certainly done things she wasn't proud of, but she'd never even killed a spider. 'It's what you could call hell Dorothy, though there's no such actual place, it doesn't exist. People make their own hell themselves when they are in their life review and can't find a way out.' She watched as Dorothy's glow subdued a little with sympathy, 'They are forgiven, but they can't find ways to forgive themselves and be rid of the guilt. They become trapped in a world of pain, reliving every element over and over and over. We can't help them. Even the watchers have to pull out, some souls have been trapped in there helpless since they entered.' She shimmied through Dorothy's lights to infuse them with her own, she could see that the conversation was causing her to feel deeply for these lost souls. 'They thought as humans that they had escaped justice, that they had been able to walk through life untrammelled amongst others, but every action has a reaction Dorothy.' Dorothy felt a compassion she'd have never once felt for a murderer in her earthly life. 'What a horrible eternity to trap yourself in.'

Calla began to discuss what would happen

during the life review. 'When you start your review Dorothy, you'll see billions and billions of orbs. Each one is attached to a moment of a life event. It could be as simple as a smile you gave someone when they were in need, or a mean comment you passed. Each orb is like a huge bubble to burst, holding just a moment, a breath. You need to choose just five positive and five negative orbs.' Dorothy nodded along while trying to visualise what on earth Calla was talking about. 'They release something called Lumai at the end. These are beautiful things Dorothy, true visual blessings, you'll see. We can fix a few things with them once your review is finished. Look for small insignificant events like a white lie or an iota of a moment of love if you like, it really doesn't matter, just choose the ones that move you in some way and effect your heart, good and bad.'

Dorothy wondered how the hell she could choose just ten orbs from billions.

She began to rise above the watchers so that she was able to settle and absorb into their beings and find out more of why they had chosen to attend. Many of the soul's lights were dense in nature and she found that these hadn't yet chosen to brave living a life themselves. Others had tried but struggled too badly with the experience and couldn't face trying again for a while. Some had lived hundreds of lives and simply wished to experience hers and Dorothy found herself languishing in those who's sweet, light, bright auras told her that they'd lived thousands.

The love and acceptance that poured from each of these souls filled her with confidence and pride. Calla had made her aware that she had previously attended many reviews of other soul's lives and that it was always a tough experience for each individual presenting themselves.

As she visited each spirit in turn, they were congratulating her, proud for her that she had lived a life and was about to share. They all knew how very difficult it was to live a life.

Each of them knew that being present in this room, was a valuable lesson for their growth, as though they had set themselves a semester of study to attend that they knew would be extremely difficult. They were aware that they would feel every emotion that Dorothy had ever felt during her lifetime. That this was the only room in this realm where negative thoughts and feelings existed, where physical pain could and would be felt.

They knew that they would feel the real anguish of sadness, jealousy, hate, pain and confusion fear and disgust exactly as Dorothy had experienced it. All the love, excitement, joys, admiration, empathy, adoration that she'd ever experienced would be theirs too.

They knew that they would feel it all in its entirety as they travelled through this life with her, every step of the way, every heartbeat, every breath. They would feel the joys and the anguish of the people whose lives she had touched. Understand why she had made certain choices and decisions. They wouldn't judge as to what they thought she should or shouldn't have done, they'd simply absorb it and support her. They understood earthly life with its subdued senses and the sense of disconnection, the lost-ness, the bewilderment of being completely and utterly alone. They all understood and acknowledged the veils and blinkers that you were bound with in the earthly realm.

They each empathised with the blind grasping of prayers to a God that they weren't really sure was there or not. They understood the complexities of trying to navigate through a life with no rationale as to its meaning with no sense as to what their lives truly represent.

The younger less experienced souls were being mentored by guides in what to expect and were being prepared for the physical sensations that they hadn't yet experienced. There was a buzz of excitement and exhilaration in the air as everyone prepared themselves and became eager to start.

A sudden and expectant hush fell. A magnificent waterfall of white pure light, a vast powerful, chasm of energy, began to pour itself into the room. The luminescent, fluid like energy, made up of billions of lights and colours began to settle itself above everyone, filling those present with awe. Dorothy felt herself gravitate towards it, gently pulled upwards, drawn into its beauty and sentient welcoming love. She felt the colours and the energy flow into her as she flowed into its vastness, and they became as one.

She looked down at all the watchers about to view her life. She could feel their love for her, their thankfulness, their connection with her, their anticipation, longing and excitement as they all began her journey. She observed them as they began to sway gently in unison. Sparkling and shimmering as though electricity were passing between them. The feelings of love from the giant swell of spangled lights above them all, filled her and her life watchers with a sense of joy. These feelings would amplify and continue to get stronger and stronger throughout the review. Dorothy could already feel herself becoming less dense, as though she were spreading outwards and upwards, becoming a part of everyone and everything. Her lights became brighter and more sparkly. She was truly in heaven. Then, suddenly and without warning, the pulsating energy shifted its position, dropped down and encompassed everyone. They all found themselves very comfortably, in residence and well cocooned in Dorothy's life.

It astounded Dorothy when she realised that she was living her life review with the exact same intensity. She was actually there, living exactly as she had done, each minute doing and saying the exact thing that she had done and said. She recognised that her consciousness was fragmented and realised that she was re-experiencing her life from every point of view, as were the other spirits. All without judgement. As the scene began to unfold and open up around them, they all watched as her mother birthed her in front of the coal fire with Jinny the midwife whom Dorothy had known in life. She watched and felt how her father had felt whist he paced around the kitchen smoking woodbine after woodbine, lighting each one from the almost smoked one. She felt the perspective from her mother, herself and Jinny. It was weird and mind blowing, though somehow, she completely accepted and understood it. Jinny rubbed little Dorothy's head with a towel, and looked into her eyes studiously, 'She's an old soul that one,' she said, and handed her to her mother.

She felt all the other's spirits sighing with pleasure as they gazed upon the precious new life about to begin her journey.

Dorothy could even sense the state of the country, plunging headward into the Great Depression as it struggled to pay for the aftereffects of World War one and the whole community was left picking up the pieces. She could feel her mother worrying and fretting about poverty as she gazed into her scrunched up baby face. And all the while, she could see herself, looking directly into her mother's eyes feeling exactly like she had when she'd lived it, and also feeling it from this new perspective.

They all watched as baby Dorothy grew and toddled her way into a small girl. They felt her hunger pangs during and after World War two when food was scarce. They all laughed uproariously as she stole a plum from the local fruit store and sneakily ate it behind her mam's back. They savoured every moment as they followed her through her schooling, then they experienced the angst of puberty as she left childhood and matured into a young woman.

They felt and absorbed the ripples of pleasure which appeared with each loving interaction that Dorothy had performed throughout her life. She glanced towards Calla who was hovering to her left and slightly separate from the watcher group, as she gently continued to guide her. She spoke silently, 'I'd certainly have smiled more if I'd known that it would have this wonderful effect.' Calla twinkled with amusement.

They witnessed her relationship with her first serious boyfriend Will and its odious ending, and they were touched as they watched her distressed state in her mam's bathroom as her spirit father lovingly sprinkled Lumai blessings all over an unknowing and deeply troubled Dorothy when she was so desperately scared and unhappy. They became immersed in the emotions at her wedding to Harold, the births of her girls, her relationship with her mam, Helen, friends and neighbours. They felt great compassion as they saw her become the architect of her own misery when picking fights with an undeserving Harold. They saw his anguish as she treated him with indifference and neglect. They understood her misery as they watched her reaction after a casual flyaway remark unknowingly caused a woman a great deal of anguish, only healing after time had blunted the edges of it. They watched as she drifted out of friends' lives without a thought for them. They journeyed with her as she navigated life.

And their emotions soared when they watched her give her all to him and treasure him tenderly. Every nuance of her life was examined.

Dorothy chuckled as she observed herself roaring laughing with her friend as she only realised just now, how much she had thoroughly enjoyed her company.

It seemed to be over in a flash, it all moved along so quickly and yet she had lived through the whole of her life again. She'd re-listened to everyone's conversations and felt the depth of what it was that they were saying from their perspectives. She'd danced all over again, she'd relived her wedding and felt Harold's joy. She'd endured her father's death with the same magnitude of grief and felt her mams and Helen's pain too, such immense waves of grief. The watchers had continued to show compassion and grace, with no judgement as they saw her deliberately cause pain with nasty words or actions. 'You never left my side Calla, I was never left alone, not for one second, I wish I'd have known that.' Calla smiled, 'No-one is ever alone Dorothy, it's simply an illusion. You wouldn't really be your authentic self if you thought you were being watched now would you?'

Suddenly, the swirling mass lifted. Loud cheers and applause filled the room. 'We're so proud Dorothy.' 'Well done.' The younger souls were amazed at how their lights had developed and flourished. They were darting around and around squealing with delight, 'Look at my lights, look at the colours.' She felt so very proud.

EMILY

Jess

'We're definitely spending the day together Emily,' Jess was instructing me on FaceTime, 'I've booked us our train tickets now, so you have no option. You need a break and I know you're off work tomorrow.' I'm fishing through my head trying to think of things to put her off. 'I've got so much to do Jess, this flat hasn't seen a duster in two weeks, and I don't like leaving Hettie for all that time.' Her face wasn't having any of it, 'You're seriously telling me that you're going to prioritise the cleaning and the dog over spending a few hours with me. Really Emily?' She knows me too well, she knows what I'll be doing. 'Tap, tap, tap, that's what you'll be doing Emily, tell the truth. Tapping away on that laptop that I can see right there behind you.' She was poking her finger at the screen trying to point behind me. 'We haven't spent the day together in ages. Have a day off please?' She was wheedling now.

So, although I have Dorothy whirling around my head as she's just stepped out of her life review,

I decide to meet up with Jess. If I could just get her to listen to me in the first place about Dorothy, then I wouldn't need to be bloody well writing it down, would I? I would be free to spend more time with her. The only trouble these days, is that I've become anxious about forgetting the bits I haven't written down yet, even though I'm also glad and relieved that I'm forgetting. It's leaving me feeling so strange. All the stuff I've written down is completely gone from my head now, so although I'm glad of the brain peace, I'm scared that it'll all go before I've finished writing the whole thing, and for some reason, this bothers me deeply. If it's there, ready to spill its guts, just waiting for me to type it out, I want to do it there and then. I can see that I'm neglecting people though, so I make the decision to go. 'Okay Jess, I give in. Atherton Train station tomorrow then? What time?'

'Come on Hettie,' I call her to heel and clip on her lead as we set off for a walk before I meet Jess at ten. I really fancied a respectable walk today, but it'll only be three or four miles before we need to get back home. I unclip her just as we reach the woods. 'Off you go girl,' and she shoots off in pursuit of a squirrel who quickly darts up a tree. I love an autumnal walk; I take deep lungful's of the petrichor aroma given off from the recent rain hitting the earth. I'd buy it if someone could bottle it. The crunchy sounds of the leaves underfoot and the sloshing sounds of water from the puddles all completely relax me. It's all so very peaceful. The paths around here are mostly tree lined and when the sun shines, it can look magical streaming through the trees and hitting the path. 'Hettie, here girl,' I call her to me to let a horse and its rider pass me by. 'Good girl,' I pat her back and fetch her a treat from my pocket. As I turn back to the path, there in front of us, are a small herd of deer crossing our path. I grab Hettie instinctively before I realise that she's just watching them as I am, no barking, no attempt to chase them. We are both just enjoying this rare sighting. It leaves me feeling all uplifted and happy. Perhaps I did need a day away from Dorothy, I think maybe Jess knows me better than I know myself.

Back at the flat, I rub Hettie down with the towel I keep in the communal area, before tapping gently on Barry's door.

'Hiya Barry,' I say in an apologetic tone before I even ask. 'Would you let her Hettie out for a wee this afternoon if you're around? It's okay if you can't though.' Mum or dad would always pop up, but it seemed daft to trail them out when Barry was always offering. 'Course I will cock, no trouble at all, I love that dog and that dog loves me,' he bent down, and ruffled Hettie's fur and she jumped up in appreciation leaving damp paw prints on his knees. 'She can stay in my flat if you're worried about leaving her.'

'Really Barry? Aw bless you, that'd be such a

relief, thanks very much. Just shove her back in my flat if she starts being a pain or if you need to go out. I'm so grateful. I'll get changed and feed her and then I'll drop her off about nine-thirty if that's okay?' 'Aye cock, that's okay, I'll just nip out and get me paper first,' he closed his door and a waft of stale beer and cigarette ends hit my nose. Hettie would stink when I picked her up, but better that than being by herself all day.

'Looking more eclectic than usual today,' shouted Jess from the top of the station steps as I walked up to greet her. 'Am I?' I laughed looking down at what I was wearing. A multicoloured hand knitted jumper which was several sizes too big, yellow jeans, admittedly also a bit big and bright blue trainers. 'I just look like a poor student,' I shrugged my shoulders. She grabbed hold of me, and we hugged tightly. 'I look like a poor student Emily, you look like a clean vagrant with no fashion sense.' I didn't care. She didn't care either. 'Actually Emily, you look quite beautiful.' Now that was funny, especially coming from the mouth of someone who really was beautiful. 'Come on, the train's due in five minutes, let's get going.' She grabbed my hand, and we ran down the short corridor and down the steps towards the platform.

'We haven't been to Manchester for at least three months,' she said as we found two seats facing each other. 'What do you fancy doing?' I looked out of the window as we started to leave the station. 'Coffee first, then a mooch around the shops maybe? See if there's anything going on? Have you had any thoughts? I looked across at her. 'I'm not fussed, I just wanted to spend the day with you really, I'm worried about you.' I frowned at her. 'Worried? About me? Why?' As though anyone needed to worry about me.

'Emily, you've not been out for weeks, you don't answer your phone or reply to any messages until we're panicking that you're dead behind the door, that's why I'm worried.'

I shook my head in denial. 'Not true actually, I've been to work every day, I've taken Hettie out every day. I went out with Beth that evening that I told you about. I'm absolutely fine, I'm just busy.' She looked directly at me, nibbling the inside of her bottom lip. She always did that when she wanted to say something that she was unsure about. 'Busy with what exactly Emily?' she asked quietly. 'You know what,' I replied, 'you know exactly what I'm busy with, so I don't know why you're asking.' I could hear the tetchiness in my voice. She glanced out of the window and sighed loudly.

'Listen Emily, I'm not the only one who's worrying. Your mum actually rang me to see if I could persuade you to get out of your flat for a day. Even she said if you're not typing, you're brooding and lost in your own world. Are you depressed Emily?'

'Depressed? I'm so far from depressed I'm

verging on elation,' I exclaimed, perhaps too loudly, causing a man to look round slowly to check whether I did indeed look depressed or elated.

'I'm writing down all the stuff that's been whizzing around in my head ever since I was a kid Jess, no one has ever given me the chance to speak about it. Not one person. Ever.' I was shaking my head as I spoke. 'I've been shut down about it my whole, entire life.' The bloke turned around again to have a good look at me, now no doubt presuming, that I'd been an abused child. 'I'm finally freeing myself Jess. Stop fretting about me and just be glad for me instead. You've never wanted to listen to me about it and now I've finally found an outlet and you're all trying to shut that down too. I can't bloody win can I?' I threw my arms up in the air with exasperation.

'For goodness sakes Emily keep your voice down,' she soothed, eyes wide with shock at my unusual outburst. 'No one is trying to stop you from doing anything. We're all just a bit worried that's all. You just seem a bit, well, how can I say it? Consumed, possessed? Haunted even.' I looked at her innocent, sweet face, 'Jess, I've been consumed, possessed and haunted for my whole entire life. I'm finally setting myself free. I wish you could understand. I wish you'd let me talk about it.'

Jess was already shaking her head, 'I'm sorry Emily, but it totally freaks me out. Honestly,

I'd hear you say stuff when we were younger, and I'd have nightmares about it for days. I kept imagining something sat on my shoulder watching me all the time. It's not that I don't believe you, because I do. It's just too weird for me and I can't bring myself to hear about it.' I smiled at her, 'You want to try being me. Anyway, now that you've extricated me from my laptop, let's just enjoy the day, yes?'

We exited the train at Victoria Station and headed straight out into the centre. 'It's lovely to know I've got you for the full day Emily,' Jess pulled me by my arm and linked me as we'd always done from being young girls. 'Snap,' I said, I really meant it too. I'd needed this day off for a while without realising it. And most importantly, and not that I mentioned it to Jess, but I felt relieved that I was still able to quickly ferret around inside my head and see Dorothy finishing her life review and looking at her orbs. I'm a strange one, I know.

'Did you eat yet?' I ask as we pass a little artisan cafe, 'because I didn't and I'm starving.' I dragged her in before she could answer. 'Oh, yummy, look at those,' she pointed to a tray of almond sprinkled croissants dusted liberally in icing sugar. 'I'm having one of those Emily, what do you fancy?' I browsed slowly, savouring each tray with its potential delight. 'Same I think, I'll get these Jess, you paid for the train tickets. Latte?'

We settled down on a little bistro set near

the window. There were leaflets and posters sellotaped haphazardly obscuring our view of the shoppers and commuters. I peeled one off whilst taking a sneaky glance at the waitress to check that she wasn't getting mad. 'The Penny. Live bands and comedy acts all day from 12pm. Gigs to suit all. Free entry. Two for one beers.' I carefully taped it back onto the window. 'We should have a gander at that, I like a live band and if the comedians are good, well we can have a laugh too.'

We ate our breakfast laughing our heads off as the heaps of icing sugar blew off as we chatted, settling on our faces giving the impression of kids after a cornet.

We mooched in and out of the shops arm in arm yattering non-stop. We let ladies rub hand cream into our hands even though they surely knew we wouldn't be purchasing their expensive wares. We ate free samples of chocolate followed by a free sample of noodles. Jess bought some bath bombs for her mum, and I bought nothing.

Fancying a beer, we headed off to The Penny just after 2pm to see if the bands and comedy acts might entertain us for a couple of hours before we headed off home.

It was one of those places that looked like it should reek of cigarettes and weed but didn't. Sticky crusty floors and a not dissimilar bar was propped up by student types. Fairly sizeable inside with chairs and tables pushed to the outside presumably so that you could get up close and personal to the acts. I shouted my order for a couple of pints over the noise of a discordant band and turned and spotted Jess waving at me to indicate were we'd be sitting.

I walked back with the pints at the side of my head pretending to cover my ears against the racket, then instantly felt guilty in case any of the band had seen me and I started to cavort instead as though I couldn't resist a dance. Jess laughed and joined in with a bit of head banging. I sat down next to her and put our pints onto sodden coasters. It had been a really great day.

'Thanks so much Jess, I'm really glad you persuaded me to come out. A change of scenery and your company has been brilliant,' I leaned in for a hug. 'Been a great day hasn't it. I think it's just been nice spending time together, catching up. I'm glad you're okay Emily.'

The next act was introduced, a comedian named Terry Trouble. I raised my eyebrows, 'I think he sounds like a children's entertainer with that name, doesn't he?' We both laughed at his first gags, but the students didn't. And when the boo's proved louder than his voice, he looked crestfallen. After just ten minutes he put his microphone on the floor and walked off the stage dejected. 'Oh, that poor man, I thought he was quite funny,' Jess looked so sorry for him. 'He's just in the wrong joint, he's too old for this venue,' I replied, 'Unfortunately he probably won't find the courage to try again after that bruising.' She nodded her agreement, 'I pity the next act after seeing that happen, I bet he's dreading it.'

The compère picked up the microphone, the piercing screech of feedback filling the room as he tapped it. 'Ladies and gentlemen, please put your hands together for our next act, comedienne, 'Bitchy Beth.' A vague applause went around the room, but me and Jess just looked at each other. It couldn't be, could it?

As the tiny figure with her tumbling blonde curls, headed confidently to centre stage, we just sat and stared, part stunned and part panicking in case she was destroyed like her predecessor.

'Don't be giving me any of that shit that you just gave him because you'll be sorry,' was her opening line.

She then proceeded to rip apart every person in front of her. Everyone laughed their heads off. She was absolutely hilarious, whipping one liner's out of thin air. The hecklers shouted abuse out but couldn't help themselves laughing at her quick-fire retorts. She was so confidently on form. She glanced around the room looking for a fresh victim. Her eyes settled on us and for a fleeting second and I glimpsed her shock, I was worried we may unnerve her. We both promptly gave her a big thumbs up sign and she regained her composure immediately, her eyes twinkling as she reached for another joke. 'She's not even glanced our way since she realised we were here,' Jess said with a worried expression. 'It'll put her off her stride, she'll come over when she's done,' I replied, quite certain that Beth would want to wind down with us.

When her gig had finished, we stood up to join in with the thunderous applause, she really had been brilliant. People were shouting 'more, more, more,' but the compère tapped the microphone loudly again and began to introduce the next act over its screeching and whining.

Beth came running over and we stood up to give her a hug. 'You were absolutely brilliant Beth,' we said together. 'How did you find out I was gigging here?' she asked incredulous, 'I haven't told anyone.' 'We didn't know,' I answered, 'We were here for the day and saw an advert for the venue, but bloody hell Beth, that was amazing. You could really go somewhere with that act, the audience laughed non-stop.' Jess set off towards the bar, 'I'll get these in, you deserve a pint after that Beth.'

She sat herself down, still a little shaky with adrenaline, 'It's my eighth gig Emily, honestly, I'm not bragging but they always laugh like that. After I'd done my fourth, I got a fair few people asking me to book in with them. I've already got the next couple of months signed up.'

I was really pleased for her, she looked so happy. 'You were always hilarious Beth, now you've got an appreciative audience instead of a terrified one.' She looked right at me, 'The only thing that stops me sleeping these days Emily, is nerves before a gig. Have you noticed I'm a good girl on Facebook these days?' I shook my head, 'Not really Beth, sorry. I'd probably wince if I saw you'd written something bad but if it's all good then it doesn't stand out. Glad you're sleeping better though.'

Jess arrived back with our drinks, fingers in two of the beers and carrying the other properly. 'I'm sorry about my fingers in your beers. They don't have trays and I couldn't get your attention to come and help.' We didn't care, we were just pleased with our pints. 'How are you getting home Beth?' Jess asked. 'Train, I presume you two are too since you're both drinking. Can I come back with you?' Jess sucked the beer from her fingers, 'Course you can Beth, you'd be more than welcome. You're our famous friend.'

She had us all howling with laughter the whole way home.

CHAPTER TWO

Dorothy

The Orbs

Her life review over, Dorothy looked at the ten orbs dancing and bouncing in front of her. Her five negatives and five positives. They all looked identical to each other, though she instinctively knew which ones were which. They are quite beautiful, she thought as she wrapped herself all around one of the squishy blobs. She held them one by one for a more detailed examination. 'Look at the amazing colours, they're astonishing. They're alive Calla, aren't they? I can feel them pulsing,' she whirled herself in and out of them. 'What incredible, beautiful things. I can feel their energy.'

'They'll help you Dorothy,' said Calla. 'You've enlightened us and allowed us all to grow by giving us your life review. These orbs are just moments for yourself now. You can relive them, enjoy them, grow from them and learn a great depth of emotion from them. Then you can repay all of it back to earth, you know,' she smiled, 'replenish someone's glow who is in need. It's always your favourite bit. You'll see what happens at the end once you've opened one and released the Lumai.' Dorothy imagined sprinkling an enchanted glitter over someone who was struggling on earth and watching them sigh with relief. Calla chuckled, 'Not quite like that Dorothy, but I enjoyed the vision. It's actually far more beautiful and breathtaking than that.'

ORB ONE

The Neighbour

Dorothy reached out and touched the first orb, it felt to be a physical thing, although it seemed fluid and squashy. It thrummed with static and lights, filled to its brim with barely contained energy. She felt thrilled and excited to be able to move on in her journey. She pressed herself into its squishy centre as it fizzed and crackled with static. Then, a bit more pressure and it burst open into billions of miniscule, animated fragments which completely surrounded her, and she found herself smack bang in a moment of a memory that had meant so much for her in her review.

'Calla?' she looked around for guidance. 'I'm back here with Tom, my old neighbour, and I'm watching my behaviour but I'm not feeling the same sense of remorse or shame or guilt, why not? I felt it so badly in the life review.' In there, the pain had been magnified, it had clung to her. Calla hovered over Dorothy, reassuring her, 'You aren't able to feel any negative emotion here on the spirit realm anywhere other than in your review Dorothy. You've already suffered and grown through that,' she soothed Dorothy with her lights, allowing their glows mingle lightly. 'Let these moments with your orbs allow you to absorb all of the feelings, the energies and the compassion you felt about your chosen situations, then you'll see what happens at the end. It's magical Dorothy. Something so very special happens and you can put all of it to good use. You'll be bequeathing all that emotion to those in need who are still living a life and need a little help.'

Dorothy allowed herself to settle fully into the moment of memory.

Tom was already in his late sixties when Dorothy and Harold moved in next door as newlyweds at number six Kerfoot Street. He was pleased to see young folk move in and hoped they'd soon start a family. He'd enjoy seeing young ones playing in the street again. On the day they moved in, he took the young couple a bunch of flowers and a welcome to your new home card as he'd seen Lizzie his wife do to other new neighbours before she'd passed away a few years ago.

A little self-consciously and hesitantly, he made his way up their path and tapped lightly on the front door with his knuckles. The door swung open immediately and Tom was greeted by a tall and smiling young man. 'Hello, I'm Tom from next door,' he blurted out uncertainly, 'it's lovely to meet you,' he said, quickly passing over his gift and card. 'Mrs Hatt,' Harold called out laughing, 'some lovely chap is bearing gifts at our doorstep. Come on in Tom, let me introduce you to my lovely new wife Dorothy.' 'No no, I won't come in,' he said, conscious of intruding on their first day in their new home. 'I just wanted to show you a warm welcome to the street. Let me know if you need anything, I'm retired now, and my wife died a couple of years back so I'm generally free if you're stuck with anything.'

Dorothy appeared from the front room. 'Come in, come in,' she motioned to Tom with her arm, 'Harold don't leave him standing at the door,' she chided gently. Tom laughed good naturedly, 'I was asked in thanks, but I just wanted to drop these flowers off to say welcome and introduce myself,' he offered his hand to shake, 'I'm Tom from next door.' Both Harold and Dorothy introduced themselves and shook hands.

'What a lovely fellow,' said Harold as they closed the door. 'Well, it's good to know we have at least one nice neighbour,' Dorothy agreed.

Over the twenty years that they knew each other up until Tom's death in 1971, they'd never had a cross word. Tom would nip round to quickly mow their lawn during summer so that they could relax more in the evenings and at weekends. He would fix the odd dripping tap or put a new plug on a fraying wireless lead. They had many over the garden wall chats.

As Caroline and later Pamela came along and grew, Tom would bring them birthday gifts, Easter eggs and Christmas presents. He offered his baby-sitting services, and the girls would clap with glee knowing that Uncle Tom would bring a quarter of sherbet pips or a couple of chocolate tools with him.

Dorothy had watched all their interactions over the years in her life review. She had felt all Tom's joy as he carried out his kindly gestures. She reached out now, to gently touch the warm glows from his aura and felt his kindness radiate through her. Dorothy watched as each smile she gave to Tom caused a ripple of pleasure through them both.

The years passed and Tom became frailer. He peered through his kitchen window hoping to glance Dorothy or Harold in the garden. He'd not spoken to a soul in a whole week. He was feeling absolutely desolate and craving a human voice, a bit of company, a little chat. The television and radio just weren't helping. He'd wished he'd kept in touch with his old friends, but once he'd married Lizzie, they'd only ever needed each other.

He'd knock on their door, that's what he'd do, he decided. He wouldn't want to annoy anyone by hounding them, but it'd be nice to just have a little chat now and then, especially to Dorothy and Harold. Though when he thought about it, he was a bit worried about looking like he was mithering them. Perhaps he'd just potter around the garden instead and hope to catch sight of them. He'd driven to the supermarket four times already this week and couldn't possibly think of anything else he needed. Even then it had just been the miserable till girl he'd spoken to. 'Lovely day today,' he'd said chirpily on one of the days. 'Yep, shame I'm stuck in here,' had been her dour reply.

He had no children to call on, and his nephew John lived in America now, so it was hard to know when to call without waking the whole household.

Last time he'd tried that, Lucy had answered the phone, 'Is there an emergency Tom? Do you have any clue what time it is over here?' she'd almost shouted. And Tom had put the phone down ashamed and embarrassed, his stomach tense and anxious. John had rung him back a couple of days later to say he'd ring Tom instead of him ringing there in future, something to do with him not grasping the time differences. It seemed he was right, thought Tom. John had laughed it off when Tom had expressed how upset he had been for waking everyone and had said that it really hadn't been a problem at all, and Lucy wasn't upset at him. But he'd not rang for over four months now.

Finally. At last. Tom spotted Dorothy. He'd been sitting at his kitchen window for almost two hours now just waiting and waiting. The chair wasn't a bit comfortable. He could see that she had a pile of wet clothing thrown over her shoulder ready for pegging out. He would simply pretend he was putting some rubbish in the bin and have a brief chat while she pegged out her washing, he wouldn't keep her, that would be enough for him. Just to hear his own voice speaking to someone. Hear a friendly voice back. He opened the back door and instantly saw Dorothy quickly bend down. He presumed she'd simply dropped a peg or a sock or something. He ambled over to the fence just in time to see her quickly scramble inside, the washing still piled high over her shoulder. He sat down in his garden chair, agitated and distressed. She'd ducked. Hid from him. Then he heard her.

'I can't even peg the bloody washing out in peace these days, honestly, I swear as soon as he hears our door opening, he appears. It's like he's perched in the kitchen waiting to pounce.'

Dorothy was getting herself ready for work a couple of days later when Peter the milkman, knocked on their door. 'I was wondering if Tom was okay?' he asked. He's not taken his milk in for a couple of days.' Dorothy felt the colour draining from her face with instant worry. 'I have a key,' she quickly volunteered as she turned and went back into the living room to obtain it from the dressing table drawer. 'I'll knock first,' she said as they walked together up the path, 'He may have just forgotten to bring it in and I don't want us to scare him.' She couldn't seem to get the key in the lock, and she realised she was shaking. 'Could you try Peter please? My hands are shaking.' Peter took the key from her and unlocked the door.

'Tom,' she called out. Then louder, 'Tom.' No reply. They made their way into the living room. Tom was sat upright in his armchair facing the television. A mug of tea lay cold and untouched on the little side table with a saucer to the side on which two digestives laid. He was stone cold dead.

Dorothy watched as the 360-degree scene all around her, fragmented into millions of diamond like shards, collected together again and then reformed themselves back into the orb. Immediately, it lit up from within, pulsing with a brilliant light and she watched in awe as scores and scores of musical notes scattered from it. She recognised these from her life review, these were the Lumai that Calla had spoken of, she remembered watching her dad's spirit sprinkling them into her muted glow when she had got home and into the bathroom after that dreadful break up with Will. Dad had showered these blessings upon her and eased her burden.

These Lumai were tangible physical things, real life blessings, the written language of music, they were dancing and alive. They each played their own celestial note, and as each note resounded, she felt herself brimming over with a sense of pride and joy. They arched and bowed and hooked onto each other, creating as they did so, their own lights and harmonious, euphonious, heavenly melodies. She knew that every of them was a wondrous, living sensation.

Dorothy knew that these were her glitter, her blessings to dish out, and that she would use these to sprinkle upon and ease a troubled life. It would be her payback to help negate some of the sorrow that she'd created when she'd lived as Dorothy. She'd be glad to do it. She would be kept busy for a while. She was pleased that she'd chosen this moment to bring back as one of her chosen orbs. The terrible feelings of guilt and regret regarding her behaviour towards Tom, had been painful for her in both her life as the living Dorothy, and during her life review. She'd definitely make amends now with all these blessings to dish out.

DOROTHY

Bestowing the Lumai

'Remember Dorothy,' advised Calla, 'You can only use your Lumai to step in to send your blessings if it doesn't interfere with someone's life plans. And you can only bestow them in the vicinity of where you lived your life.'

She was as excited as Dorothy was to watch her bestow these treasures on to those still on the earthly plain and in need of a caring hand. 'I know, I know, I'm still choosing,' she was whizzing in and out of people's auras.

Some people were grieving or desperately unhappy or scared but she wasn't able to step in because they'd chosen this lesson, it felt so difficult not to help. Suffering was suffering and it was difficult to watch and ignore.

She searched carefully for those who were deeply unhappy, those whose lives weren't running to plan because of an accident, or maybe another person's intervention had scuppered the life plan. She hunted for those who were suffering from something they hadn't chosen and whose souls were taking on an unexpected lesson that they hadn't prepared for. It could send a spirit and any life plan completely off kilter.

She looked at all her precious Lumai that were surrounding her, each one singing and chorusing pure love. Such wonderful things. She pushed herself into their midst and let their lights dance within her and invigorate her. She felt herself absorbing their compassion and love, gently compelling her to disseminate them to her chosen souls so that they could carry out their vocation. Dorothy understood that she could release the Lumai into someone, but that she didn't have any jurisdiction about the outcome they might cause, only that they would greatly help. It seemed that the Lumai themselves knew the best thing to do.

'Dorothy, they don't have to be used for people in dire need you know, as you said, suffering is suffering, you could just help out with a toothache or stop an old lady falling.' Calla was laughing at Dorothy's inability to make a decision. 'I know, but Calla, only ten people to help out of all these needy souls. It's an impossible choice. I just want to give them to the first ten people I see.'

'Well, there's nothing to stop you, but come on, do choose, we've got too many exciting things ahead.'

LUMAI ONE

Rachel Billington

The first choice that Dorothy settled on was that of Rachel Billington. She'd felt intrigued that there were already many souls hovering above and around her. 'I want to look a little more closely at this girl Calla,' she'd said. It would be wonderful to offer her Lumai to someone where she could really make a difference, her own hard-won blessings bestowed upon someone in dire need.

It was Friday 18th of May, and something dreadful had happened just three days prior which had wrecked Rachel's world. Dorothy and Calla watched pityingly as she sat on her bed.
This girl's pain was palpable, she rocked herself to and fro, to and fro, with seemingly no respite from her pain. Dorothy caressed her aura, it was so very muted and still, it barely had any lustre to it at all. Her lights were a murky green blur that barely lifted off her shoulders and yet Dorothy sensed that she was a good and kindly soul. She

lingered there a while to look at the girl's future. It was was horrendous and painful. Everything she did was blighted with what had happened and all because of a simple accident. She pulled away as she continued to watch the scene below her with absolute compassion. 'Oh gosh Calla, this poor, poor girl, I'll have to help her.'

Both Calla and Dorothy watched as Sepha, Rachel's spirit guide, imparted devotion and love onto her charge. She worked relentlessly, selflessly, pushing her own lights into Rachel's aura, sending visions of calm and serene images into this lost soul. Neither of them were aware of Dorothy and Calla above, nor the multitudes of spirits around, trying to reach the girl with their love and blessings.

Three days previously and Rachel had herself a very busy day planned. Tuesdays were always busy days for her, but as usual, she was perfectly organised and had it all worked out. Alarm set for 6.30am, showered and ready by 7am, baby up, bathed and having his breakfast by 7.30am. 'You need to be organised when you're a working single mummy,' she'd told a very cranky Joshua when she'd lifted him from his cot. 'Nah mama, nah,' he'd grappled with her sleepily to try and clamber back in. She twirled him around the room in her arms. 'Mama, has her big boy a bubbly, bubble, bath ready, whooooo.' She whipped out his dummy and kissed his sloppy wet deliciousness.

She started her work as a receptionist at the local doctor's surgery at 8.30am and although Joshua usually went to nursery whilst she was at work, today, Phil, his dad was off work and was taking him for the day. 'Daddy is coming for you today baby. A lovely day with daddy, yes?' 'Dada,' he burbled, he was starting to understand her and repeat what she was saying now that he was almost eighteen months old.

She carried him into the bathroom, whipped off his pyjamas and saturated nappy and plonked him in the bath. God bless him, she thought. She absolutely adored everything about him. 'Look at the cuteness of you my big lad,' she squeezed his fat little legs, 'look at my big boy.' He giggled and pointed at his bottle on the sink. 'Ah you want your bottle, do you? Kisses for mama first then.' He whipped out his dummy and leaned in for a kiss. 'Mwahhh,' he dutifully complied and pointed again, 'Boc-boc mama.'

She waited until his head was thrown back drinking his warm milk and gently poured water over his blond curls. 'Weeee, weeee, the water is coming to eat up your curls, yummy, yummy.' He giggled at the game as he always did. She made a foamy blob on his head with shampoo and laughed at the picture of him. She'd take a photo quickly before she rinsed it all off, you lost moments like this forever if you didn't capture them right away. She knew her camera was loaded with film and just a couple of strides away in her bedroom. She'd only be gone for one second, he was safe enough now not to tipple over. She took one last glance to make certain that he was stable. 'One minute baba, mama is just going to get my camera.'

She quickly ran the three steps to her bedroom, grabbed it and headed back. As she ran back into the bathroom, she glanced a quick view of him still sat sploshing about as she'd been sure he would be. Unfortunately, in her rush, she'd caught her foot in his pyjamas, tripped and hit her head hard on the sink.

She woke to the sound of the phone ringing downstairs. She couldn't quite figure out how she could manage to get down there and answer it. She couldn't figure out why she was on the bathroom floor either, or what all the blood was about. She lay down again too tired to think about it. Bang, bang, bang, bang, bang. 'What was all that noise?' she sat up feeling completely groggy. The phone was ringing again, it was Phil, she could hear him leaving a message, 'Bloody hell Rachel, pick up the phone, you've got me worried to death here. I'm about to break your door down if you don't answer. It's half-nine and you were supposed to be dropping Josh at eightish.'

She slowly pushed herself up to a standing position using the toilet for support. 'I'm coming, I'm coming,' she muttered. Why was she covered in blood though? She was still feeling so very muzzy and confused, she glanced at the bath. Her entire body froze. She started to scream, 'No, no, no, no.' Her little Joshua, his little innocent naked body, face down in perfectly still, bubble free water, his little arms and legs limply hanging. 'No, no, no, no, noooo,' she was screaming and screaming and screaming. She grabbed his body up and out of the water and flipped him over in her arms. He was completely grey and floppy. 'Joshua, please, Joshua baby, nooooo, nooooooo, help me, please, please, nooooo, help me,' She continued to scream and scream, his small, cold, grey, wet, lifeless body hugged tightly to her.

Phil had started to break down the door as soon as he had heard her first screams. She was still screaming now as he was racing up the stairs. 'I'm here Rachel, I'm here.' He ran into the bathroom and took in the scene with confusion. Rachel was sat on the floor leaning against the bath with the baby in her arms. There was blood everywhere and a huge gash on Rachel's forehead with blood dripping down all over a wet Joshua. 'Bloody Hell Rach, what's happened? Stop screaming for God's sake, you'll terrify him.' Breathless now and with his heart hammering in his chest he reached out to take Joshua from her. 'Give him here, you're getting blood all over him.' She shook her head slowly, her eyes wild. He reached out again to take Joshua, nodding gently. Rachel was white as a sheet and clinging tightly to him, rocking and rocking herself. She released her grip on him and allowed him to gently roll onto her lap. Phil's mouth dropped open and his eyes became full with terror and he joined in with the screams as he saw his sons dead face.

Three days later, as Dorothy and Calla surveyed the scene, Rachel was sat alone on her bed, her knees to her chest. Her eyes were both black and she had a huge bump to her forehead and ten blue stitches. All around her were Joshua's clothes, blankets, toys and photographs. The phone rang downstairs, it was her mum, 'Rachel, I know you can hear this. I'm on my way back. I know you want to be left alone but I can't do it.' She'd only managed to drive a mile and it didn't feel right.

'Whatever mum,' was her flat reply into thin air. She was completely pole-axed by shock and grief and tortured by self-reproach. 'It was all my fault baby, I shouldn't have left you, not for one second,' she sniffed loudly and wiped her tears with his little vest. 'My poor trusting baby. How can I live without you? How can I bury you?' She kissed his little curly blond head in photograph after photograph. She gently picked up each item of his clothing and his blankets to smell and inhale his baby scent as deeply as she could. Her whole being was tense with grief. She'd never, ever get over this. Never stop missing her precious boy. Never get rid of the guilt or imagining him reaching out to her as he slid under the water. She sobbed and sobbed until she could barely catch her breath.

Dorothy swept herself into her aura. Thick and sticky with hardly any room for movement. 'You poor wretched soul Rachel, I can help you. I choose you.' She smiled at Calla, expanded her whole light being and gathered together an abundance of melodious, exquisite, Lumai. She pulled them tenderly and with great joy, straight into Rachel.

On Tuesday the 15th of May 1990, Rachel Billington had slept straight through her alarm. She woke at 7.30am. 'Damn it, damn it,' she shouted at herself in a temper. Joshua had woken her shouting from his room, 'Mama, mama, boc-boc mama.' She ran straight to him. 'Good morning my precious curly top, no time for a bath today I'm afraid.' He giggled and held his arms out to be lifted from his cot. 'Ahhhh, I love you so much baby. And guess what? Daddy is having you today you lucky lad.'

Dorothy's lights burgeoned and mushroomed into a vast colossal expanse, glittering and whirling and filling her with bliss. Calla looked on with pride. 'I told you that you always like this bit the most.' They hugged with exhilaration, their radiance sparkling and newly enriched.

ORB TWO

The Inheritance

Orb two appeared exactly as the others did, apart from the first one which had stopped pulsing after it had released its Lumai. She gently held it to herself and caressed it tenderly, feeling its life force as it reverberated within. She was so very proud of this moment in her life, all the watchers had luxuriated in the mighty spangle of lights that it had created. She wished that we could know all this when you were actually living a life. Imagine the joy you could create. She squeezed tightly. A huge burst of vividly coloured sparkles exploded outwards, and Dorothy found herself hovering over herself in her kitchen.

She was just about to sit down to tea at the kitchen table with Harold and the girls. 'Yes, yes, yes,' Caroline shouted out, 'Pamela, come on, it's fish and chips.' Pamela's bounding footsteps reverberated as she hit each stair. Dorothy collected the cutlery and the salt and vinegar from the kitchenette and plonked it on the table, automatically saying, 'Not too much salt Pamela.'

'I won't mum, I'm not a baby now,' she promised. Just as Dorothy put her bum on the seat, they heard a brisk knocking on the living room window, followed by the front door opening and in walked Gladys, Dorothy's mother. 'I've got awful news,' she imparted as she stood at the kitchen door, a cotton hanky wiping her nose and pushing it up underneath her glasses to mop up her tears. 'Our Bessie's dead Dorothy.'

'Oh, mam no, whatever happened? When? How? Sit yourself down mam,' Dorothy ushered her backwards into the front room. 'Harold love, put the kettle on please,' she called out as she plumped up a cushion on the couch in readiness for her mam to sit down on. 'I've called at our Helen's on the way here and let her know, she's all shaken up or she'd have come with me.' Salty, hot tears made another exit and slid down towards her wobbling chin. 'I know she was a fair bit older than me, but 72 is still not that old really, is it? And she looked fighting fit, didn't she? Ambulance men said it was her heart given out, nowt could be done, dead before they arrived, they'd said.' A fresh wave of tears and snot began. 'In the street too, she'd have been so embarrassed.' Dorothy found herself shaking her head slowly as the news settled in her, 'I only visited with the kids on Sunday, and she was absolutely fine then. She was on about buying one of those coloured televisions. I can't believe she's gone. Poor aunty Bessie'

Months later, Dorothy arrived home from the supermarket, to find a thick, weighty, expensive envelope. Yates Solicitors, Leigh, the imprinted stamp on the front of stated, giving away the contents. She'd been expecting this. She opened it carefully so as not to damage the letter inside and quickly scanned the contents. She needed to attend there, something about aunty Bessie's will. She rang and made an appointment for the following morning.

Sitting across the cluttered desk from her, Mr Yates himself was opening and closing his mouth. Dorothy wasn't hearing any of his words though. She'd lost any ability to concentrate when he'd spoken his opening line.

£1800. All for her. An absolute fortune. Not a bean to Helen, and just bits of furniture left to her mam. No explanations given. 'What the hell?' thought Dorothy, and in less than a millisecond she'd spent the lot. She'd pay off the mortgage, buy a new couch, get those new wall to wall carpets in all the rooms, fresh lino in the bathroom and kitchen. She'd even learn to drive and buy her and Harold a car, and why not have one of those new package holidays to Spain? A fridge? Crikey, they were rich. She looked at the solicitor, 'I had no clue she had any money, not really, I knew she wasn't short, but this is a shock.'

Dorothy got off the bus one stop early and called in at her mam's. 'She left me everything mam, everything. It'll break our Helen's heart. I'm not telling her, I can't.'

Gladys shook her head miserably. 'I always knew Dorothy, she told me years ago. I said it wasn't right, especially since our Helen has always been so fond of her. I said it'd cause trouble between the two of you. But she'd said it was her money and she could leave it to whoever she liked. She always had a soft spot for you though Dorothy, you knew that.'

It was all bursting out of her head by the time Harold got home from work. Other than picking up the girls from school, she'd done nothing. She'd spent the afternoon staring into space, her mind working overtime. But already, she'd devised a plan. She ran it round and round in her head, still uncertain on whether to do it or not. She kept picturing all the things she could buy, all that money. She'd never see money like that in her life again. Then she pictured Helen, already living on the breadline and renting a house from the council.

So, as Harold walked in, she announced it, 'Aunty Bessie left me £900 in her will.' It just came out. A big fat lie. 'Bloody hell Dorothy, we can almost pay the mortgage off with that, or pay some off and buy a fridge or one of those new coloured televisions.' Good old aunty Bessie.' He was smiling all over his face.

Dorothy called in at her mams after she'd dropped the girls off at school the following morning. 'Now mam, you must never, ever let on to our Helen about any of this. I don't want her to think badly of aunty Bessie, and I don't want her beholden to me. I haven't even told Harold. I'm just going to bob into the solicitors now and tell him to send me and Helen £900 each but to keep quiet about what really happened.'

Gladys grabbed hold of Dorothy in an unusual display of affection. 'You're an absolute belter Dorothy, I'm beyond proud of you and it'll never cross my lips as God is my witness.' Dorothy hugged her back, 'Mam, if I hadn't done this, I'd have just condemned myself to a permanent life of guilt. I'd have been scared to spend it for fear of our Helen asking how I'd afforded things. It's a fact of life that you can never rely on people to do the right thing, but our Helen, she'd have definitely done this for me if it had been the other way round wouldn't she?'

The vision that Dorothy was so lost in, exploded into fragments. She'd been so proud of herself both in life and at her review for this kind thing that she'd done. And now, watching as the harmony of Lumai sang out their melodies, surrounding her and lighting the sky with their brilliance, she was gratified that even more joy would be gained from it.

LUMAI TWO

Hilary Bastion

Dorothy smiled at Calla. 'I've found my next recipient.' There down below, lay on her couch, eyes staring right through them both, was Hilary Bastion. Dorothy swept over her aura. 'Oh Calla, this poor woman. Her life isn't supposed to be like this.' They could see her guide Zadra keenly working hard to help, relentlessly and determinedly pushing her own dazzling lights into Hilary's aura where they'd simply peter out into a dim glow, her silent words of advice unheeded.

'It's been two years Calla and she's still struggling. She's tried, but she's lost all hope. If you've lost hope, then there's nothing left is there?'

Exactly two years ago to this day, Hilary had been very happily married to Guy. And Guy had been very happily married to Hilary, or so she'd thought. Until she got in from work and found him hanging in their front room. Cold and blue. His navy tongue engorged and bulging from his mouth. Their white painted kitchen chair on its side where he'd kicked it from under himself in order to take that final, fatal step. She'd replayed the exact scene that she'd found over and over and over. It carouselled unbidden around her head for months.

It no longer had the power to make her convulse into helpless, incapable sobs. It would still present itself unsought into her head, but it no longer had the command that could shock her from her sleep or make her stand impotent and shell shocked at the supermarket checkout. It could no longer bring her to her knees. She could replay the whole scene now at will. Every detail of it, without any emotion, like a film constantly rewound and rewatched, it had lost its allure.

Instead, Hilary filled her days lay on her couch torturing herself over and over. Relentless, enduring recriminations about why she hadn't seen it coming. Her beloved husband and she hadn't noticed that he was so miserable that he wanted to die. What did she miss? There was no suicide note to tell her why. The police had determined that there didn't appear to be any outside factors at play, so no drugs or threats that they were aware of.

They'd only struggled with their finances as much as the next young couple and anyway, both their parents would have helped out if money were an issue. There didn't appear to be anyone else in the equation, no evidence of any affair.

She'd searched the house from top to bottom, even climbing into the attic to see if she could find anything, anything at all, but there was nothing. They'd not had a fall out, in fact they'd made love the night before. They were making plans for a summer holiday and Guy had even circled a couple of package holidays to Spain in the travel agent magazine that he'd fancied. The whole situation was unfathomable. She recalled that his mood had been buoyant in the whole week before he'd died, and now she wondered if that was because he didn't have anything to cause him any worry, knowing that he was going to be dead soon.

For the first couple of months, Guy's friends would appear one by one or in small groups to offer their condolences and support, but Hilary quizzed them in such depth, eyes wide and looking for reasons with every word that they uttered, that they'd stopped coming. They'd felt cornered and out of their depth when a new barrage of questions came their way fuelled by a new notion that she was harbouring.

She turned up six times at Guy's office where he had worked as a conveyancing solicitor, demanding that they tell her that he was stressed with work or that they'd overloaded him with cases. In the end, and very reluctantly, they'd told her that they'd have no option but to call the police if she kept turning up.

She had never been back to work. She couldn't

face it. All those sympathetic smiles, no thanks.
All her friends bar Carol had given up on her, her phone never rang for chats or with invites. She was a social pariah. She didn't blame anyone, she completely got it, who'd want to spend any time with a guilt-ridden woman, who could no longer join in happy, nonchalant, chit chat?
Carol was the only person who turned up week in, week out.
At first, she'd tried to get Hilary to do small steps, a trip to the local shop or a short stroll. As the months wore on, she'd tried asking her to meet with a small group of friends, or to come out for lunch or dinner. It all fell on deaf ears. She just couldn't muster up any enthusiasm for anything. She did eventually persuade her to see her GP and had kindly attended the surgery with her on appointment day, only to hear Hilary say that she'd accept the sleeping pills he'd offered because she'd thought these might be of use, but it was a no to counselling and a no to anti-depressants.
'Of course I'm depressed doctor, my husband killed himself, all the pills in the world won't make that pain go away, will they?' The kind doctor nodded and said it may take the edge off the pain and to come back if she felt worse or changed her mind.
'Why did he do it though Carol? If I just knew the reason, then I'm sure I'd eventually let him go.' Carol had learned not to respond with an

answer, just to nod sagely with her sympathetic expression on. 'Hilary,' she ventured warily, 'It's been two years now. I'm not saying you shouldn't still grieve, because of course you should, you lost your husband. I'm simply saying that you're punishing yourself looking for an answer that you won't ever get. You need to take a few baby steps back to some semblance of normality.' Already Hilary was shaking her head, but Carol continued undeterred, 'I've booked us a weekend away this Saturday, just me and you, nothing busy, a secluded cottage in the lakes. A change of scenery for you.'

'I don't think so Carol, I can't face it,' she really did feel gratitude to her kind friend. 'You're so sweet to me, even now, after two whole years of morbid, morose, depressed, misery greeting you every time you visit me.'

'You don't need to face anything Hilary, I'll pack, I'll drive, I'll shop,' she got up to put the kettle on. 'You'd be doing me a massive favour actually, I really need a couple of days away. I'm worn out with one thing and another and it's only a couple of days.'

She returned from the kitchen with their steaming brews and handed Hilary hers. 'Please consider it Hilary, for my sake if not for your own.' But already, she could see from her expression that she had no intention of accepting.

Hilary knew that she wouldn't press it any

further, she knew that once she had said no, it was useless to start hounding her. She'd just end up closing herself down and the whole visit would be a disaster. They'd done that a time or two. So instead, they spent the rest of the afternoon chatting pleasantly about Carol's work problems and her recent decorating. Hilary had nothing to talk about.

She wearily climbed the stairs that evening to bed, every step an effort. God knows she'd tried to cope with it all. She was heartsick with trying. Day in and day out of constantly trying. It'd been so long now, two years, and the pain was still there in the pit of her belly, relentless and all consuming. It never left her, never gave her a moments peace. Like a coiled spring, the agony lay in her chest while she slept and the minute she started to wake, it quickly uncoiled like a big dirty fist, squeezing the life out of her. Well, it didn't matter any longer. She wouldn't have to face another morning.

She opened her bedside drawer, shifted the magazines she'd put on top to hide her secrets and lifted out her stash of tablets and suicide notes. She propped the notes up by the lamp. Each one gave a very clear picture of why she had chosen this. She couldn't bear for anyone to go through the same pain as she'd done, so she told them straight. She told them that they had done everything perfectly, and that not one thing they could have done would have prevented her from doing this. She told them she loved them. Each note had taken her a few goes to get just right, and she'd burned the first few tries for fear of them being found. She'd been buying pills for weeks and weeks and popping them out of their strips and into a paper bag for ease of use when the time came. These, along with the sleeping tablets given to her two years ago, would definitely do the job.

She fetched a glass of water from the bathroom and then climbed into bed. She sat herself up, propped a pillow behind her head and tipped the pills onto the duvet which had dented in a perfect bowl between her legs. She tipped in her tablets, then she began to scoop them up in her hand and post them into her mouth to drink them down. Handful after handful. She never had a doubt. She'd be free of the pain soon and found herself wondering why she hadn't had the guts to do it before now. Once they were finished, she pulled the pillow from behind her head, plumped it up, and lay back and waited. She dozed off to sleep.

Dorothy reached up and collected a cloud of harmonising Lumai. They filled her with an indescribable joy, they danced and sang out their tunes, their bright lights filled with love, and she tenderly pulled them down into Hilary's sleeping frame.

She and Calla watched as the hazy, fatigued and flat aura, started to replenish itself into an abundance of bright, mesmerising, delightful luminosities.

Hilary woke the next morning feeling odd. She lay there a while and waited for the usual stomach drop as she remembered how shit her life was. Something felt different though. She threw back the bedding. There was vomit everywhere. All over the floor, her pillow, her duvet. Part dissolved tablets, whole tablets, white foam. And she was still alive. She couldn't decide if that made her happy or sad. She pottered off to the kitchen in her bare feet. 'Good Lord, this floor is cold,' she shouted out, running back to the bedroom for her slippers. She smiled as she tugged them on. 'I'm smiling, oh my word I'm smiling.' She ran over to her dressing table and looked in the mirror. Yes, she was definitely smiling. She had no idea how or why, but she'd woken without the sensation of a breeze block in her belly. In fact, she felt light and energised, ready to face the world again. She had no idea that grief could just dissipate overnight but by God she was relieved.

She pottered off back to the kitchen and put the kettle on. This morning, she didn't linger over Guy's untouched mug. She gently lifted it and put it onto a higher shelf. She couldn't think why she'd been punishing herself for so long keep looking at it each morning, lamenting on how he'd never drink from it again. She leisurely sipped on her coffee, amazed to feel so well, then remembered her dear friends invite. She'd clean up the mess in the bedroom later and burn those letters, for now she had an important call to make. She made herself a fresh brew and carried it into the front room. She walked over to the telephone and dialled a number.

'Carol, it's me, I'm coming with you to the lakes on Saturday if you'll still have me.'

Dorothy and Calla swayed and danced with euphoria. 'Ah Calla, look at her lights, she's positively glowing. To fix that poor girl is just the best feeling ever.' They swept in and out of each other's lights, shining and sparkling. Dorothy felt such pride. She was laughing with exhilaration, 'Let me find my next person quickly please, because this feeling is just so absolutely amazing. It's worth living life after life just to be able to do this for someone. Just look at how happy she is, she's completely aglow.' Calla laughed along with her, 'Come on then, let's get hunting.'

ORB THREE

The Cruel Streak

This orb appeared exactly as the others did. All squishy and enchanting. A divine and super charged globe bursting with colour and raw energy. She squashed it to her, waiting for the shower of this moment of memory that she had selected so carefully. She knew exactly what it contained. She'd endured a lot of pain during her life review watching and absorbing this moment. She'd have done anything at that time to go back and alter her behaviour, say something different. The watchers had felt her pain and embarrassment and they had sent waves of love, affection and support up towards her where she had absorbed it gratefully and allowed it to lighten her load.

She'd actually felt her own venom, her intrinsic hatred. She could taste its acrid bitterness and it proved a very difficult watch. Her heart had ached as she saw her own aura darken as she spat out her obnoxious words. And she'd watched Harold absorb what she'd said, and she felt his hurt, felt his pain. She watched his confusion and the shock etched on his face as he walked out of their bedroom to escape her unwarranted vitriol.

Dorothy couldn't pinpoint exactly when it had started. It had ebbed and flowed throughout their marriage. They'd had good years and bad years. It didn't begin suddenly one day or following a row. Nothing had stoked the fire. Her hostility towards him just seemed to start as minor irritations and then build and grow with no rationale behind them. The feelings of deep loathing had just seemed to start in her, flourish, and then gather momentum. Poor Harold.

When they'd first met, he was a confident man. A clever and emotionally intelligent man, he'd known instinctively how to woo her, how to care for her. He'd never thought that she'd agree to come dancing and go courting with him because she was a real looker and he'd known he wasn't. And yet, unbelievably, she had, and he couldn't have been prouder than when Dorothy was on his arm.

When Dorothy and Helen had been in their late teens, they'd while away time on their beds, writing lists of essential criteria that any prospective husband would have to meet.

'Handsome is number one on my list Dorothy,' Helen would shout over to Dorothy, 'What's yours?' 'Obviously wealthy Helen,' she laugh in answer, 'Although it's a joint first with handsome.'

As she matured, she soon became skilled at weeding out the chaff. Within the first two dates, she'd know if her new suitor was a good earner, motivated to buy their own home, wanted to spend all their time with her, or wanted children. She dropped them like a rock if they didn't fit her bill.

Prior to Harold and before she'd turned twenty, she'd met Will. Devilishly handsome, charming, good career prospects and he could dance with the best of them. He'd ticked each and every one of her boxes. Dorothy spent hours practising her marriage proposal acceptance in the mirror and draping herself in white cotton bed linen to see what she would look like as Will's bride. She became proficient at signing her new name, Mrs Dorothy Harrison. Life was a permanent joy.

Exactly ten months later and her life no longer felt harmonious, and Dorothy was petrified. Her monthly was over a week late.

'Oh God Helen, what will I do?' she wrung her hands together in the sanctuary of their bedroom. Helen would keep her secret. 'How sure are you?' asked Helen, 'How late?' Dorothy paced the room. 'About a week I suppose, I'm not really sure, maybe ten days. Will promised he'd be careful and now I'm in trouble,' she began to cry, and Helen rushed over and cuddled her. 'What will mam say? She'll be disgusted with me. I've let everyone down. I'm glad dad's not alive to see me disgrace the family. I'm so scared Helen, and Granny Annie, it'll kill her,' a new wail came forth. 'Have you told Will yet?' Helen asked, 'You'll just have to get married straight away. Everyone does it, just look at how many babies come early Dorothy, no one ever says anything about it.' She pulled her sister close and stroked her hair. 'Hilda Brown had only been married three months when her George came. He was so called early, but he managed to weigh in at eight pounds. It'll all work out fine, you'll see.' Dorothy extricated herself from the hug and kind words and sat on the edge of her bed.

'I'm meeting him this evening,' she sniffed, gently stroking the pink eiderdown. 'We were supposed to be going dancing, but I'll persuade him I have a headache and take him somewhere quiet. I suppose at least this might speed up his proposal.' They both giggled. 'Not a word to anyone Helen,' implored Dorothy. Helen zipped up her lips with her fingers, 'Let me know what Will says, wake me if I'm asleep.'

Dorothy could see Will waiting as her bus pulled into the station. So darned handsome. He looked up, cigarette dangling from his lips, and performed a big, exaggerated bow for her. Usually, she'd giggle and blush, but today, her belly was knotted with tension. She'd casually tell him that she wasn't up for dancing tonight because of her headache. She'd take him to the George and Dragon and find a quiet corner where he'd tell her to stop fretting and that they'd get married next month.

'You don't look dressed for dancing,' he said frowning as he offered his out hand to help her alight from the bus. 'I thought we were going to the Garrick tonight?' Dorothy sighed, 'I know Will, but I have this awful head. I thought we'd just have a drink in the George tonight if you don't mind.' Will let go of her hand, 'I really fancied a dance tonight Dorothy, you should have stayed home if you're not feeling well. I'd soon have realised you weren't coming.' His expression was sullen, like a small, petulant child.

She couldn't hold it in any longer. Here he was, acting like a child and she was bursting with the need to tell him they were expecting one. 'I'm pregnant Will.' There, it was out, she'd said it. Not in the way that she had hoped to, but at least it was out of her now. Will stood stock still. Motionless. Eyes wide and mouth open. 'Pregnant?' he asked under his breath. 'You can't be, I was careful. Are you certain?' he shook his head in denial. He walked a couple of steps in order to lean on a shop front for support and Dorothy followed him. He placed his hands on her shoulders and faced her. She felt a wave of tears course down her cheeks. She knew she'd be okay now. He'd cuddle her and tell her it would all be fine and not to fret. He looked right into her eyes, 'How do I know it's mine though?'

Dorothy felt as though the world had lost its axis. Her stomach dropped like a brick. She screamed loudly, uncaring who would hear, 'What? What did you just say? What do you mean how do I know it's yours? Of course it's yours as you damn well know. How dare you say that to me.' She pushed him as hard as she could back towards the shop front and began to run back towards the station, sobbing as she went. 'You're trying to trick me into marrying you and I'm not having it,' he was shouting out now, 'it's definitely not mine.'

Dorothy got back onto the exact same seat on the exact same bus she had just got off five minutes previously. 'Well that was a flying visit love,' said the conductress, 'that'll be tuppence please.' She rolled out a ticket and pressed it into Dorothy's hand along with a large cotton handkerchief. 'There's plenty more fish in the sea love, a pretty girl like you won't be left on the shelf for long.' She shook with sobs on the empty bus all the way home.

She let herself in carefully, planning to sneak quietly straight through the hall and into the downstairs bathroom. She would sort her face out before her mam could start asking questions. She had just about closed and locked the door before she heard her. 'That you Helen?' mams voice sounded out in the hall. She took a deep breath, 'No mam, it's me, I've come home, I've got a rotten head.' She heard her mam start to walk away, 'I'll get you a couple of aspirin love.' She looked at her reflection in the mirror. She looked a mess. She was a mess. 'Oh God please help me.' She mouthed silently.

She just needed a wee before she could wash her face. She whipped her dress up, pulled her knicks down and there she saw, with blessed relief, her monthly.

Dorothy's tick box had changed after that. Genuine, kind and trustworthy now took the lead places and the lovely Harold ticked them all. Not in the same league as Will looks wise, but he more than made up for that with his kind nature. She'd met him out dancing a couple of months after the Will business and had fallen for him immediately. They were inseparable. She'd ever so cautiously explained why she wouldn't sleep with him, she was worried that he'd send her packing when she'd explained that she wasn't pure, but he'd completely understood and agreed to wait until they were married. She'd never spoken to Will since that awful night, but she saw him once in the town centre around five months later when she'd caught him looking at her belly questioningly. She didn't owe him an explanation. He revolted her.

Within twelve months, she and Harold were man and wife moving into their first home. They were ecstatically happy. All her dreams had come true at just twenty-two years old. Married to a perfect man and in her own home, what a result. Five years later and their family felt complete with the arrival of Caroline and Pamela.

Ten years later, Dorothy realised that she'd flinched as Harold walked past her and bent down to tenderly kiss her neck as she'd sat cross legged on the couch reading the Sunday express. 'Did you just flinch Dorothy Hatt?' he asked laughingly, 'I'll make you pay for that.' He gently pushed her over and climbed on top of her, pushing his stubbly face into her neck and kissing her. 'Get off me Harold, the girls could walk in at any moment,' she was pushing him off her. 'They're still fast asleep, we'll be lucky if we see them before eleven,' he said, taking the opportunity to nibble on her ear. 'No, really, get off,' she said louder now. She was pushing his head away with both hands. 'Bloody hell Dorothy, what's the matter with you? You should have had another hour if you're still tired. Got out of the wrong side of bed, did we?' He got up and walked off to the kitchen feeling a bit dejected. 'I'll make you a stronger brew Dorothy, wake you up a bit.'

Even at the time she'd known he didn't deserve the way she rejected him. He was still the exact same lovely Harold. But she'd started to build a repulsion for him, and she couldn't seem to stop herself. He'd started to lose his hair and insisted on growing one side longer so he could tease it over the bald patch. In a morning it would be splayed on the pillow making her stomach contract. Worse still was when they made love and it flapped and flailed with his every thrust and she was unable to concentrate on anything else. She listened as he supped every cup of tea and slurped each mouthful, then she'd gag as she washed his mug with the dried dribbles down the side. She'd prepare tea for him each evening then find herself having to leave the table three or four times due to the tension she felt watching him eat. He put salt on his food before he had even tasted it. He put a morsel of each of the foods on his fork before he'd eat it. His irritations were endless.

She could feel her mounting anger. The way he'd eat his toast, putting it down between bites and then rubbing his thumb and fingers together to discard imagined crumbs, the flaky bit of skin that appeared every so often at the side of his nose, his freckled shoulders, the way he haphazardly left his toothbrush so that it sometimes disgustingly touched hers, it was all repulsive. She never hid her repulsion, even if she didn't speak of it, her face with its sour, joyless disposition told the story. Harold, always unsure what he had done to cause her to feel such revulsion of him, would quietly retreat from the situation. Yet, still he loved her, still touched her shoulder tenderly as he walked past. He always presumed she was tired, or it was the time of the month.

He never felt downtrodden, or hen pecked. He

just tried harder to please her and laughed off her comments because he loved her so very much.

They'd been having a relatively good day. Harold had mowed the lawn and weeded the small flower bed at the bottom of the garden. It all looked quite lovely, and Dorothy had made a pot of tea to take into the garden where they could enjoy a brew and a rich tea and admire his efforts. The last efforts of the sun shone down on them, and they both sat back warmed by it, knowing that in a week or two it would be too cool to sit out.

After such a lovely evening, Harold was in a cheerful, happy mood. He was ready for bed though. He looked over to Dorothy sat in her chair under the window with her head stuck in a Catherine Cookson novel. He watched her a while, watched as her eyes flicked from line to line captivated by the words. She looked beautiful, her silky brown hair settling in waves just below her shoulders. He could make out the outline of her breasts under her blouse as she breathed in and out.

'Are you ready for bed love?' She looked up, dazed to be lifted from the streets of Newcastle and back in her own living room. 'Sorry?' Harold walked over to the television to switch it off. 'I said are you ready for bed, I'm off now, we're all locked up when you're ready.' Dorothy folded the corner of the page and reached over to the small table to put it down. She pushed out both arms wide and stretched herself. 'Come on, let me help you,' Harold laughed at her, grabbed both hands and pulled her to standing position. 'I was watching you while you read Dorothy. You're really beautiful you know. I'm a very lucky man.' She laughed, 'If you say so Harold, if you say so.'

Dorothy sat on the toilet having a wee while half-heartedly watching Harold as he brushed his teeth. It was something in the way he rinsed his mouth after he'd finished that caused her mood to switch. He'd spat out the water so that it splattered all over the sink. I mean, why would you do that? Why wouldn't you just lean down and spit out? She looked at the sink with disgust. That spit has no doubt landed on all of our toothbrushes hundreds of times. The thought made her gag. 'You've just spat all over everything Harold. Do you spit out like that every time you brush your teeth? All over mine and the girls' toothbrushes? It's disgusting.' Harold looked taken aback. 'Dorothy what on earth are you talking about? I simply brushed my teeth. Please don't start a row tonight, we've had a lovely day.' He walked off to their bedroom. He was in bed, his head under the covers when she climbed in. She turned off her bedside lamp and snuggled down as far away from him as was possible, pulling up the blankets to her chin. He flipped himself over and started to wrap his arms around her. 'Come here Dorothy, don't fall out with me over a little thing like that.' She let out a loud snort of derision, then shot out of bed, her anger radiating through her as she fought to control her mouth, 'Get your hands off me you repulsive man. How can you think that spitting all over my toothbrush is okay? You don't even care.'

Harold lay back in the bed throwing his hands up in defeat. 'Okay I'm sorry, I really am, I hadn't realised. Get back into bed Dorothy.' He moved back over to his side to give her space patting the bed to welcome her back in. 'You disgust me you do. All your horrible little habits are already torturous to watch and now there's an even more disgusting one that I didn't even know about. You make me cringe even coming within a foot of you Harold Hatt. I've never been attracted to you, ever. I should never have married you with your bald head and flappy hair. You can barely manage to change a plug or put a new light bulb in you're that pathetic. I wish I'd have married Will Harrison instead.'

The scene shattered into shards of dazzling, intense splinters. Brighter in colour than any she had seen before. The Lumai sprang from its centre and immediately began a chorus of harmonious melody. Such agony this moment had caused her in her life review, she had been tortured with the pain she had inflicted. Her lovely Harold hadn't ever deserved any of it. Now, with all these Lumai blessings to bestow, she could put right her wrongs. She would gladly pay her debts back.

LUMAI THREE

Natalie Urmston

Dorothy looked over at Calla. 'I've found my next soul.' Calla could see that she was highly animated. Her lights bounced from her dramatically, filling Calla with a sense of pride. She so loved watching Dorothy as she spent her hard won Lumai. 'I can make this poor kid happy again, can't I?' They looked down at Natalie. Youth was a trying time. Endor her guide was tenderly soothing her, expertly weaving his own lights into hers, sending his precious blessings to a soul who couldn't hear.

'Well Calla, she'll hear my blessings loud and clear.' Dorothy reached out and gathered an abundance of singing Lumai and delicately nudged them into Natalie's aura. She waited for the reaction. Nothing. She looked to Calla who was tinkling with laughter. 'Be patient Dorothy. The Lumai always know best. Let's watch and learn.'

Natalie had set her school alarm an hour earlier than was usual. The bike ride would take around

45 minutes and then she'd have to get it locked up in time for registration once she'd got there. She climbed out reluctantly from underneath her duvet and padded over to the window. Pouring down.

She was going to wash her hair this morning, but it seemed pointless. She'd be drenched when she finally arrived at school anyway.

She really didn't fancy biking to school every day but couldn't think of an alternative. If only it wasn't so far away. She'd already moved school once because of bullying so she couldn't possibly tell her mum and dad the same thing was happening to her again. What the hell was wrong with her? Did she look like a victim? She looked completely normal from what she could muster. Was it the way she held herself? Or her voice? Or her hair? Or her shoes? What she said? What she didn't say?'

She'd braved it at her old school all the way through year eight right up until the summer holidays so that she wouldn't be starting her new one mid-term. She didn't want it obvious that she was moving due to being bullied and this way seemed fail safe.

She had to catch two buses for this new one, but that had seemed a small price to pay. On her first day, the form teacher Mr Forbes, had introduced her to the class and asked that Sarah and Olivia show her the ropes and orientate her. They'd been lovely. She'd even opened up to them about the bullying at her last school. They'd been really interested and sympathetic.

She could see the fretful face of her parents when she'd arrived home that evening but was able to reassure them and tell them quite truthfully that she'd made two lovely new friends.

On her second morning, she had run over to greet them, but Sarah quickly explained that she and Olivia had only been asked to show her around for one day, so she'd have to find someone else to hang around with. Her face had turned beetroot red, 'Oh okay then, no problem.' Her insides twisted painfully, and her heart raced. How absolutely mortifying. They obviously hadn't wanted to be with her yesterday either. She'd felt like such an idiot.

On day three, she'd got off the first bus and was in the queue for the second when she heard their loud voices behind her, mocking her. 'Fancy having to catch two buses to school because the school nearby can't stand the sight of you.' A peal of laughter. 'No wonder with a face like that, I think she should be banned from our school too.' More laughter.

Over the weeks she tried to disarm them by charming them, 'Hey you two, I've got cakes for the journey, I just saw them in that bakery and thought we could share them.' She opened up the box to give them a view of the delights. Olivia looked inside, reached down as though to take one, then instead, knocked the whole box clean out of her hand, laughing as they splattered all over the floor. Her dinner money wasted and now not even a cake to plug the gap. 'If we wanted to look like a pair of overweight cows like you do, then we'd eat that shit for breakfast too.'

A younger student bent down to help her pick the mess up. 'They're awful bullies those two. If it's not you, it's someone else. They started on me when I'd only been here a month,' she looked at Natalie with incredulity, 'Who would do that? For one whole week they picked on me relentlessly for the entire bus journey. Then one day, I punched Sarah right in the face. She gave me a good hiding in return, but it put her off picking on me ever again, perhaps try that?' Natalie wished she had that sort of courage.

She tried offering to do their homework for them. 'Go away thicko,' Sarah shoved her over. 'Never get on this bus again or life in school will get harder still. Get it freak?' So, she hid at the back of the queue and carefully watched where they sat before she got on and hid some more. 'Poooo, what's that stink everywhere?' shouted Olivia loudly one morning. The pair of them walked around sniffing loudly. Other kids laughing their heads off. 'It's getting stronger and stronger,' sniffed Sarah. 'Oh yuck, surprise, surprise its Urmston here, stinking the whole bus out again.'

They'd grab hold of her hair and yank it as they walked by, 'Oops, must have got caught in my bag,' they'd laugh.

One day in class they told everyone to keep a tight hold of their purse because they'd seen someone stealing. Then they both looked directly at her. She turned bright red. 'See her guilt,' they sneered, 'she's even had the decency to blush. Thieving bitch.'

Every day it was a new torment a new threat, a covert punch, a new demand. She felt completely alone. Isolated and unsafe. A constant feeling of anxiety, dread and panic filled her days until she was safely cocooned at home. And even then, her thoughts would be taken over by thinking up ways of how to make it stop.

So, she'd decided that her mornings and afternoons would be far less stressful not having to face them on the bus journey and that a long bike ride would be easier. So, bike ride done, she sat in registration drenched wet through, already dreading her journey home but glad of the respite from her tormentors.

'I'm not sure why, but there was no fishy body odour on the bus this morning was there Olivia?' Sarah and the rest of the class, chortled with laughter.

Mr Forbes introduced a new girl. 'Sarah and Olivia, would you do the honours again please? Help Amber settle in?' He looked at them over the top of his glasses. 'Yes sir,' they chorused, all smiles and batting eyelashes. Poor unaware Amber, Natalie already felt sorry for her. They'd spend the whole day being sweet and friendly, pulling what information they could from her and then they'd use it to relentlessly beat her down. She'd been there, done that.

Throughout the course of the day, she observed them as they giggled and laughed together. Three heads locked together sharing secrets. 'We're the three musketeers,' shouted Olivia. It had been Sarah who'd shouted that old chestnut out when Natalie had been falling for their plan. Poor Amber.

The following day, drenched again after her bike ride, she was sat on a bench near the safety of her form room, watching as Amber had made her way over to them. She was cringing inside as she watched Amber nod along as Sarah said her spiel, and then she watched her slowly walk away. She'd kept a covert eye on her, expecting her to scuttle away embarrassed as she had done. Her body wasn't slumped with dejection though, in fact she laughed out loud and walked over towards her. 'Hi, I'm Amber, I'm new here.' Natalie looked up in surprise. 'Yes, I saw you yesterday in registration. I'm Nat.'

Amber nodded over towards Sarah and Olivia. 'The toxic twosome over yonder have disowned me after only one day now that they've done the handsome Mr Forbes bidding.'

Unfortunately, they'd both spotted the nod in their direction, and it was just the cue they'd been waiting for. They began to march over.

Natalie felt her stomach begin to squeeze with anxiety. Oh God she really didn't need this. More fodder for the bullies.

'Did you just point at us?' Sarah shouted aggressively, her face scowling as she neared. 'Are you talking about us you bitch, after we made you so welcome on your first day too?' Natalie got up to leave. 'Sit down bitch.' Olivia pushed her by the shoulders, and she slapped back down onto the bench.

'Let me give you a bit of advice Amber love,' sneered Sarah sarcastically, 'you really don't want to befriend this wimpy little nothingness here, in fact if you do, you'll be the first fool because as you can see, no one else is interested.' Natalie felt the injustice deeply, how could anyone befriend her when these two constantly scared them away with threats? She couldn't say it out loud though. She was too busy quaking in her boots.

'And don't forget we know all your little secrets now Amber,' Sarah tapped the side of her nose with the secrets left unsaid.

Dorothy and Calla continued to watch the lengthy scene as it unfolded below them. 'Why haven't my Lumai worked Calla? She's still being bullied and so is the new girl now. Her aura is exactly the same as it was last night, it's all stringy and flat.' Calla motioned towards them, 'Yes but look at Amber's, it's magnificent, so full of power. Her colours are breaching the aura.

This girl is an old soul and I think your Lumai have brought her to Natalie.'

Amber stood up. Not a shred of nerves about her. Natalie was terrified. They'd beat Amber up and then her just for being in the wrong place. Sarah tried to shove Amber to force her sit her back down, but Amber had been expecting it and held her ground.

'Do not ever push me again,' she grabbed hold of Sarah's arm and dug her fingers in deeply. 'Get off my arm you idiot,' she tried to pull away. 'You'll say sorry to Nat before I let go.' Natalie was panic stricken,' Oh no, honestly, it's absolutely fine. I'm okay Amber thanks, just let her go please.'

Olivia started to help extricate Ambers fingers from her friend's arm. 'Let her go you adopted freak. No wonder your parents didn't want you?' Amber simply laughed her head off, not a scared bone in her body. She let go of Sarah, then grabbed Olivia's arm, digging her fingers in deeply and knowing there'd be bruising there tomorrow.

'Let me go you bitch, you're hurting me.' she wriggled herself free.

Natalie noticed that they'd both stepped back a little and Amber was the one laughing and in control. She watched in astonishment as Amber took a quick step forward as though she were going to land a punch on one of them. They stepped back. 'No wonder you got expelled from your last school, you're definitely a psycho, they were right with that diagnosis.'

Amber laughed loudly again. They started to become visibly flustered.

'Listen you disgusting pair of dirty souls. I saw straight through you both yesterday. All the ammunition you thought you'd collected on me. Well, I made it all up. Now, moving forward, I've decided that I quite like this girl here,' she pointed down to Natalie who was cowering behind her rucksack for fear of a stray punch, 'So, if I see or hear anything, and I mean anything at all that even vaguely upsets her, I'll smash your heads together. We can try it out now if you like. Go on. Try one of your insults, you won't get a second chance.' Natalie watched as Amber roughly and dominantly pushed herself between them, goading them, daring them. Olivia appeared flustered and unsure. She really didn't fancy walking round with a busted lip from this weird one. 'Come on Sarah, we've got more important things to deal with than this rubbish.' They walked off.

Calla and Dorothy watched as a small flame of light began to flicker gently within Natalie's aura. They watched together as it ignited and exploded as hope began to fill her lovely soul. They saw as Amber's glow connected with it, completely unaware that she nourished it with her own. By the time they had reached registration, Natalie's aura had become a whirling kaleidoscope of colour.

Dorothy and Calla twirled around in delight, laughing and dancing, thrilled as to how her Lumai had done her bidding. Their own spirits grew and magnified. 'Gosh Calla, I'm addicted to doing this. I think I'm going to have to live another thousand lives.'

ORB FOUR

The Jitterbug

Dorothy reached out to the floating orb. It fizzed and crackled with bright colours emanating around it. She was thrilled to be bursting this one. She had absolutely rejoiced in this moment of memory. It had been barely anything in her actual life but reliving it had been so wonderful. The watchers had all joined in and were jitterbugging all over the place, laughing and laughing and the whole place was alive with glittering, bright splinters of new lights. It was simply, one of those moments that was so much fun, they'd had to replay it over, again and again and they danced and danced. 'If I'd known about the reaction it would cause, I'd have danced my whole life,' Dorothy shouted out to anyone who was listening.

She squashed it to her. Whoosh, a bright shock of light and the whole scene was back. Back in the kitchen at Kerfoot Street.

Dorothy watched herself as she stood side by side with Harold. They were both leant over the kitchen sink facing the window as Dorothy washed the pots and Harold dried them. It had become their evening ritual years ago. The radio was playing a slow melody, and both were swaying together in time to the music. 'That glass has still got bubbles in the bottom of it, dry it properly please Harold.' She was feeling playful, he could tell from her tone. 'Well, that's still dirty,' said Harold in retaliation and flung a clean dinner plate back into the washing up bowl. It caused a surge of foamy water to slosh out which had drenched Dorothy's chest and arms. She stepped back without a word, looking downwards to survey her dripping arms and drenched blouse. She let out a long sigh, leisurely ran more water into the bowl along with a hearty squeeze of washing liquid and swished it around innocently until the bubbles were high.

As Dorothy watched the scene, she sensed Harold tensing, a bit unsure as to whether he'd misread her mood. But just then, Dorothy delved into the bowl with both hands, grabbed a huge pile of bubbles and slopped the mess straight onto Harold's head.

She watched herself as she laughed uproariously running off behind the kitchen table in a vain attempt to escape his retaliation. He'd filled a mug to the brim and slung the contents at her, resulting in a perfect splat of her face. 'I'll kill you for that,' she squealed, grabbing the tea-towel and soaking up what she could from her hair and face as she headed swiftly for the sink. She dunked the mug back in and launched the water straight towards him, promptly hitting the washing that was drying on the ceiling clothes airer. 'That's not funny Harold, it was all but dry,' she shouted. 'Good job it was you that wet them and not me then, wasn't it?' he said as he tipped a fresh mug straight over her head. She burst out laughing. 'What a sight for sore eyes I must look.' she said as she slung the tea-towel into the water and whipped it straight across the room where it slapped a perfect hit to Harold's head. 'Bullseye,' she shouted and danced on the spot with glee. Harold headed back to the sink for more ammunition and turned the wireless volume knob as he passed by, causing noisy music to fill the air. The water fight continued until the pair of them were drenched wet through and they could barely walk without slipping. They were hanging onto each other, laughing and laughing and laughing with each other. The wireless was blaring with music when the opening chords of T-Rex, I love to Boogie, filled the kitchen. 'I absolutely love this song,' Dorothy shouted over the music. Come on, have a jive with me Harold.' They bopped and bopped, frenetically and madly, completely lost in the music. They lost themselves with the music and with each other, remembering times of youth and laughter. Together.

When the record had finished, Harold

breathlessly turned off the wireless and pulled Dorothy to him. He looked at her. Sopping wet through, right down to her slippers. 'I love you, Dorothy Hatt.' And she leaned right into him and looked him dead in the eyes, 'And I love you too Harold.'

The scene evaporated in a flutter of heavenly Lumai. Hundreds of thousands of them, dancing and jingling in the air. They sang a chorus of divine rapture and Dorothy was utterly entranced. She couldn't wait to share these out.

LUMAI FOUR

Matthew Davey

Dorothy hovered over Matthew's glow. It was vast and brightly coloured but so very quiet and still. Even the aura's that she had witnessed previously that had been dulled and flattened had managed to move a little bit. Dorothy swirled into it to have a closer look around. 'It's beautiful in here, soft with lots of beautiful, swirled colours of warmth, yet there's no movement at all. It's as though it's just stopped, like a static tornado. I'll have to help Calla, this poor guy is stricken with guilt and most certainly in need of my Lumai.

Matthew and Maggie were walking around the charred and wet floor of what had once been their home. The stench of pungent smoke had already started to cling to them. 'All our stuff gone. Everything we owned burned to ashes,' Maggie was sobbing, 'all the baby's stuff too, she hasn't even got a pram or a cot.' A fresh wave of tears coursed down her cheeks. 'We got out with our lives Maggie, and all of this can be rebuilt or re-bought, these are just things. We still have each other and Charlotte,' he pulled her to him, 'I keep running through it all in my head, the heat, the flames. But more than that, the fear that I wouldn't be able to get you two out. I keep reliving it all.' The unbidden memory of her howling like an injured dog as she watched the flames rip through their home, haunted him day and night. She stroked his face tenderly. 'I know that Matthew, I do, and I'm really grateful, it's just that I feel so powerless. So utterly lost. I can't think where to begin to get us sorted again.'

He was shaking his head, 'If only I'd just put the bloody smoke alarm battery back in.'

Maggie kicked a piece of sodden burnt plastic over to see if she could identify it, 'You can't keep blaming yourself for that, it was the middle of the night. I can bet most people would wait until morning to hunt around for a new battery. It was driving us daft listening to its stupid beeps every couple of minutes.' He looked up to where the ceiling should have been. He could see huge swathes of sky.

He didn't want to say anything to Maggie, but he was worried sick about it all too. They'd had to borrow clothes for themselves and Charlotte to get them through this first week. The firemen hadn't let them in until now to see if they could salvage anything. Now that they were in, all their hopes were dashed. Not one thing here could be saved. They weren't allowed to go up the stairs, what was left of them, due to health and safety concerns but Matthew knew already that there would be nothing left.

Small things that you never really thought about kept hitting them anew day after day. At first it had been nappies and dummies and toothbrushes, all the basic necessities they needed to survive. Then as each day passed, came thoughts of the practical things like a hairdryer and a kettle. How would they manage to replace everything? The insurance list was getting longer and longer and still she was adding more and more of what she could remember each day. She would burst into tears as she realised more things that were lost. Charlotte's first portrait, all of their photos, her cats' ashes, all gone and all irreplaceable. Matthew fretted about his work tools and thick winter work jackets. They had both been so very grateful to her mum who'd taken them in. It wasn't ideal to be in a tiny bedroom with only bunk beds, but it was safe, and mum was so sensible with her words which kept Maggie anchored to reality and enabled her darkest days to be elevated by love and care.

Dorothy reached out beyond the acrid, dirty scene in front of her and pulled her Lumai in. Each little sparkling quaver sang a unique harmony of love as they danced above them daintily. She gathered them within her own aura and jubilated. 'Oh Calla, I wish I could tell every human to relish every moment, they have no idea of the joys to come, or how precious and unique their life is.'

She tenderly leant down and dispatched the Lumai into Matthew's glow. They watched as it began to flourish and gleam and the harrowing, grimy scene evaporated and gave way to a bedroom.

Matthew was deep in sleep. He found his dream being invaded, disturbed by something, a noise perhaps? He sat up bleary eyed. The baby was restless in her cot. Perhaps that's what had woken him. He lay down again and fell straight back into a dream. He was disturbed again and sat up irritated. 'It's the smoke alarm battery Matthew, I keep hearing it beep every couple of minutes or so,' Maggie said quietly for fear of waking Charlotte. He sighed loudly, 'Bloody Hell, of all times to start beeping, I'm knackered. I'll go and change the battery, or it'll have us up all night.' Maggie lay back down, 'Don't change it tonight, it'll be fine, just take the old one out and I'll put a fresh one in tomorrow.'

Matthew headed downstairs and pulled the pouffe underneath the offending alarm. It beeped loudly and annoyingly. He reached up and unclipped the battery. Peace at last. He began to head for the stairs when he stopped suddenly. Damn it, he couldn't leave it without a battery, and it would only take a minute. He went to the kitchen which still felt warm with the heat being given out from the tumble dryer, but he was still shivering as he replaced the battery.

'All sorted now,' he said as he grabbed hold of Maggie and quickly spooned her to steal her warmth.' She yelped quietly but laughingly, 'Oh bloody hell Matthew you're frozen, get off me.'

They woke disturbed again. Beep, beep, beep, beep, beep. 'That bloody thing again! I'm going to smash it off the bloody ceiling.' Matthew grabbed his dressing-gown; he didn't fancy freezing to death again. Beep, beep, beep, beep. It was piercing his tired head. He opened the front room door and instantly smelled acrid, pungent smoke. He screamed out 'Maggie, there's a fire, there's a fire, get the baby and get out.' He was running up the stairs as fast as he could, 'Maggie, get out, we're on fire, the house is on fire.' She'd heard the sheer panic in his voice and was already at the top of the stairs with Charlotte in her arms. 'Oh God Matthew, I can smell it.' He reached out for the baby, 'Give her to me, come on hurry up, we need to get out, we'll go next door and ring the fire brigade, the fire is in the kitchen, but the doors closed so hopefully it'll be contained until they arrive.

'It would have been a very different story without a smoke alarm sir,' said the fireman as they began to install huge fans to blow out the worst of the smoke and inspect the damage. 'You're very lucky indeed, just a little smoke damage to the kitchen which can be sorted with a bit of paint. You'll need a new tumble dryer though.'

'Oh Calla, I absolutely love this. What clever little Lumai they are.' She whirled herself around, laughing loudly, her lights fizzing and popping. Calla laughed with her, 'I love to see them too Dorothy. Now come on, let's find your next recipient.'

ORB FIVE

The Colleague

Dorothy had left school at fifteen-year-old and had been thrilled to secure a small office job at the local mill. She knew she wanted to attract a decent sort of bloke as a husband and this way, she could dress prettily instead of looking like the women who worked in the mill. They had wisps of cotton all over them and in their hair by the time they had finished their shift. They may have earned more than her, but Dorothy very definitely felt superior.

She mostly worked with Mary who had kindly shown her the ropes and helped her to understand the filing system and the correct way to answer the telephone and how to transfer calls to Mr Traynor. All the women looked after her and said she was a sweetheart who soon got the hang of things. Dorothy loved it and looked forward to going to work every morning.

When she was sixteen, Mary retired. In her place would be Annie, a school leaver this term and Mr Traynor had given Dorothy the responsibility of settling her in. She'd been beyond thrilled.

'Mam, on Monday we have a new girl starting and Mr Traynor has asked me to train her up,' she looked from mam to dad beaming with pride over tea on the Friday evening. 'Well done love, it's because you're conscientious and hard working.' Dad was proud of her, and mam had nodded along, 'They're lucky to have her aren't they Johnny?'

On Monday morning she put on her prettiest outfit and a little blusher so she would look professional when she met her new colleague. It would be great to have someone near her own age to chat with. She was outside the office door ten minutes early as usual when Mr Traynor arrived to unlock.

'Our new girl starts today Dorothy, don't forget you're showing her what's what.' She looked up at him surprised, 'Mr Traynor of course I haven't forgotten, it's all I've thought about all weekend. I'm really looking forward to meeting her and showing her the ropes.' He nodded along as she spoke, 'Good girl Dorothy, I knew I could rely on you. I'll have my cup of tea and biscuit's when you're ready please.'

Mr Taylor disappeared into his room and Dorothy headed to the small kitchen. She heard a sturdy knock on the door and knew it must be the new girl because everyone else just walked straight in.

There, to Dorothy's shock, was a fifteen-year-old girl who looked like she'd just stepped off the front cover of a magazine. Dorothy thought back to when she'd first arrived here, quiet and mousey and wouldn't say boo to a goose. 'Good morning I'm Annie Bold, bold by name and bold by nature,' she opened her red lipsticked mouth, flashed a set of pure white Hollywood gnashers to laugh uproariously and then promptly and confidently sashayed herself through the office. Dorothy instantaneously hated her with her shoulder pads and A line skirt which were utterly incongruous with office surroundings. Who the hell did she think she was? She opened and closed her mouth a few times, but nothing came out. It wasn't supposed to be like this, she was supposed to feel superior and in charge. Instead, she felt small and insignificant.

'I'm Dorothy, I'm going to be supervising you and showing you the ropes.' Annie burst out laughing, 'You? You're a kid, you're younger than I am surely?' Dorothy felt herself blushing, 'Well for your information, I'm coming up to seventeen and I've been here eighteen months. Mr Traynor has asked me to train you.' She could feel that she was becoming defensive and continued curtly, 'Come on then, this will be your desk, put your bag in that drawer. In winter, your coat needs to be hung up there,' she pointed to the rail. 'Mr Traynor likes a tidy office.' She walked her through the room, pointing out who sits where, the kitchen, the toilets and the vast filing cabinets.

Mr Traynor opened his door, 'Dorothy, where on earth is my cup of tea? I've been kept waiting for ten minutes now.' Dorothy was horrified, 'Oh I'm so sorry Mr Traynor, I was distracted with showing our new girl around, I'll get it straight away.' She looked at Annie, 'Come with me, I'll show you how he likes his tea.' Annie put her bottom lip down, 'Bloody hell, he says jump and you jump. He'd be waiting longer than ten minutes if it was down to me to make it.' Dorothy looked at her angrily, 'Well it will be up to you because this is the first job, and you'll do it every morning. I've never let him down once and now thanks to you, I have. I just hope he isn't too upset with me.'

As the staff came in, Dorothy introduced Annie to them. 'Oooh look at you, you pretty little thing,' said Agnes. 'Wow, we have a Hollywood star in our midst,' said Betty.

Every day for two weeks she arrived looking glamorous with a different outfit on. Dorothy looked her up and down on the Friday morning as she walked in. 'You certainly have a lot of clothes Annie, I only have three dresses in my entire wardrobe,' said Dorothy on the Friday, 'Seems a big waste of money to me when people are hungry.' Annie simply winked at her, 'It costs an arm and a leg to look like this Dorothy, I have to beg, borrow and steal off mum and dad to look this good. I can wrap dad round my little finger though.' She shook her head to throw her hair back over her shoulder. Dorothy had begun to harbour a visceral loathing for her, this stupid girl who showed no discernible talents other than physical beauty, but she already seemed to have the rest of the staff fawning over her. Dorothy decided there and then that she would make it her personal crusade to tarnish her reputation and ruthlessly get her elbowed out. It arrived quicker than she'd anticipated.

Today was pay day. It was Dorothy's job to collect the little brown wage packets from Mr Traynor and hand them out to the staff. 'Thank God I get paid at last, it's been a pain having to work a week in hand,' Annie said, as she reached for her envelope. 'Don't open it Annie, can you see the snipped off corner just there?' she pointed, 'You count the notes first through that, then if any is missing, you can say so without ever having opened it. It tells you on the front what should be in it.' Annie glanced at the front, 'Bloody hell, four quid? That's not much for all that work, is it?' Dorothy snorted derisively, 'I've not actually seen you do much work Annie.'

Mr Traynor's door opened, and Dorothy hurriedly put her wage packet down on the desk in front of her so that she could quickly assist him with whatever he needed. Annie sniggered, 'Quick, quick, Mr Traynor has opened his door, teacher's pet needs to run as fast as she can to help. Lord knows what he thinks when he's just trying to nip for a quick pee.' Dorothy was furious, 'Just carry on with the stocktake. At least I actually earn my wage here unlike you.'

Dorothy and Annie spent the next couple of hours lifting box after box of files as they continued with the stocktaking. At ten to five, Mr Traynor's door opened as usual. He liked to take a walk around on a Friday afternoon to make sure that everything was just as it should be. The staff were all sitting with their handbags on their knees in readiness for Mr Traynor to give them the go ahead to go home. Dorothy suddenly remembered her pay packet. She walked over to the desk she'd put it down on, grateful that she'd remembered. Her mam would be wanting her keep money. It wasn't there, someone must have accidentally picked it up. 'Has anyone seen my pay packet?' she shouted out, 'I left it on this desk.' Everyone was shaking their heads. 'Annie, you saw me put it here, did you see where it went?' There were no thieves in the office so there was no intent to be suspicious of her, but her demeanour caused Dorothy to suspect she'd taken it. 'I never saw you put it down Dorothy, it could have ended up in one of those boxes we were in and out of.' She was flustered and beetroot red. 'Did you take my money Annie? Because you certainly look guilty.'

Mr Traynor walked back into the office from his inspection. 'What's going on here then? What's this upset?' Dorothy began to babble, 'I put my wage packet here this morning and now it's gone. Annie is acting all suspicious, but nothing has ever gone missing here before she came.'

Mr Traynor looked at her incredulously, 'Dorothy, you can't just accuse someone of something so vile.' He looked around at Annie all red faced and starting to cry. 'This is easy to fix. Empty out your bag Annie.' Annie shook her head. She couldn't possibly empty her bag in front of everyone. She was on her monthly and her Dr White's were in there. She couldn't face the embarrassment of tipping them out in front of everyone. 'I can't Mr Traynor, my bag has private stuff in it. And anyway, if I'd nicked her wages, I wouldn't just put them in my bag, would I?' He looked right at her. 'And where in the world would you put them, Annie?'

They thought she was a thief, she'd never stolen a thing in her life and now this stuck up, snooty Dorothy was trying to make out that she was. She flung her handbag across the desk at him, 'There, check it,' she couldn't have been more embarrassed as she watched him tip the contents across the desk. He started to put everything back in. 'I'll do it,' she snatched the bag from him and hurriedly began putting her sanitary towels back in. 'Are you happy now?' she angrily looked at Dorothy.

Dorothy raised her eyebrows, 'Well my wage packet is still missing, you were the last one to see it and you said you wouldn't hide it in your bag if you had stolen it. I suspect it's down your bra or somewhere even more nasty.' Annie burst into tears. 'I haven't taken your money. I'm not a thief and I will never set foot inside this office ever again in my life. I have put up with your jealousy and withering criticisms for two whole weeks Dorothy Gough and this is the final straw.' She flounced out, slamming the door behind her. 'Good riddance,' shouted Dorothy, 'She definitely took it. And now I have no keep to give to mam and she'll go mad.'

'Dorothy, just go into the kitchen for a moment while I quickly discuss something with the staff please,' Mr Traynor asked. When Dorothy came out, they were all smiling. A little pile of money had been placed on her desk. 'A little gift to make up for what she's taken Dorothy, no need to pay it back, we've all chucked in.' What an absolute relief. 'Thank you so very much, you're all so kind,' she could feel her lip wobbling and tears threatening. 'At least we found out early on about her before she had a chance to pinch anything else. No wonder she's always dressed nicely when it's all bought with ill-gotten gains.' Secretly, she was glad to see the back of her. Lazy and loud mouthed, she just didn't suit an office of this calibre.

On Monday morning she arrived at the office ten minutes early as usual. She headed straight to the kitchen to make Mr Traynor's tea. While the kettle boiled, she went to the filing cabinet to get the last box down ready for stocktaking. She saw it there. A manilla wage envelope just peeping out from underneath the typewriter. Her stomach dropped with horror. She picked it up and shoved it quickly into her bra. She couldn't possibly let people know she'd made such a dreadful mistake.

The scene shattered outwards in a million, glittering fragments. A huge cloud of humming, glistening, singing Lumai shot into the air chorusing a heavenly melody.

Dorothy shot over to Calla. 'That guilt never left me for my entire life. I accused an innocent person of theft and then I kept all that money the others raised for me. If only I'd have just admitted it straight away.' Calla smiled, 'Just know that you learned Dorothy, that's all that's expected, and now you have these gorgeous Lumai to gift to someone in need.

LUMAI FIVE

Brian Simpson

Dorothy and Calla hovered over the scene. They noted Coria, Brian's spirit guide as she gently soothed his heavy greyed aura. They watched as she immersed herself within it, pouring so much of herself and her love into him. His aura mass was vast and airy, signalling a beautiful life being lived, though its dulled ash appearance was indicative of his current terrible raw grief.

Dorothy swept herself into it to seek out the explanation. She could instantly feel the pain, the guilt and the torment. He despised himself more than any person could understand. Immediately she reappeared by Calla's side. 'My new candidate Calla,' she stated, 'this poor man is a tortured soul through no fault of his own. I'd like to help him.'

Brian Simpson had woken up that very morning all prepared for the day ahead. He'd kissed his wife Janet, and tenderly ruffled his son Michael's hair as he'd said goodbye before he'd set off for his interview. 'Good luck Brian, not that you need it, they will be doing themselves a misdeed if they don't take you on,' she'd planted another kiss on his lips. 'Thanks for your vote of confidence Janet, I feel nervous but prepared. I love you. See you later then, bye son.'

Winter was losing her hold and the watery sun offered snatches of hope that spring would soon make her appearance. The roads were clear and dry. He should make the journey in an hour and his appointment was an hour and a half away, so plenty time to park up, calm any nerves and find his bearings. He was beyond excited. 'This will be a dream come true if I get this post Janet,' he'd said last night. 'It's all I've ever worked for.' She had smiled at him, pleased that he'd finally got a chance at his dream job.

He hung his jacket on a hanger and hooked it over the back seat door. He didn't want to look crumpled and give the wrong first impression. He set off on his journey. He had studied his map closely last night and roughly sketched one out for his journey, even though he virtually knew the route off by heart now. He just hoped he'd miss any traffic and could find a parking spot.

He put the radio on to distract himself from overthinking about questions his interviewers may ask, but then turned it off again when he realised he was shouting the potential questions over it in his head. He needed peace not music. The journey was mostly motorway, so he settled down at a steady 68 miles per hour. No traffic, he'd definitely be there on time so that was a worry less for him. He relaxed into the journey.

He pulled off the motorway fifty minutes later and was now only a ten-minute drive away, he felt his belly lurch with a sudden influx of butterflies. 'Breathe Brian, slow breaths, in and out, in and out,' it always calmed him down when he told himself to concentrate on his breathing.

He could see a small traffic build up in the town, but he still had loads of time, so it didn't cause him to panic. He looked at his watch, 8:45. School traffic. He knew it would soon peter out and he'd still have a good thirty minutes left to complete a ten-minute journey.

He glanced down at his hand drawn map. He'd be taking the next left after these lights, and it looked to him as though all this traffic was heading straight on so that was good. He definitely didn't need to fret about being late now. He turned the corner, he guessed he was around five minutes away now. He'd be able to completely compose himself in the car now before he went in.

He put his foot down and settled into a relaxed 30 miles per hour.

It all seemed to happen so quickly and yet in slow motion at the same time. A kid on a bike just shot out of the side street and straight in front of him. He'd watched as the lad looked up and right at him, eyes wide with terror as he'd realised his predicament, desperately trying to steer away from the collision but knowing he had no escape. Brian had slammed his brakes straight to the floor screaming out as he did so. The sounds had been awful. The thud had been dull and heavy. A body being hit by a car. A young lads body. A metal scraping noise echoed on for far too long and Brian still tightly gripping his steering wheel, watched as the lad's bike skidded on its side and straight under the wheels of a bus coming from the opposite direction. His heart was hammering in his chest. He could hear it. He was panting heavily.

He could hear car horns blaring as the drivers in either direction became frustrated with the unseen hold up. He watched as a panicking woman ran over as though she was going to help but instead, just stood in front of the car covering her face, wide eyed with shock.

He couldn't move. He wanted to get out of his car and check that the lad as okay, but his hands were held fast to the steering wheel and his feet were still pressed to the floor. He couldn't remember what to do to stop the car rolling forward. A man ran over. He'd help the lad surely. Brian watched wide eyed as he looked at the kid on the ground and turned away quickly. Brian saw the pain portrayed on his face and watched him as he began rubbing at his head with both hands. He watched as he began to steer the woman away shaking his head. Car doors began to open in the backlogs of traffic and people began to appear by the car. Someone took charge, a suited gentleman called out, 'Has anyone rang for an ambulance and the police? Move back now please people, nothing can be done here I'm afraid.' Brian could hear the sounds of sirens in the distance. He'd keep the brakes pressed down and his hands tight on the steering wheel until the police told him it would be safe to let go. His heart continued to beat really fast. His thighs and hands were vibrating with the effort of keeping the car still. He thought he might vomit as he felt the bile rise in his throat.

The bus driver was walking in circles shaking his head, the kids bike crumpled underneath the front wheels. Brian could see its passengers looking through their windows at the road in front of his car. They'd get upset, look away and then look back again. A terrified Brian watched them all.

A brisk knocking at his window caused him to look to his right. A policeman. 'Sir, open your door please?' Brian looked at him, 'Officer, I can't move. I'm stuck.' The policeman looked at Brian and felt such sympathy. How did you ever get over killing a young kid? No wonder he was shocked. 'Sir, reach over and put the gear stick in neutral and the handbrake on.' Brian did as he was asked. Then he let the clutch and brake pedal up and switched off the engine. His arms and legs shook with relief. He opened the car door. 'Is he dead? Please tell me he isn't dead? I can't look. He just pedalled straight out of the side street. I had no chance of stopping, you ask anyone,' he was sobbing now. 'Oh God, I can't believe this has happened, that poor lad.'

He was brought home that evening by the police. 'Oh Brian come here, you poor, poor thing.' Janet had pulled him to her to hug his pain away, she'd spent the entire day crying and panicking. Brian had spent the whole day in a cell. He'd been breath tested and questioned. His car had been impounded as evidence. The police were all lovely and sympathetic but remained impartial until they had more evidence from the many witnesses. Janet had rung the hospice to tell them of the accident and that Brian wouldn't be attending for his interview.

He held her close to him, seeking comfort in her love and familiarity, 'I'm never going to get over this,' he told her. 'It doesn't matter what the circumstances were, I killed a child Janet.' He broke down wailing.

Dorothy smiled down at this lovely man who would have taken the Bridge of Care Hospice to its peak by managing to streamline its operations and then deliver the best of care to its patients. She wouldn't know what her Lumai would offer but she hoped it would be enough for him to continue on his original life plan. 'It's horrendous Calla how an accident can cause a life to become completely upended isn't it?

Hopefully, these will help to put him on the right path again.'

She reached herself out and gathered the dancing lights of her Lumai together, she drew them down tenderly and watched as they distributed themselves throughout poor Brian's greyed and fogged aura. They lit it up with flashes of bright swirling colours and disseminated into his aura.

Dorothy watched incredulously as the scene in front of her suddenly dissipated. She was in an entirely different scene, a different place and it was a day earlier. She turned in puzzlement to Calla. 'Huh? Where did Brian go? I wanted to see what my Lumai did.' Calla laughed. 'Dorothy, I've told you. They'll do what they need to do. You'll get an outcome, just watch and wait. You should definitely consider a few patience lessons.' Dorothy laughed, 'I was just excited to see what they did and instead we're shipped off to a new scene, and a new person.'

They found themselves over 13-year-old Judd Brown. A vast, multicoloured and glorious glow reached way above his head. Dorothy languished within it for a while. He was in the process of carrying his mum from her bed to her wheelchair. 'I'm so sorry Judd, you shouldn't be having to do this for me.' He was laughing, 'I'm a big strong lad now mum. The carers said they may be behind this morning, and you know how you hate to be laid in bed for so long. Honestly mum, it's no trouble at all.' He stuck a cushion behind her back just as she liked it. 'I'll go to the chemist for your antibiotics before I go to school so that you can get started on them straight away.'

Alice looked at her son, her eyes filled with sadness that her accident had ended up causing him to be her carer. 'You're a good lad Judd,' she reached out and gently stroked his arm. 'Rubbish,' he replied laughing, 'I charge a fiver an hour so you're in my debt forever.' He stroked her cheek lovingly. 'I have to go now though because I'll be late for school if I don't. Do you need me to do anything else before I go?' She took a quick glance around. 'No, everything is where I need it. Be careful on those roads lad and I'll see you in a bit.'

Judd went through the back door and to the shed. He took hold of the handlebars of his pushbike but felt that there was something wrong. He looked down at the wheels and spotted that the back one had a puncture. 'Damn it,' he spoke aloud.

He went back inside. 'Mum, I'm sorry but your antibiotics will have to wait until after school unless you can get someone else to pick them up for you. My bike's got a puncture, so I won't be able to use it today.'

The scene evaporated. Dorothy was excited now. She knew she'd be back over Brian. 'There he is Calla, there he is.' Brian was just about to leave for his interview at the hospice. His aura glowed beautifully. Dorothy and Calla whirled in and out of it with delight. 'See Dorothy, patience is a virtue.' They both giggled. Calla was spinning away thoroughly relishing the aura full of Lumai. Dorothy was already on her way, 'Calla, come on, we need to find my next nominee. People are suffering out there now so come on, hurry up.' They laughed together as they went in search of their next lost soul.

EMILY

The Medium

'Fancy a night at the club next Thursday Emily? There's a medium show on. I really fancy it, and didn't you used to be into stuff like that when you were younger?' Beth was on FaceTime and Jess was sat at the side of me on my bed. She snorted. 'Used to be? That's a laugh.' I elbowed her, I rarely said anything about it these days and I don't think Beth was ever aware really.

'Well, I'm game,' I looked at Jess to see what she thought, she was screwing her face up. 'I'm always a bit scared of stuff like that.' Beth was eager, 'Come on Jess, it'll be a laugh,' she put on a deep spooky voice, 'Does anyone know an old lady with a name beginning with B, no, P, no C?' We were all laughing at her mimicry. 'Okay then, count me in but if it scares me witless, I'm sleeping here.' Jess cheered. 'I'll book us in, it's only a tenner and the medium has really good reviews.'

The following Thursday I walked up to the club, I could see Beth and Jess howling with laughter on the steps. It made me chuckle before I even found out what they were laughing about. 'What's so funny guys?' I asked as I neared. Jess looked mortified but was still laughing. 'Sorry Emily, it's Beth, she's completely inappropriate but so bloody funny with it. We were laughing about you, well, more your dress sense. Then you walked up with that 'get-up' on, and we couldn't compose ourselves.' I looked down at my 'get-up,' I had no clue what they were talking about, but it still made me laugh. 'You look like you've put an Edwardian ladies' frock on, with a five-year-old's pink tights and finished the look with a pair of ten pin bowling shoes,' Jess was bent double again laughing her head off and Jess couldn't control herself. The sight of them set me off too, though I was laughing more at the sight of them laughing than my hilarious 'get-up.' It was a great way to start the night though, even if I was the butt of the joke, they knew I wouldn't care.

We paid Beth for the tickets and found seats near the front, 'Beth no heckling or I'm leaving,' I had to warn her because it would be just the sort of thing she'd do for a laugh. 'I definitely won't,' she looked at me, long blonde curls covering one eye, 'I know what that feels like from their end these days.'

The club filled up. We'd seen the queues start building at the bar, so we'd got ourselves three pints in to keep us going. There were leaflets dotted about so I picked one up and read it. Four mediums. I didn't doubt that there was another life after this one obviously, but I couldn't help but wonder how many of them were charlatans. First one was up, we'd soon find out. 'I hope they pick me out,' said Beth, hoping for a fortune telling that would tell her of successes to come on the comedy circuit. 'Well, they'd better not pick on me because I'm going to do a runner if I find any spirits lurking around me,' said Jess, her eyes wide.

He pointed out a woman in the back of the room. 'Have you lost someone love? I have a man here telling me his wife is here and to tell her he loves her. Name begins with a J, I think? Or it might be a G? I'm definitely getting this message for someone over in that area.' We were all looking over, 'Oh I hope someone recognises that,' said Beth, completely enthralled. No-one seemed to pick up on it and he moved his finger around the room giving vague messages until someone from the other side of the room latched on in hope, 'I think you're describing my dad there, that's just something he would have said,' and sure enough, the woman cried, and the medium said he was thrilled to be able to share his gift.

The second medium appeared. 'Wow, now she does look mystical,' said Jess. 'How does she?' I asked, I could just see an overly made-up woman with bleached hair and a local accent. 'Get in the moment Emily,' she dug her elbow in me, 'It's all magical and I'm loving it.' The medium had been sat on a chair but now she stood up. 'Well, she's certainly dressed for the part,' I laughed. She was in a red, crushed velvet hooded robe. 'And you thought I had no dress sense.'

She did the same shouting out stuff and a vague pointing, but then she did an abrupt turn and looked straight at me. 'I'm getting told I must speak to you,' she said. I was suddenly all ears, my mouth was dry and I wanted to sip my pint but I waited excitedly. 'I am speaking to your guide, he says his name is Michael and you need to be wary of a male with the initial P. Does that mean anything to you at all?' I felt utterly deflated. 'Nope,' I said, 'Not a thing.' Luckily, the woman behind me felt it might have been a message for her, so all was well.

The third medium Gary entered the stage. He wandered around for what seemed an age. Apparently, he was connecting and picking up the vibrations from the other side. He pointed out a man in the middle of the club, 'I've got a Terence here. He says you dropped a note in his grave on the day he was buried.' The man simply broke down in front of us all, his voice was strained with trying to respond, 'That's my brother, no one in the world knows that I did that. Thank you so very, very much.'

He looked at us three. I heard Beth and Jess take a sharp intake of breath. 'You, the girl in the dress, yes you,' he said as I pressed my hand to my chest to ascertain that he definitely meant me. Twice in one night, it had been worth my precious tenner. 'I have your guide here, her name is Calla, she says carry on writing. Does that mean anything to you?' I sat with my mouth wide open, my heart banging in my chest. I looked at Jess, who had heard me mention that name so often. 'Yes, it does, it means so very much to me. Thank you so much.' I was shaking as I grabbed my pint, completely overcome with emotion. 'She says be careful of a fall.' Then, just like that, he was pointing at someone else.

We enjoyed the rest of the night chatting to others who had received messages. One guy laughed in my face when I said I completely believed mine. 'It's a load of codswallop,' he said, all knowing, 'When you're dead, you're dead.' I didn't argue and when Jess kept looking at me shaking her head with disbelief that he'd correctly guessed the name of the guide I'd been trying to tell her about for years, I simply shrugged my shoulders and nodded. I was worried about a fall though. I'd be extra careful when I was walking home and especially on the stairwell, and I wouldn't climb on anything high. 'Thanks Calla, I've waited all my life for a message from you,' I whispered into my pint.

ORB SIX

The Resentment

The pulsing orb was directly above her, whirling and firing with its power and filled to capacity with its precious Lumai. Her blessings to bestow. She gathered it to her, caressing it tenderly and delicately. She could feel its vitality. She surrounded it with her lights, pulled it to her centre and burst it.

This had felt so much more than just a moment in both the actual living through it and during her life review. Resentment and jealousy had been prominent features throughout the majorities of her lives, and she had chosen this moment as a perfect soul lesson. The scene opened up around her. She looked to Calla questioningly, 'This isn't where I expected to be.' Calla smiled at her, 'You saw all this in your review Dorothy, though the orb will not show you the exact moment that was important for you, it will instead show you the most important repercussion that was felt from your actions. Each action causes ripples, doesn't it? Her pain was greater than your pain.'

She had met Louise on her very first day at school. They naturally gravitated to the other, holding hands at playtime and mopping up each other's tears as they bravely waved goodbye to their mummies each morning. 'I think you two girls must be joined at the hip,' Miss Whitaker the dinner lady said, which had made them giggle. As they grew, Gladys and Beryl their mums, got to know each other at the school gates. 'Louise would like Dorothy to come for tea after school on Friday if that's okay with you,' offered Beryl, 'I'll pick them up together and bring her home around six-thirty should we say?' She looked at Gladys for approval. Gladys smiled, 'They'll absolutely love that, the pair of them will be over the moon.'

That was the start of it for Dorothy. Eight years old and afflicted with her first taste of envy, which culminated eventually, into resentment. She skipped up the street hand in hand with Louise, beyond excited at this new venture with her best friend. 'It's this one here, come on Dorothy, I'll show you my room,' Louise was dragging her up the path excitedly. Dorothy stared open mouthed. It was the biggest house she had ever seen. It was set right back from the road with a path of steps leading to the huge front door. Either side of the path was the vast garden with its multiple trees and heaving flower beds promising an even bigger garden at the back if the side gate was anything to go by. Dorothy would never, ever be able to bring Louise for tea at her house. She'd be too ashamed after seeing this. She'd hate it if Louise thought she was poor.

'Come on, come on,' Louise was laughing, 'Why are you standing still?' she pulled on her arm to get her moving again. Once inside and Dorothy felt worse as she watched Louise bombing off excitedly up the grand central staircase gesturing excitedly for her to hurry up.

Her bedroom was a resentment inducing delight. Pink and vast, a huge furniture filled dolls house stood under the bay window with shelf upon shelf of jigsaws and books, dolls and toys adorning every wall. A silver cross pram complete with doll, pillow and blankets was being bounced by Louise, completely unaware of her beloved friends reasoning for not wanting to play with anything.

'I'm too hungry to play Louise.' Dorothy announced, suddenly dissatisfied with her lot in life.

Tea was served by Beryl on a large oak table on matching crockery and special child sized silver cutlery. There was a jug of milk on the table and not the milk bottle that was always on Dorothy's. The salt and pepper pots were in delicate china pots instead of the cartons that they were purchased in, and Beryl sipped tea delicately from a teacup with a saucer and not from a mug. The little fairy cakes were presented on a china stand instead of from a paper bag. Dorothy felt swamped and overcome by these huge differences in how they lived, and she didn't like it one bit.

'I want to go home now please Mrs Barnes, I'm missing mam.'

Dorothy started to notice things about Louise now that she had previously paid no heed to. Like how when their cardigans developed a hole, hers was darned carefully but Louise would appear in a new one. When Dorothy had showed up at school with her new red leather double buckled shoes, that she'd had to go to such devious lengths to obtain, Louise had turned up with an identical pair the day after. Just like that! No waiting until the old pair had worn out, no hanging on until payday, or waiting her turn. It stuck resolutely in Dorothy's craw.

Louise never noticed or commented on the darned clothes, she never mentioned that Dorothy lived in a small, terraced house or that her family were poor. She didn't care, she just liked Dorothy.

Dorothy also loved Louise dearly and couldn't help but want to be with her, but she just simply could not bear for her to have more things than her, nicer things, bigger things, more expensive things. It ate her up inside and she'd do mean little things to ease the feelings.

When they were seventeen years old, their

parents had allowed them to go for a weekend away to Morecambe and stay in Louise's parent's apartment on the seafront. It was all they could talk about for weeks. They had discussed endlessly the clothes and shoes they'd be taking, where they'd visit and what they would do with their days.

They'd caught the train even though Louise's dad had offered to drive them there, 'No thanks dad, it's all part of the fun.' Louise had said, so he'd kindly given them the train fare and enough for a taxi from the station to the apartment.

Dorothy unpacked the moment they arrived, carefully hanging her dresses in the wardrobe and folding her cardigans and blouses so that they wouldn't looked creased. 'Well, I can't be bothered with all that malarkey,' announced Louise, 'The creases will just drop out when I put them on. Mum usually unpacks for me because I'm just too lazy.' They both laughed as she simply unzipped her suitcase, laid it open and stated, 'That's my unpacking done.'

'Come on, let's make every second count, let's go for a walk along the front. We can get fish and chips on our way back. I'm already famished,' Dorothy looked at Louise. 'Okay, I'm not wearing the same stuff I've travelled in though, I'm going to put a dress on.' Dorothy watched as she started to pull clothes out from the case. It all looked new. 'I thought we'd decided what we were bringing to wear Louise? We've been discussing it for weeks,' Dorothy felt the familiar grip of jealousy claim its hold in the bottom of her belly. 'Oh, Dorothy I know, but dad took me shopping for new outfits and I simply couldn't resist, and you know what you're like with your silly green-eyed remarks, so I didn't mention it to you. I'm sorry.'

She didn't look sorry though and now, next to her, she'd look less fashionable. 'Louise, it's just that we'd decided, I'd have bought a new dress if I'd known. Anyway, it's done now. Come on, let's get a move on.' Even to herself, Dorothy found it impossible to admit that she was envious.

After a full and fun day, they called at the chippy and headed back home. They plonked themselves down on the bed, a heaving serving of fish and chips still in paper on their laps and using fingers instead of cutlery they munched on their fish suppers and reminisced about their day and what they planned to do tomorrow.

In the morning, Dorothy awoke to the sound of Louise sobbing quietly, she rubbed her eyes and sat up, guilt already settling like a brick in her gullet. 'What's the matter Louise? What's happened?' Louise looked at her, tears pouring down her face, 'Look,' she nodded downwards towards her suitcase. Dorothy peered over the edge of the bed and looked at the sorry mess. A pile of cold, greasy fish and chips lay in all four corners of the suitcase, grease visibly and silently seeping into the contents. 'Oh, you silly thing Louise, you must have knocked them off when we fell asleep.' Louise looked her dead in the eye, 'Yes, and then gravity must have played havoc with them, squashed them down and repositioned them into each corner.'

Dorothy dramatically pressed her hand to her chest. 'What are you insinuating Louise?' She laughed loudly as though Louise were obviously joking. Louise, her face a picture of hurt bewilderment raised her voice for the first time ever at her dear friend, 'Dorothy Gough, don't sit there chortling in your superior contemptuous way. I know you did this.' Her voice was louder than Dorothy had ever heard it as years of growing antipathy exploded from her mouth. 'All my life I have tried to ignore your constant jealousy because I love you. I've always made considerable efforts to forgive you, but this behaviour?' She sniffed loudly as more tears fell angrily, 'This, I can't do.' Dorothy stuttered and stumbled, and Louise simply watched as she babbled on in the most embarrassing way. 'I'm done Dorothy, I'm finally done. I'd rather gargle with razor blades than ever speak to you again.'

Dorothy had expected the Lumai to appear at this point. She'd never forgiven herself for the callous way she'd treated her lovely friend, each memory was etched deeply and painfully in her head. She had never even bothered to apologise. Redemption was unlikely when she considered all the snide things that she had done due to her petty jealousy. She was nasty and didn't deserve to be forgiven. Louise had kept to her word and never spoken to her after that, there was never any malice from her, just perhaps a deserved degree of contempt.

At her life review she had felt her beloved friend's sense of betrayal and hopelessness. She wondered when the Lumai would release.

Calla stayed close within Dorothy's aura whilst they continued to watch the scene. Louise arrived home already in tears as she walked up the steps to her front door a day earlier than planned. 'Louise is that you?' her mum was calling out as she came from the living room. 'Oh my word, what's happened? Are you okay? Is Dorothy okay?' she rushed towards Louise. Louise knelt down and began to open the suitcase, 'Look mum, this is what she did. You haven't a clue about the depth of her jealousy and the little snide things she's done over the years, it's worse than ever. But I adore her you see, so I just always tried hard to overlook it.' She was sobbing now, 'But this, this is the last straw, and I will never, ever speak to her again.' She opened the suitcase fully and watched her mum's horror-stricken face as she saw the congealed food melded with her daughter's belongings.

The scene evaporated and the Lumai exploded from it in a flutter of euphonious, extravaganza, each of them humming and parading their tuneful note and loving light. 'It'll feel wonderful to dispense these Calla, look at them dance. Come on, help me choose someone.'

LUMAI SIX

Susan Baycroft

Dorothy looked down at Susan's aura. Thick, treacly, dull and yet quite vast. 'I'm intrigued Calla, I've never seen an aura before that's in such a poor state, yet so large.' She stretched out her glow and wrapped herself in the woman's lights. She found herself whizzing right back in time. Susan, a young woman at the altar, her aura pulsating and glowing as she took her marriage vows in the little registry office. She looked into the eyes of her husband Dean, whose lights were drab and diminutive.

Dorothy witnessed as she gave birth two years later to the delightful Deborah, but already this life was spiralling out of control. The husband was abusing and controlling, criticising the way she looked, how she cooked, how she mothered. He was slowly suffocating her.

He had been rude to her friends and her parents and now they refused to visit. When Susan took it upon herself to visit them, that caused him to raise his fists as a threat and so she became socially isolated too. He took himself off for regular nights out, returning in the early hours stinking of cheap perfume and with a belly full of beer which always escalated his temper and Susan would keep as quiet as possible during the beatings so that Deborah slept through them. In the morning, the growing Deborah would help her mum to save face by pretending she believed how she had fallen downstairs in the dark or had clumsily walked into a door. By the time she was twenty-eight years old, she was completely downtrodden.

One evening, Dean was out on the town, Deborah was fast asleep, and Susan was looking for a snack to eat in the kitchen. Her gaze stopped on the unopened whiskey bottle in the cupboard. He hated whiskey, it had been gifted by his manager and had stood there since Christmas. He wouldn't miss it and it was years since she'd enjoyed a drop. She poured a small glass and she sniffed into its depths, enjoying the aroma of its woody and fruity notes. Gosh, she'd forgotten how delicious it was. Four glasses later and she crawled unsteadily up the stairs and climbed into bed. She barely felt the beating that night. In fact, if it hadn't been for the bruising on her neck and cheek, she'd have felt certain that a beating hadn't even occurred.

After that, she had started to buy regular bottles. For a couple of years, she managed to convince herself, ostrich like, that it was almost a medication to numb her husband's fists, and besides, it was so relaxing. It stopped her being quite so scared when Dean was due home from work or when he decided she was doing something wrong or hadn't put the right clothes out for him.

By the time Deborah had reached seventeen, Susan was losing whole days in blackouts. She would wake up in a soiled bed and vomit all around her, or suddenly sit up under the dining room table, her cheek adhered to a pile of dried vomit, wondering how the hell she had got there. When Dean had finally left her after waking up covered in her excrement and beating her black and blue, Susan had felt nothing only joyous relief. She could stop drinking now and properly care for Deborah. She sat down with her the same afternoon. 'Deb, I'm free of him at last. I know you've heard me say it too many times before, but now he's gone and I'm not living my life scared to death, I'll definitely be able to stop drinking.' Deborah felt a little hope rise in her heart again. Her mum, despite this horrible problem, had a heart of gold. She had never once, even with her huge problems, let her down. She had attended every school event and had never been late picking her up from school. She'd wear sunglasses in the winter and long sleeves in the summer, pretending that she hadn't heard the snide remarks from the other mums at the gates. 'I'll help you mum. Now that dad's gone you really don't need it.' She hugged her tightly and prayed hard, then immediately felt her hopes dashed. 'I may as well finish that half a bottle since it's paid for, but after that, I promise you, I'll never touch another drop.'

They sat together on the sofa that evening watching television and Deborah watched as her mum slowly drank the half bottle until she had supped the last drop. She lifted the bottle to her lips and caught the last dregs on her tongue. 'I could just do with another couple of glasses really. You know, to celebrate my new sobriety and being free and everything. Just one last blow out to get me through.' Deborah felt her stomach sink, 'Mum, you have just drunk half a bottle, you know that much would put a grown man on his back, don't you? Why don't we go to bed now and then you can enjoy your first morning in years without a hangover?'

Susan knew that she was right but there was such a burning desire to get just another glass or two inside her. She'd be okay then. 'Well, I've been hiding bottles here and there for years, so I'll just check everywhere I can think of and if I can't find any, we'll go to bed. Deal?' She proceeded to turn the house upside down, emptying cupboard after cupboard leaving Deborah to sort her mess out. 'Well, looks like it's time for bed then,' said Deborah, her heart aching as took herself upstairs. She knew that she'd hear the front door open and close before she'd even managed to brush her teeth.

Susan woke up, she couldn't figure out where she was, so she closed her eyes again to have a think. The floor was cold, so she must be on the kitchen floor again. She put her hand to her face, her eye socket was tender and there was blood coming from somewhere. She sat herself up. It was nighttime. She looked around, she was in the middle of the town and lay on the hard floor. 'Think Susan think,' she said aloud, trying desperately to muster up any memory from her foggy head. She stood up and wandered over to a bench. She felt wet. She ran her hand down the back of her legs. She was completely soiled. She remembered leaving Deborah at home to nip for a small bottle of Whiskey. Her stomach clenched as she tried to evade the thoughts of her upset daughter. She'd let her down again. If she went home, she could get straight in bed and perhaps Deborah may just think they'd gone up to bed together after all. She would have to take a shower first though because she absolutely stunk rotten.

'Damn it,' the living room light was on, Deborah would have known by now that she had sneaked out after all. Oh well, what's done is done. She let herself in. 'Oh, mum thank God, thank God,' Deborah was flying towards her. 'I'm so sorry sweetheart, I just couldn't manage without another couple of glasses. I'm truly sorry,' she hugged her daughter to her. 'Where on earth have you been? You have a black eye, and your nose is bleeding, mum we've been searching everywhere for you,' Deborah was sobbing now.

'I'm so sorry, I thought you'd have just gone to sleep and not realised I'd sneaked out. I promise I'll make it up to you. I know I've disgraced myself again, but I'd prefer not to dwell on it and anyway, I'm definitely going to stop from today.' Deborah looked at her dishevelled, broken mum, 'Mum, you've been gone for five days.'

Later that day, fraught with anxieties and uncertainties, Susan made her way to the doctor's surgery. She was scared witless about how she could continue her life without a drink, but the kind man had promised her that help was available and how stepping foot in his surgery was the very first step to recovery. She hadn't told Deborah, she couldn't bear to see the anguish on her face if she failed again.

On her way home, she saw St Joseph's church. 'What harm can it do to ask for a few blessings and a bit of help and guidance?' she wondered out loud. She'd not stepped foot in there for about twenty years. She walked in, there was already a mass in progress, so she took a pew at the very back, knelt and began to pray. 'Please Lord, please help me. I need to stop drinking. I just want this horrible life to stop. I want to have a mundane, ordinary life. I want to be a mother to Deborah. Please, I'm begging you with all my heart and soul, please help me to find that elusive inner reserve of strength that I'm really in need of. Amen'

Dorothy looked up towards her Lumai, 'Come on my precious little angels, do your magic.' She gently gathered them to her and nudged them into the deserving Susan.

She and Calla watched together as the Lumai invaded that broken, dismal aura and danced around until it glowed and sparkled. They watched as Susan looked up puzzled but innately aware that something miraculous had happened, the etched pain on her face easing off into a smile as she realised that her plea's had been answered. They watched as she re-emerged from the church with shifted priorities.

Dorothy blazed with a whirl of lights and colours shooting from her. 'I just bloody love this Calla.'

ORB SEVEN

The Smile

This orb looked exactly the same as the others. She watched it hovering in front of her, pulsing and trembling with static charge. Its colour was vibrant and lustrous, it was alive with emotion. She pulled it towards her in anticipation, feeling its life force, sensing its spirit. She crushed it to herself. With a whoosh, she was within her chosen moment.

A simple moment fastened together either side by the wretchedness of grief. A tender smile between a father and daughter. A tender smile that when relived in the life review room, resulted in such a flurry of emotion so intense among the watchers, that it triggered a tsunami of electricity and lights and caused Dorothy to feel both proud and gratified. That such a simple, heartfelt, tender smile could elicit that response, was a wonder to behold.

Dorothy had just turned seventeen years old when she'd learned that her beloved dad was terminally ill. She'd not noticed that he'd been coughing more than usual, or that he'd lost weight, or that his couple of weeks off work had melded into a couple of months. He was her dad, of course he'd get better. Neither herself nor Helen had been told that he and their mam had made multiple trips to the doctors and the infirmary.

'Dorothy, would you just nip into Leigh please and get your dad a piece of that cod he likes from the market?' her mam had asked her one Saturday morning. She looked up from her magazine and towards her mam sat on the couch supping her morning mug of tea, 'I thought you were cooking a stew? We always have a stew on Saturdays. Why do you want cod dad?' Dorothy looked at him in puzzlement as he sat on his comfy chair opposite her enjoying his morning woodbine with his mug of tea and the paper. 'You're breaking our great tradition of beef stew for Saturday tea dad,' she laughed.

'Gladys, I didn't say I wanted a piece of cod, I just said I didn't fancy stew,' he was looking at her mam and shaking his head, 'and I don't fancy cod either as it happens.' Her mam took a deep breath and let it out in a big, exasperated sigh. 'Well, you have to eat summat Johnny and a piece of fish will do you no harm.' Dorothy heard a twang of panic in her mam's voice and looked back again at her dad. She put her magazine down and sat up properly. She looked from her mam to her dad. Something was wrong. They weren't telling her something.

'Why have you no appetite dad?' she asked him, accusatory. 'Mam, why has he no appetite?' She looked from one to the other and could feel her heart begin to start pounding. 'Why are you not answering me?' she looked again from one to the other waiting for either of them to reassure her quickly. In a second, they'd laugh and tell her to hold her horses and that he'd just got a stomach upset. But they didn't. Dad looked at mam and nodded, silently consenting to some sort of agreement to let mam spill their secrets. 'Go and get our Helen from upstairs love,' she put her empty mug on the small side table and motioned for Johnny to join her on the couch. Dorothy shot to the hall and bounded up the stairs yelling as she ran, 'Helen, Helen, get up Helen, something's wrong with dad.' Helen, startled from her sleep was pushing her blankets back and grabbing her dressing gown as Dorothy entered her room. 'What's happened? Is he okay? Is he poorly?' Her sleepy face was panicked. 'Mam wants to speak to us, well they both do actually, but something's really wrong Helen and I'm scared.'

Dorothy and Helen knelt together on the rug in front of the gas fire directly in front of their mam and dad. 'Go on then, tell us what's wrong,' Dorothy offered, but something in her gut really didn't wish to hear the news.

'Well,' her dad started, 'you know I've been off work with this cough?' They both nodded along rapidly. 'Well, it seems it's serious. Seems it's not good news really. Well, how can I best put it?'

He looked to Gladys for a bit of help. 'Well, your dad isn't well girls.'

Dorothy threw her hands up in the air. 'Well, that's just told us precisely nothing.' Helen, always the calmer of them both, gently pulled Dorothy's hand down. 'Can you be a little more specific mam, we're really scared here you know.' They watched anxiously as their dad looked to their mam, he started to speak, 'The bottom line is, well, it's cancer. They can't do anything because its spread you see. It started in my lung, and now it's in my liver and lymph nodes. I've got a few months left is all.' His lip was wobbly. Dorothy shot up and hugged him, tears already pouring down her face. This was her worst nightmare, her beloved dad. 'Are they sure dad? There must be treatments for it, you're only young.' Her mam interjected, 'We've been for every test possible over the last four months Dorothy, there was talk of taking the lung out at one point, but it's spread too much so it can't be done.' Her voice was shaky and thin.

'So how long then dad, have they said anything?' Helen was brave enough to broach what Dorothy needed to know. Dad looked directly at Dorothy with his answer, 'Weeks, probably not months, I'm so sorry girls.' He stood and walked back over to his comfy chair and lit another woodbine.

Helen wandered back upstairs shell-shocked,

and mam wandered into the kitchen to prepare a fresh pot of tea. Dorothy wondered how you could do normal things when your whole world had just had its rug ripped from underneath it.

'I'm going to the market for that cod. Mam's right dad, you do need to eat, and it will do you good.' She'd needed to get out of the house and get some fresh air. How on earth could her mam and dad have been acting normally for all this time? How had she not noticed that her dad had lost so much weight and was barely eating? She shouted up the stairs, 'I'm nipping into Leigh Helen, do you want anything?' Helen opened her bedroom door and stuck her red eyed, crying face out, 'No ta sis.' She went to the kitchen to find her mam sat down and staring into space. She sat down next to her. She'd hug her but her mam wasn't one for hugs unlike dad, 'Mam, do you need anything else from Leigh? Can you think of anything that he might fancy?' Her mam sighed quietly and patted Dorothy's hand, 'I don't think so love.'

Within three weeks, mam had bought a single bed and put it in the front room to save dad trying to drag his weary body up and downstairs when he'd needed a lie down. He'd said no for a week but had finally caved in when Dorothy had found him sat on the stairs after she'd come home from work. He'd been stuck there for over an hour, too exhausted to move. 'I'm sorry love, I thought your mam would've been back ages ago.

She only nipped out to your aunty Bessie's to give her a birthday card, she must have got chatting.'

So now, he was safely ensconced in the front room with everything he needed on the lamp table beside him and all the surplus furniture was stacked up here and there throughout the rest of the house. Doctor Ellis called in every day to see how he was doing and to ask mam if she was still coping and managing okay. 'Help is there if you need it Mrs Gough,' he'd said kindly. But in truth, they enjoyed looking after him themselves. Dorothy would buy him an egg custard tart on her way home from work and her mam said the only reason that he ate it was to please her. 'Good,' she'd said, 'I'm happy to make him feel an obligation to me if it means we can get something in his belly.'

A few days later, Dorothy could see a real decline. She watched him sleeping like a baby, as though he hadn't a care in the world. He seemed to spend most of the day sleeping now. He'd barely touched a mouthful of food in days. His drinks were taken away cold and replenished with hot tea until they too turned cold. Doctor Ellis had said that morning that it was only a matter of days now.

Dorothy sat beside him and stroked his hand. 'I'm here dad.' He opened his eyes and blinked rapidly trying to get his bearings. He tried to speak but his mouth was too dry. 'Let me sit you up a bit dad, let's give you a sip of water then you can speak.' She gently put her arm behind his shoulders and sat him a little more upright. He took a small sip of the proffered water then lay back down, exhausted with all the effort it had taken. 'Light me a woodbine up please love, would you?' Dorothy tipped a cigarette from its packet, put it in her mouth, lit it then put it to her dad's lips. He took a small puff. 'That's enough love, thanks.' Dorothy put the cigarette out, took off her slippers and climbed into the bed. 'Budge up dad you fat pig,' she wriggled herself in slowly until they were squashed up together side by side. She'd always been his favourite, not that he'd ever said it of course, not in so many words, but she just knew. They fit each other like a jigsaw, perfectly slotting together. She pulled the covers up under their chins. He was chuckling away. She turned onto her side to get a better view of him. 'Dad,' she whispered. He turned to look at her. 'I bloody love you dad and I'm going to miss you for my whole entire life.' He looked her right in the eyes, his mouth dry and his voice frail and hoarse, whispered back, 'I'll watch over you if I can my precious girl. I love the bones of you.' They tenderly smiled at each other, glad in their hearts that nothing had been left unsaid.

Dorothy was so completely absorbed in the moment that she'd thought it was all actually happening and that she was still living, when the scene had disintegrated into smithereens. She was instantly surrounded by a magnificent flurry of sparkling, singing Lumai. 'Oh Calla, look at all these,' she danced in and out of them, feeling their love and sweetness passing through her very being. 'I'm going to have to find someone very special and very much in need to be able to bestow these.'

LUMAI SEVEN

Warren Hill

Dorothy hovered over the scene. It was pitiful and heart-rending. All those ripples of pain reaching out and infecting so many souls made Dorothy's aura feel lacklustre. The whole family was tortured. She stroked the young lad's aura, reaching in so that she could see what had led to this moment. He was a kind soul, his glows were light and clean and dispersed with slivers of golds and reds, it was just really still, almost static. 'Poor boy,' said Calla, his aura really is quite beautiful, but it should be bouncing with vigour at this stage of life.'
'Dad, when will I have big muscles like you?' Warren was watching his dad as he lifted his younger brother Todd onto his shoulders on their way to the park. 'When you're a man like me,' he pushed both his arms into the air and ran forward with Todd bouncing around on his shoulders, 'Because I'm superman, my big muscles help me to fly.' Warren ran after him laughing.

He was thirteen now, but his muscles didn't appear to be making much of a show, the fat around his belly and the tops of his legs did though, he could feel it all wobbling as he ran.

The following year and he had begun to notice that lots of his friends had now started to develop and thicken out, but he looked in desperation at his own body in the mirror every night, what a mess it was. What was wrong with him? A chump. A plump, weak and pudgy boy, completely not the right sort of body for attracting the girls. He hated himself. He'd have to do something about it.

'Dad, can I join that gym over the bridge?' Anita and Mike were sat cuddled up on the sofa watching television, Todd between them half asleep. 'If you want to lad, what are you thinking? To get fitter or bulk up a little?' He lifted his arm to show his dad, 'Well I'd like these little peas to grow into tennis balls,' he was laughing and squeezing his biceps. 'But mostly to lose a bit of weight and get fitter.' Mike laughed, 'Well you look okay to me lad, but nip in tomorrow after school and check out the prices and opening times, yes it's okay with us isn't it Anita?' She looked up at Warren, 'Course it is son. It doesn't do anyone any harm looking after themselves, good for you.'

Warren headed back upstairs to his bedroom, whipped off his shirt to have a last look at the blob thing reflected. From now on, this body would begin to look like a proper body, a decent one that he wouldn't be so ashamed about, he'd be lean and muscular. He'd attract all the girls. He'd stop eating chocolate on his way to school and he'd stop eating all those crisps after tea. He felt a real determination that things would change, roll on tomorrow and let the new Warren commence. He felt so buoyed and determined.

One month later and he was thrilled with the results. He could see his belly slowly disappearing. He weighed himself. 'Mum, mum,' he was shouting with excitement, I've lost 10 pounds.' Anita walked from her bedroom into the bathroom where Warren was stood in his pyjama bottoms on the scales, she laughed with pleasure at her son's achievement and sense of pride. 'Well done lad, you deserve it with all that training and careful eating. And I must say, I do think you look healthier for it. I'm so very proud of you Warren.' She pulled him to her, and they hugged. 'Thanks for helping mum, the gym, the healthy snacks and meals, it's kind of you.' She rubbed his chin, 'You'll be shaving next, I'll have a tall, lean, muscular bloke in the house, and I'll be wondering where my little Warren disappeared to.'

Six months later and Warren stood on the scales and was ecstatic with his results. He didn't weigh monthly any longer like the manager at the gym had advised him, he weighed each morning instead. He could keep a better watch then in case he put a bit on. He didn't bother telling mum or dad either. They'd started to comment negatively as though it was a bad thing. He went back to his bedroom to look at himself.

He was over fourteen now. He was still growing, so any height increase would be great at making him look decent. He ran his hands down his belly. There was still so much fat. His legs were still fat at the top too. He was pleased with the three stone loss, but it wasn't really reflected in the mirror from what he could see. Never mind, he was doing okay so far, so he'd just have to try harder. He'd increase his daily run from five to six miles, and he'd cut out breakfast too.

Anita's stomach did an involuntary lurch when she heard him coming downstairs a good hour before school. She knew he'd be in his running gear and that he'd sneak out before she got the chance to try to stop him. It was crucifying her. She always seemed to say the wrong thing which usually culminated in a row and then Warren grew more anxious and stayed in his room more. Then she'd hear him, feet pounding on the floor doing more exercise. She could barely function knowing that her son was killing himself.

She waited until she'd heard the front door slam and took herself upstairs to his room to change his bedding. It would definitely cause a row when he got home but his bed hadn't been changed for weeks now and he hadn't done it despite her repeatedly asking.

She whipped off the duvet cover and the pillowcase cover's and quickly replaced them with fresh ones. Then she changed the bottom sheet. As she tucked the fresh one in, her fingertips caught the edge of something. She felt deeper and pulled it out. A box of laxatives. 'Oh my God no, please no. I can't take any more.' She burst into floods of tears. She had completely upended the mattress and there, hundreds and hundreds of boxes of them lay, some empty boxes and strips, some full. She grabbed the wastepaper basket and swiped them all in. He'd be furious with her, but she didn't care any longer, he was going to die if this carried on. She left the mattress on its side, took the waste with her and slammed the door behind her. She'd expected an almighty row to break out when he discovered what she had found. Instead, she just heard his music and the sounds of his feet reverberating on the ceiling as he ran and ran and ran on the spot.

Mum and dad had sat him down the same evening. 'Warren, why don't we make an appointment at the doctors for you. She might be able to give you something to make you feel less anxious, we won't mention the exercise or the food issues.' It was a new idea they'd decided upon since every other suggestion had failed. He'd simply walked off back to his room agitated with the pair of them interfering. If he wanted to see the doctor about anything, it'd be for sleeping tablets, he just couldn't seem to drift off at all with his mind working overtime. Even if he did drift off, he was often woken by hungers pangs.

Twelve months later and his life was a mess. He'd be okay if it wasn't for mum and dad. They just didn't understand at all. It's like they actually wanted a whale for a son. They'd stopped paying for his gym membership and that had absolutely infuriated him. 'How can I get fit if you're punishing me like that, why would you do that to me?' He'd showed himself up by crying and shoved his dad so hard that he'd fallen into the wall. 'Warren what the hell is wrong with you? You're acting like a mad man,' his mum had looked at him with that stupid expression that she kept having when she said she was worrying about him. He really didn't want to listen to their whining that he wasn't well, of course he was well, he'd be fine as soon as he just lost that last stone and looked like what he was supposed to look like. Well, they could cancel his gym sessions, but they couldn't stop him running and they couldn't stop him eating less either. Anyway, he'd got so stressed one day when dad had tried to stop him from doing his run that he'd passed out, crumpled up on the floor like a cheap suit, spark out. So now they just let him continue. God if he couldn't run, he'd die for sure. He set off, he felt exhausted today as though he could barely pick up his feet never mind run.

He'd be okay though once he set off, he could always muster up those reserves of strength. And anyway, once he'd lost some more of this weight, he'd have less to carry around and it'd get easier. So, like a mantra in his head telling him to take just one more step, and despite the breathlessness and dizziness, he ran his planned six miles. He weighed himself the moment he arrived home. Yes, a pound down, what a relief. Mum was making a fry up as she always did on a Saturday. Sometimes, he went mad at her because it was obviously just to tempt him and he would have to sit in his bedroom with the window open, his stomach clenched with pain and hunger, trying not to inhale the delicious aromas. Today though, he'd allow himself a decent breakfast, he deserved one after that run and he'd only eaten an apple, ten peas and a really small tomato the day before. His mum had tried to cause a row about it when he said he'd eaten a sandwich on his way home from school and wasn't hungry, but he'd become the master of deflection and he'd almost spat the words at her, 'So now I'm a liar am I? He hated hurting them both, but he just couldn't risk them jeopardising his weight loss.

'I'm sorry about before dad, I don't know what possessed me to push you.' He began to sit himself down at the dining table. 'It's okay lad, I know you were upset, we're all upset.' He stopped talking after he caught Anita's eyes, and she was shaking her head as if to shut him up. He supposed she was right, he'd not mention anything that could trigger the lad. He rarely sat down at the table and when he did, he always ate. So, I'll be quiet and let him eat. Hopefully, he'd realise what he was missing and be okay again. They tried to make a conversation, but it was stilted and tense. Anita and Mike found themselves accidentally staring at Warren as though to will him to eat just one more mouthful. They found themselves slowly relaxing and catching each other's eyes with optimism as he ate two slices of bacon, a fried egg, a good portion of beans and a couple of slices of toast. He'd cut off all the fat from the bacon of course and he'd carefully cut the yolk out, but it was still a reasonable breakfast. Anita and Mike looked at each other and dared to hope but made no comment. They'd learned the hard way that any words of encouragement always backfired and sent him into a spin and sometimes he then refused to eat for days.

'Mum, I don't think Warren's well, I just heard him being sick in the bathroom.' Nine-year-old oblivious Todd had no idea of the horror of his words. Mike shot upstairs with Anita in pursuit. 'Warren, open this door right now, this has gone on long enough.' He didn't even get the chance to get to the door before his dad had smashed it off its hinges. There, they looked down in shock at their beloved, emaciated, exhausted, naked boy as he squatted down on the scales, his vertebrae jutting out, his hip bones protruding and his shoulders so emaciated that they looked like a coat hanger. He could see his mum's eyes wide with terror. His dad was rocking to and fro with his hands on his head watching helplessly as his son looked from one to the other of them slowly, his face ashen, disorientated and shaken. He looked so deeply ashamed, tears pouring down his face. 'I don't know how to stop.'

Dorothy gathered up the fluttering Lumai. She gently pulled them as they sparked and twinkled, and she granted them straight into Warren's lovely aura. Calla swirled around excited. 'I so adore watching this bit Dorothy. How very proud you must feel.'

They watched as the young man's aura suddenly lifted and grew as he gained a new strength to start to fight this wretched disease. They watched his future as he fought determinedly and doggedly as he battled his way to health and wellness over the next twelve months. They watched with joy as the family healed together.

ORB EIGHT

The Flowers

She looked at the ten orbs bouncing in front of her. Only three orbs containing Lumai were left, and they were pulsing and throbbing with their unspent energy. She knew she could relive all these moments whenever she chose, but she knew that you were only able to release the Lumai on this first viewing. She pulled one down and crushed it to her, watching in amazement as an explosion of lights propelled her into her chosen moment.

Dorothy was sat at the traffic lights waiting for them to turn green. She could see the old lady about to step foot in the road, so she kept her foot on the brake pedal. Sure enough, the old lady started to cross. She had an oversized black umbrella held aloft in one hand, protecting her against the driving rain and she dragged along a black and white polka dotted shopping trolley with the other. Its lightness obvious as its wheels bounced off the kerb and into the road, giving away the clue that it was empty.

Dorothy headed to the market car park, pleased to see that she wouldn't have to fight for a space for once. Perhaps she'd have to come shopping this early in future instead of her usual preference of housework first and shopping later. Then, after she'd bought most of her stuff, she'd nip to buy a bunch of flowers and a card for her old mam for Mother's Day.

She definitely wouldn't be hanging around browsing, it was heaving down and blowing a gale. She called in at the market first to buy meat from the butcher. They always had a friendly chat and Harold liked the lamb chops from there. Fish counter next and then finally fruit and veg. Her arms were aching now. She'd go back to the car to deposit this lot and then she'd get the rest of the stuff she needed and nip into a cafe for a bowl of soup and a sandwich.

She was just giving the waitress her order and lighting up a much-deserved cigarette, when in walked the lady she had seen a couple of hours ago at the traffic lights. She was heaving with all of her might trying to pull the trolley up and over the step into the shop. Dorothy rested her cigarette in the ashtray and got up to help her. 'Come here love, I'll do it,' she took the handle and pulled it up. 'Goodness me, that's got a fair bit of weight in it,' she laughed. The old lady quietly thanked her and found herself a seat. Dorothy continued smoking her cigarette as she watched the old woman with her back to her. She was literally starting to steam in the heat of the cafe. She'd removed her coat, and it hung limply over the back of her chair and Dorothy could see that her clothing underneath had become wet. Poor woman needed a better coat.

Dorothy had just started on her soup as the old woman, pot of tea finished, started to pull her coat on and brave the weather again. She looked out of the window. You wouldn't catch her leaving just yet, the rain was pelting down, and the wind howled and threw the rain sideways at the shop window. She'd finish her lunch and pot of tea, then nip back to the car to offload these bags, she only had a card and flowers to buy now, but she didn't want to risk them getting squashed with all this other stuff.

She hung around and eked the last of her tea out as long as possible hoping that the driving rain would soon settle, but the waitress was getting irritated with her taking a table up when there were customers waiting. So, a little annoyed since she was a regular customer, she paid her bill without tipping as she usually did and headed out into the pelting downpour.

As she reached the car, she saw the old woman again. 'Oh, bloody hell, that poor woman,' she said out loud as she watched her trying to heave the weighted trolley up a kerb. She placed the shopping bags in the boot and made her way over to the woman. 'Hello again love,' she said brightly, 'You're struggling with that thing today, aren't you? Come here, let me help.'

The old woman let go of the handle and Dorothy heaved it up the kerb. 'Have you far to go love?'

The woman reached out to take the handle again, 'Well I've done my shopping at last, just got to get home now. Thanks for your help though. Again,' she continued quietly, 'I think I'd have still been trying to get into the cafe if it hadn't been for you.'

'Have you far to go?' Dorothy asked. The woman looked up, 'Oh just a mile or two. I'm used to it now love, I've been doing this for years.' Dorothy thought how she still needed to go for her card and flowers but something in her couldn't let this old woman struggle home. 'Well, I'm all finished now so I can take you home. I'm parked just there,' she pointed. 'Oh, would you love? I'd be beyond grateful. I hadn't expected the weather to be so bad. It's March for goodness sakes, the country should be positively bursting with the promise of spring.' Dorothy heaved the drenched trolley over to her car. 'Go on, get yourself in and I'll put your shopping and brolly in the boot.'

She started to drive and had to stop almost immediately to rub the windscreen free of steam with her chamois. She glanced at the woman's face. She looked so sad. Probably around seventy-five or thereabouts, Dorothy guessed. 'It'll be okay when the heating kicks in, are you comfortable love?'

'My name's Edith, and yes, I most definitely am. My day started rotten, you know, the kind of day where it's hard to even stand up straight. But now, with this unexpected act of kindness, the world feels lighter again. I'm grateful in more ways than you know.' Dorothy glanced over, 'Well I'm Dorothy, and I'm glad to help.' They arrived less than ten minutes later, and Dorothy sent the woman ahead to open the door. 'I'll get your stuff, you go in.'

She dragged the weighty trolley over the porch step and into the warmth of the front room. 'And this is Donald,' Edith announced. Dorothy looked at the single bed along the far wall. It could have been the same scene from her youth when she'd watched her dad take his last breaths all those years ago. There, lay the dying Donald who was clearly meticulously well cared for with snacks and glasses prepared for him while Edith had gone to shop. He waved a thin, pale hand in her direction and offered a faint voiced hello.

Dorothy drove the two miles back into the town centre. She bought a card for her mum, then visited the florist where she purchased two huge bouquets of flowers. She drove through the still driving rain in the opposite direction to home and straight to Edith's house. She knocked on the door and presented Edith with the bunch of flowers. 'For you, because you're doing an amazing job.'

The whole scene suddenly gave way as it

fragmented into shards of brilliant, radiant illuminations. The Lumai erupted from it in a cloud of melodic rapture, filling the air around Calla and herself with tangible love. She pulled them to her. I adore these little things. 'Come on Calla, my favourite gifting bit is coming up.'

LUMAI EIGHT

Pauline Monaghan

'Look at this woman Calla,' Dorothy called out as she lingered over Pauline Monaghan's sleeping frame cuddled up close to her husband Bob. 'Her aura is beautiful, it's colourful, airy and bright. I'm not sure why she called to me.' She tenderly interlaced herself with the aura, filling herself full of the woman's history.

Pauline had thought she'd noticed something a little odd around five years ago after having picked her mum up ready to do their weekly shop. Her mum had knocked on the car window. 'Pauline, I can't find my purse anywhere, I've looked high and low.' So, they'd both gone back inside and prepared themselves to carry out a further high and low hunt, when Pauline saw it, there, in plain sight on the coffee table. 'Ha, mum, you're losing your marbles,' they'd both laughed, and her mum had said couldn't think why she hadn't seen it.

A month later and she'd forgotten that they always went shopping together on Fridays and wasn't ready when Pauline had peeped her horn outside.

'Are you okay mum,' she had asked once they had finally set off, 'Are you feeling poorly at all? Is your memory okay?' Marjorie had cocked her head in surprise, 'Why do you ask that? It's the first time I've forgotten anything.' Pauline reminded her about the incident the month before. 'I don't remember that at all. Are you sure? Was it not Bob's mum and you're mixing us up?' She furrowed her brow. 'Perhaps there is something wrong. I'm worrying a bit now though.' Pauline patted her hand. 'Don't worry mum, it's probably nothing. Let's just get you an appointment with your doctor though just in case. Sometimes these things just need nipping in the bud.'

They had always had a wonderful relationship. She was a perfect mum and a perfect grandma. All the grandchildren adored her. They were all in their thirties now, but still visited her and invited her to their homes and any for any special occasions that cropped up. She was a wonderful human. She was always calm in a crisis, always there if you needed her, and to make you want to spend time with her more than anything, was her infectious personality. She was hilarious fun to be with, gigglier than any school child and Pauline simply loved the bones of her.

She'd been to see the doctor who did a couple of

tests and announced that she was fit and well and to come back if she got worse.

Within twelve months it definitely did get worse, when repeated incidents had kept cropping up and Marjorie had received the devastating blow that she was suffering from Alzheimer's disease. 'Oh, just put me in a home Pauline. I don't want to be a burden to anyone,' she'd said stoically on the way home from the hospital. 'Mum, that will never happen,' Pauline was shaking her head, 'Not in a million years. When the time comes that you can't live alone, you'll be moving in with me and Bob.' Marjorie chuckled, 'Best see what Bob has to say about that one won't we? He might not be chuffed about a mad old woman taking over his home.' They both laughed, but it never reached their eyes.

Pauline watched the slow theft of her mum. She watched as it stole everything, ravaged every little part of her. It almost stole her marriage. She'd moved her mum in when she'd started to wander outside at night. She'd left it as long as she could knowing that her mum would feel even more lost in her and Bob's home than she did in her own. She lied awake each night anxious about allowing sleep to come in case her mum had tried to get out again. She woke one night to Bob shouting, 'For crying out loud Pauline, I can't keep putting up with this shit,' as her naked mum was trying to climb into bed with them with wet, soiled underwear clutched in her hands.

And then death finally claimed her. People were sending sympathy cards and ringing her with their condolences about the death of her poor mum, but Pauline felt pure relief. She felt free. She could take a shower now without bringing her mum into the bathroom with her for fear she'd wander off or cause herself an injury. She could go shopping without making sure Bob was home to manage her mum for an hour. She could do a weekly wash instead of a daily one. She could enjoy her grandchildren again, the garden, baking, life.

A week after the funeral and Pauline and Bob were relaxing in front of the television. An actress was portraying a person with dementia and Pauline started to think of her mum. 'I'm struggling to remember mum Bob, every time I think of her, I can only picture this confused woman who fights me every time I'm trying to help her. I can't remember my real mum.' Bob rubbed her knee, 'It's because that confused old woman was around for the last five years Pauline, it'll all come back love. It's like your mum died all those years ago really, isn't it?' Pauline wished she'd said goodbye to her then, before she was lost.

Three weeks after the funeral and Pauline was still low. 'I was hoping I'd remember a bit more of her Bob, but still, I can't find her in my head. It's really getting me down.' Bob, turned over to face her, thumping his pillow to plump it up, 'Try to get some sleep love, I'll think of a few things you did together to jog your memory and we can chat about it in the morning.' He kissed her forehead.

Dorothy wondered why Marjorie hadn't visited Pauline in her dreams. 'Come on Calla, let's go find her.' They entered the library and located the hospital. 'I presume she's still in her cocoon Dorothy, otherwise she would have done a dream visitation. She's probably still savouring the bliss.'

They found her beautiful soul recovering and recuperating in the soft blackness. 'Can we still help Pauline now? Because we can't intrude while she's here, can we?' Dorothy looked toward Calla in puzzlement. 'Trust in the Lumai Dorothy, I've told you, they always know what's best.'

'Well, she isn't my most desperate candidate Calla,' said Dorothy as they hovered back over Pauline but she's sad and she's so very deserving. I'm glad to be able to help her.' She reached up and drew a huge collection of her precious Lumai into herself. She sparkled with delight as they sang within her. Calla laughed, 'Come on Dorothy, share them nicely now.' Dorothy chuckled, released them gently from her aura then stretched up and gathered the cloud of tinkling Lumai, and gently cast them into Marjorie's luminescent glow.

They watched together as Marjorie, lights ablaze,

edged herself under the covers of Pauline's dream, gliding herself through the gossamer veil as she reached out to her beloved daughter. They watched as they chatted away and hugged and remembered and danced together. Two wonderful souls. They laughed and reminisced and Pauline, oblivious that she was sleeping, relished the much-missed company of her mum. And they still watched as the morning sun rose and Pauline woke with clear pictures of her beloved mum. 'I dreamt of mum Bob, I really felt I was with her all night. I feel so relieved, she was young again and it was mum before she forgot who she was. It's as though she came to me in a dream to let me know she's okay.' Bob was smiling at her, he pulled her to him to let her lie on his shoulder, 'I'm glad she came to you Pauline, you deserve it.' He kissed the top of her head, 'she'll know how well you looked after her.' 'That was the least dramatic outcome of my Lumai gifts Calla, but just feeling the absolute relief for that kind woman, who gave up five whole years of her life to look after someone who didn't even recognise her, fills me with such love and joy.' And Calla laughed as she watched her spinning off, into the stratosphere, leaving a trail of sparkles behind her.

ORB NINE

The Kestre

1

This had been a beautiful moment to enjoy in the life review room. She'd created much fun with the watchers in there. They'd been whooping and laughing enjoying the moment with her. It was another moment that wasn't particularly precious during her life. Like most human memories, the actual moments seep away, and you vaguely remember a pleasant day out. In the life review room, each moment is vivid and alive. The emotion is there and then.

Dorothy had been on her way to catch the bus for school when she first saw it. She didn't think she'd have noticed it at all but for a gap in the traffic allowing the unusual noise, a sort of flapping sound to attract her attention. She glanced up. There, midway up the fence was a huge bird completely tangled up in barbed wire. 'Oh no, you poor thing.' She looked around for someone to stop and help but this stretch always quiet, and the traffic was too fast for a driver to even spot that there was a problem.

She plonked her bag on the floor and tried to reach up. Not a chance. She put her foot in the metal fencing to give herself an extra few inches, but then she was having to hang on with one hand and she needed two to release the poor bird. 'Damn it, sorry bird, I can't reach you.' She'd have to wait until dad was home tonight and get him to come and help get him down. The weather was cold but at least it was dry so he wouldn't get drenched too. She'd have gone for her mam, but she was terrified of birds and anyway, she was walking Helen to school. She looked up at his little face, he just blinked at her, he'd long since lost his struggle. A vein of melancholy started to clutch at her belly. She was about to climb down and give up when a passing motorist pulled onto the pavement.

'Hello love,' he was walking over, 'I passed a few minutes ago and saw you struggling, it was only after I'd driven past that I realised you were trying to help a trapped bird, so I came back. Bloody hell that's a big un. It's a kestrel I think.'

Dorothy felt such relief, 'Oh thanks so much for stopping, I was just about to give up. I was planning on coming back tonight with my dad, but he'd have been so scared and in pain all that time.' He looked at her and smiled, 'He wouldn't have survived in this cold love, the brass monkeys have already put their thermals on.' She smiled back nonplussed. Then, her knight in shining armour reached up and began the grisly task of unravelling the barbs. 'He's got himself into a right tangle here,' then he yelped as a barb punctured his thumb. The bird didn't even attempt to move. 'I think he's really injured love, doesn't look like there's any fight left in him.' Then he unwound a long piece of wire, and the bird was suddenly free. The man held it aloft hoping it would take flight. He looked at Dorothy, 'He needs a vet I'd say. Anyway, I'm late for work so there you go,' and he just plonked the massive thing into her arms and walked off.

Part relieved and part panicked Dorothy now had no idea what to do. Mam and dad definitely didn't have money to pay a vet bill. She considered just walking to the field and leaving him there, at least he had a chance to live now that he was free. She looked at him in her arms, 'You're absolutely exhausted, aren't you? I can't just plonk you in a field.' She carefully bent down keeping a secure hold on the floppy dead weight bird and scooped her school bag up with three of her fingers that were free and set off back home. She'd just have to put him in the shed in a box for now and hope her mam didn't find out.

Her arms were in agony by the time she'd reached home and put him on the floor in the shed. 'I'm coming back little fellow, I'm just going to find you some food and water.' She retrieved the key from underneath the plant pot and let herself in. She took two towels from the airing cupboard and two bowls from the kitchen.

She had no clue what a kestrel ate and needed to be certain it was something her mam wouldn't miss, she'd go absolutely bonkers if she knew there was a bird in the shed.

Finally, she headed back to her charge. She pulled a large plastic container that dad had used for various jobs, and she lined it with a thick towel, then she lifted the kestrel, plonked him on top and covered him snugly with the second. She put the bowl of water and the bowl of sardines in tomato sauce right next to him. 'There you go birdy, you're definitely in a better state than when I found you thirty minutes ago.' She closed the shed door and hurried off to school running straight into her mam at the front gate. 'Dorothy, what are you doing here? Are you okay? You left before me and Helen.' The lie broke out of Dorothy's mouth before she had even formulated it in her head. 'I packed all the wrong books mam, I thought it was Thursday not Friday and when I remembered, I had to come back and sort the right ones out.' Her mam had laughed, 'Oh you dozy devil, go on then off you go, you're already late.'

All day long she'd been distracted, she'd told anyone who would listen about her exciting discovery that morning. The girls were mostly disinterested but the boys were all asking if they could come round and see it. 'No, at least not yet. If mam finds out about him, she'll go crazy and make me get rid of him. I'll be able to sneak you in though when she goes to bingo next Thursday.' She was absolutely itching to get home. She could barely think straight never mind study, she only ate a few bites of her lunch and was beside herself with excitement as the school bell rang signalling the end of the day. She ran all the way home.

Mam was already home and preparing tea, Helen was sat on the couch watching television. She was dying to go straight to the shed, but her mum would wonder why. She just couldn't risk any suspicion. She'd wait until it was a bit darker when her mam closed the curtains, and the shed wouldn't be in view.

'For goodness sakes Dorothy, sit still, you're a real fidget tonight, what's the matter with you?' Gladys was getting irritated with her, but she couldn't keep still she was that desperate to check on the bird. 'And why are you separating your food like that?' Dorothy had been slicing little portions of meat up for the bird unaware that mam had even noticed. 'It's a bit fatty that bit mam,' she'd lied.

She'd taken her plate into the kitchen and deposited the scraps of meat into a bit of tin foil. She drew the curtains and hoped that didn't arouse her mam's suspicions and she quietly let herself out. He was sat in the corner of the shed. He hadn't eaten any food that she could make out but at least he seemed to have more energy. She walked slowly over to stroke him, and he let out such a squawk, that it made her yelp in fright and worry that her mam might come outside to see what all the noise was. She put the meat scraps in his bowl and looked around for her dad's trowel, one of the lads at school had told her to dig worms for him. She found her little bucket and spade set which would do nicely to collect them in. Thirty minutes and ten worms later and mam came outside, 'Dorothy what on earth are you doing? We've been looking everywhere for you.' Dorothy looked up from her spot in the flowerbed. 'Sorry mam, I'm digging for worms, one of the lads at school has an injured bird in his shed and I promised I'd help. Gladys scrunched her face up, 'Yuck, well rather you than me.'

It became much easier to get out now because mam had no suspicion when she was coming and going to and from the garden. And Keith, a fine name for a bird she'd thought, was going from strength to strength. He was bombing around now, and one wing was completely out and able to flap, the other went from being limp, to slowly moving about. There was bird poo absolutely all over the place though, when she finally let him go free, she'd have to spend hours in here cleaning it all out.

Dad joined her at the back door, 'I'll help today Dorothy, I'll collect worms with you,' he said kindly. She couldn't lie to her dad. She looked down sheepishly, 'Dad, I'm not collecting worms for a lad at school, I found an injured bird and he's in our shed.' She looked up at him with absolutely no idea how he would respond. 'Dorothy Gough your mam would go mad! But I won't,' he smiled at her in collusion, 'Come on then, let's have a gander.' She felt her shoulders drop with relief. 'He's gorgeous dad, he's miles better too. He could barely lift his head when I first brought him home and now he's running around flapping one of them and the other is improving. He's called Keith.' Johnny laughed at her chattering excitement, 'And breathe Dorothy.' They entered the shed where Keith had managed to flap himself onto a low shelf.

'It's beautiful Dorothy, but you can't call it Keith because she's a girl,' they both laughed. 'Sorry Keith,' she said, 'I'll name her, hmmmm, Kathy instead then. How did you know she was a girl dad? You've not even looked at her hardly.' Dad looked up to where Kathy was perching, one wing stretched and the healing wing moving cautiously. 'It's her size love and her colouring, she'll be a lot darker brown than a male.' Dorothy loved how he was so knowledgeable. He'd been a keen birdwatcher as a boy. 'She's a young one too, you can tell with the colour of her feathers see, they're all streaky, they'll be plain when she's matured. What have you been feeding her on?' Dorothy picked up a couple of bowls and showed him. 'Sardines, worms, meat, I just keep bringing in different things. I've got the lads from school bringing me worms in exchange for a look at her tomorrow. Do you think she'll get better dad?'

'Well, she's certainly improved from what she was when you first brought her home from what you've said, so let's just keep our fingers crossed and your mam out.'

Dorothy was so pleased the following evening when Kathy had both wings out and was running and flapping. 'Oh, look at you, look at you, I'm so proud,' she dropped a fresh cache of worms into the dish and watched in awe as she swished her wings powerfully. The lads would be really chuffed to see her later.

'You off to bingo later love?' Dad had shouted to mam whilst giving Dorothy a knowing look, he was aware that her excited worm collecting friends from school would be coming soon. 'I certainly am. Do you want me to get you a fish supper on my ways home?' He patted his belly, 'There's always room for more in here.

'Do you think we'll be able to release her soon dad? She seems strong now.' They were in cahoots together in the front room. Then they both looked towards the kitchen as the sound of screams hit their ears. They shot up from the couch as one and bolted into the kitchen. Mam was outside screaming and screaming. They scrambled for the kitchen door and ran out together. There, was the most hilarious sight they had ever seen. Mam was running around the garden being chased and repeatedly cornered by a huge angry bird. No matter which way she ran to try to get back to the kitchen, Kathy cut her off. She took great bouncing strides and flapped her massive wingspan powerfully as she chased her perceived intruder.

Mam was screeching and hysterical and pathetically waving both arms in front of her in some sort of attempt to scare her away. Dorothy and her dad were bent double with laughter, tears streaming down their faces. They watched the spectacle and clutched their stomachs, each new scream setting them off more. The more she darted about, the more the bird ran at her and the more she screamed. They could barely stand up for laughing. It was the funniest thing they'd ever seen.

Dorothy and Calla were laughing together, remembering how all the watchers had howled at it in the life review, their lights fizzing and crackling when the scene dissolved and evaporated.

The Lumai exploded out like tiny hummingbirds, filling the air with their music notes and love. Dorothy was still laughing. 'I'm definitely going to rewatch that scene again and again Calla. Those lads were so disappointed that she'd flown off, and then dad, ever so charmingly asked them to help clean the shed up and they did. And poor mam didn't end up going to bingo that evening either, but she soon forgave us.' She gathered up her cherished Lumai and pulled them into her, savouring the deliciousness that they imparted within her.

LUMAI NINE

Derek Rudd

Calla amused herself watching Dorothy whizzing in and out of the aura's of the living as she shot through them beyond the speed of light. She was so excited, and it really pleased Calla to watch her choose with such passion. Some souls would bestow their Lumai on those who were right in the midst of the depths of sorrow, but Dorothy would examine them completely. She'd run through their entire life, she simply understood and absorbed their distress of the moment and then she gently assisted. She'd make a great guide soon. She simply connected with each of them on a spiritual level and deeply loved them all.

She hovered over Derek. He'd been in and out of trouble the whole of his life. 'He'll regret that when he arrives at the life review room won't he Calla,' Dorothy had laughed.

He was seventy-two now with only another seven years of his life left. He looked utterly bereft. He just sat there staring into space. His aura was far from the best she'd ever seen, but he'd lived a pretty selfish life. It was flat and quite dull with echoes of beige and mustard. She could see that there had been growth over the last few years and that he'd felt a deep love for the first time in his adult life. His guide Lu was trying to soothe him, but it was as though she was blocked. She swept herself in for a closer look around before she made a firm decision with her precious Lumai.

For the last eight years he'd not been in any trouble whatsoever. Not because he'd wanted to change his ways or his morals, but because of Boss. Boss the Jack Russell, who'd arrived at his grimy flat as a ten-week-old puppy, stolen from a garden and placed with Derek as a temporary measure and a few quid, until he could be sold.

Derek had taken hold of the tiny, whistling bundle with its warm squirmy body and for the first time in his entire life, he'd felt a real connection, a warmth to something living. He'd already bought a dog food supply planned to last for a couple of weeks until the dog was moved on, but the anxious pup was turning his nose up at it.

He couldn't decide if it was because the poor thing was simply scared or because the food smelled unappetising, so he decided to nip back out and buy the little fellow a different brand and a ball for him to play with. He found an old blanket in the airing cupboard that had been left by the previous tenant and he placed it on the floor near the fire. 'Come on dog, stay here for a bit and I'll go and get you a new ball.' He patted the floor, and the pup warily came towards him with his tail between his legs. Derek arrived back home less than an hour later with a variety of food, treats and toys. His heart soared when this happy little pup padded towards him wagging his stubby white tale in a welcome.

Derek had planned to rob a house that evening, he'd seen a television yesterday while doing a quick recce, and he'd seen that a stupid couple had left their light on and curtains open. 'Bloody fools, showing off your wares, I'll have that tonight and it'll have made me a bob or two before bed.' But he didn't fancy leaving the puppy now, what if he got arrested and there was no one to feed it? 'Bloody hell puppy, it's as though you're the boss. That's your name now. Come here Boss,' and Boss came padding over, lay down on his back and wriggled away happily when he got a belly rub.

Terry, the bloke who'd robbed him from the garden, came to pick him up to sell him to his new owner. Derek answered the door, 'Nah mate, he got out last week and I couldn't find him anywhere. Sorry.' But Terry, who wasn't a fool, heard the pup scratching and mewling from the kitchen. Derek laughed at the giveaway, 'Okay, I've still got him, how much were you selling him on for then? Terry said fifty quid, Derek said thirty take it or leave it, and Terry took it.

'Oh, you bad boy Boss, you're costing me an arm and a leg, come to daddy,' and Boss bounded over, dove straight onto Derek and smothered him in puppy breath kisses.

He never committed another crime after that. There was too much of a fear of being sent back inside and he worried too much that Boss wouldn't have anyone decent to take care of him. They walked miles and miles together and had met loads of other dog walkers who had become friendly. Boss had really helped to turn his life around. For the last eight years, that dog had been his life, he'd been what Derek lived for.

He had looked out of his window this morning to see a sprinkling of snow on the ground and people up and down the street defrosting their cars. Gone were the autumnal days which he had begun to adore since having Boss, and winter had well and truly sunk its teeth in. He made himself a mug of tea sweetened with honey and Boss sat on his knee while he drank it waiting patiently for the last sup that Derek always gave to him.

He wrapped himself up in a couple of layers of warm layers in readiness for their morning walk as he felt the cold more easily these days. Boss had never taken to wearing a jacket and had just squirmed and wriggled so much when Derek tried to insist on one, that he didn't even bother trying these days. He put the lead on, and they headed off to the park. 'Bloody hell it's freezing Boss,' he looked down at the dog who seemed completely oblivious to the cold. 'You'll soon warm up playing fetch though.' Boss's ears pricked up and Derek smiled.

They walked around the field that adjoined the park and Boss happily played fetch with his ball. No matter how far they walked or how many times he fetched his ball, Derek had not once in his life tired him out. 'I wish I had his energy,' shouted Brenda, from across the field. Derek had laughed, 'Me too.'

They set off for home. 'Come on boy, let's get your lead back on. Boss bounded over aware that he'd receive a treat and a pat on the head.'

They headed back towards the main road. The sun was bright now and Derek was conscious that the pavement surface was wet and slippy due to the partly melted ice. He'd slow down his stride a little to be sure his feet didn't slip. He rounded the bend, only two minutes away from home now where he'd get them both breakfast and then settle down to watch a bit of telly before their afternoon walk.

The cars coming round the bend were driving really slowly due to the slippy road, and Derek watched as the drivers were hit by a sudden shaft of sunlight and had to lift their hand to pull down their windscreen visors. 'Glad I'm not a driver Boss,' he said looking down. As he looked up again, instinct caused him to leap to one side as the car on the bend left the road and skidded up and on to the pavement. He sat still, shocked and dazed but thankfully unhurt. It had all happened so fast. The young driver shot out of his car, 'I'm so sorry mate, are you okay? I lost control on the ice, I was trying to steer away but it just kept coming towards you.'

A few people had started to gather around. 'My dog, my dog, where's my dog?' he was looking around wide eyed trying to get to his feet, a clammy desperation etched on his face.

A lady on the other side of the car shouted over, 'I've got him Derek,' it was Brenda. Thank God he knew someone, he was so shaken he couldn't think straight. She walked over to where an embarrassed Derek was trying to pull himself up. Her face was streaming with tears, she held Boss in her arms, lead dangling freely. 'There's not a mark on him Derek, but he hasn't made it.' He sat back down on the pavement. His precious dog. It couldn't be true. He overheard someone say he was a lucky man, he looked up, 'Lucky? Lucky you're saying? My dog's dead.' Then he howled with raw grief. Some of the bystanders couldn't help but cry with him. A kind man offered to carry Boss home while Brenda retrieved her own dog from where he was secured to a railing and then she walked with Derek back to his flat. He'd never experienced pain like it. An agony gripped his stomach. His precious dog. He looked over at the man carrying his limp body. He loved that dog more than life itself. He would never recover from this loss, never. Fresh tears poured down his face. 'I'm so very sorry Derek, I really don't know what to say to you.' Brenda still crying herself, linked his arm.

Dorothy gathered up her Lumai, they fizzed and hummed, and the love was pulsing through them and throughout her. She waved them gently into Derek as he sat lost in his grief staring into space. 'I wonder what they'll do Calla. Perhaps they'll send a new puppy for him to love?'

They watched as the Lumai began to sparkle and fizz in Derek's glow. Then, the whole scene evaporated and reformed.

Derek was putting his mug of tea on the floor, the last of its honeyed dregs saved lovingly for his treasured dog. 'It's looking mighty cold out there this morning Boss. We'll have our breakfast before our walk this morning, let the air warm up a bit.'

Calla and Dorothy whooped with delight. 'It's not as though he hadn't cared before and now has a sudden appreciation for the dog, is it? He's always absolutely loved the bones of him and couldn't possibly ever appreciate him any more than he did. He truly does love that little dog more than he loves himself. I'm so very glad that I chose Derek.'

ORB TEN

The Red Buckled Shoes

Dorothy watched her final precious orb in front of her vibrating with life. The others now all hovering above her still, but not crackling with life as this one was. She was glad she'd saved this one until last. She would squash this one to her now and let it reveal its delights. She held it tenderly and let its fizz and static crackle flood through her. Then she pulled its thrumming weight towards her, squashed and burst it. She was instantly within the scene of a throng of busy shoppers muscling through the town centre. This moment had never caused any lasting damage in anyone's life, but it had been Helen's sweet little innocent face that she had wanted to bring back from her life review. That poor little face with its expression of utter disappointment, all caused by a scheming Dorothy. Some of the watchers had even chuckled at first given that Dorothy was just a child, but Dorothy hadn't, she'd known it was wrong even then at eleven years old. She'd felt

Helen's upset. She'd felt the ripples of worry from mam and dad. This moment, for whatever reason she had chosen it, was very precious to her.

So, just eleven years old and being trudged reluctantly in the pouring rain, to get Helen's feet measured for new shoes. 'But you said you can't even afford any until next month mam, so why couldn't we have just come next month instead? We're all getting drenched wet through for no good reason.' Dorothy had a face of thunder as Gladys looked down at her, 'Dorothy, not that it has anything at all to do with you, but if we get Helen's feet measured today, I might be able to pick a bargain up before next month, but I'll need to know her size, won't I?' She pushed her along with the small of her back, 'You need to learn a little patience young lady. Look at the state of poor Helen's shoes, there's more hole than sole.' Dorothy didn't need to look, she knew because she'd seen the holes getting bigger and bigger each week. Helen began to hop with one leg held up behind her, 'See, look Dorothy, you can see my wet sock.' Dorothy looked in the opposite direction.

They went into the shop, at last, a warm dry place. She pulled her hood down and followed mam to the counter. The friendly shop assistant said she'd measure Helen's feet in a moment and to spend the time waiting by browsing the shoes. That's when she saw them. The most beautiful pair of red patent leather, double buckled shoes. They were absolutely delightful, exactly Dorothy's taste and colour. She lifted them from the shelf and held them aloft, 'Mam, mam, look at these.' Helen turned and began to walk over, smiling, pleased that Dorothy was trying to find her a pair. 'Not for you stupid, for me. Mam, mam, please can I have these?' Gladys walked over, 'Lovely Dorothy, but we're here to get Helen measured and I've no money to buy her any, never mind buy you a pair who doesn't need them.' She took the shoes from Dorothy and put them back on the shelf. 'Come on Helen, the lady is ready to measure you.'

Dorothy ran straight to her dad as he walked in from work that same evening. 'Dad, there's some red shoes that I've seen in Leigh, and I love them so much. Mam said she's no money, but would you buy them for me? Please dad, please.' He laughed at her and ruffled her hair, 'Sorry love, I've not a spare shilling never mind enough for a pair of shoes, and anyway, it's our Helen who needs shoes isn't it?'

She hated Helen now. If she'd never been born, then those lovely red shoes would have been hers. She kicked her shin under the table. 'Ouch Dorothy, that was my leg you kicked then,' she looked up, 'Say you're sorry then? Mam, our Dorothy just kicked my leg and didn't say sorry.'

Dad looked up from his tea, 'No squabbling at the table.' He knew why Dorothy had kicked Helen, but it didn't make it acceptable, 'Say sorry to your sister, it's not her fault that she needs new shoes now is it?' He gave his best stern look to Dorothy. 'I really, really want them though dad,' tears began to form at the corner of her eyes. Gladys shook her head, 'We all want what we can't have. I wouldn't mind a new pair of shoes for myself either.'

Dorothy went to bed that night picturing the double buckled shoes on her feet. She imagined how they'd look with her best dress. She pictured the image of herself in her red shorts, a perfect match with the lovely red shoes. Before she'd fallen asleep, she had made herself a plan.

In the morning, she went downstairs and into the kitchen, she took a knife from the kitchenette cutlery drawer and headed straight into the bathroom. She removed her shoe and began to scratch away at the leather of the buckle. She wouldn't completely cut it off, that would be too obvious, and she'd be in an awful lot of trouble.

A week later and daily scratching had left it hanging on by mere threads. She took in a deep breath, willed herself not to blush and as nonchalantly as she could, began to edge herself into her mam and dad's conversation. 'Have you seen my shoes mam? The buckle is about to fall completely off.' She removed the shoe and pushed the offending buckle towards them. Gladys stood up and snatched the shoe from Dorothy. 'You nasty girl, you selfish little madam. How could you do this?' She was shouting now and holding the shoe in front of Johnny's face. 'Look what she's done Johnny, she's deliberately snapped them so that she could get those bloody red shoes.' She launched the shoe across the room. 'Well, I'll tell you one thing Dorothy Gough, you will wear those shoes. I will put an elastic band around them to hold them on if I must, but there's no way you're getting any shoes before your sister,' she stormed out and went straight up the stairs to calm herself down. Dorothy looked at her dads upset face, 'I didn't do anything dad, they just wore out.' His sad expression told her he didn't believe her, but he drew her in for a cuddle nonetheless. 'That was a really silly thing to do Dorothy, there's no money. If we had any money, we'd just buy you the things you want. But to do this, well you've disappointed me is all I have to say.'

The buckle snapped off completely at school a few days later. Dorothy tried to hide it from her mam, but this proved impossible when she tried to walk and just kept stepping out of the whole shoe.

The following Saturday, mam had sat Helen down and explained that there was no option but to wait another week or so for her new shoes. She just accepted it. She didn't fuss. She stayed at home with dad while Dorothy and her mam had gone into Leigh. The lady had measured her feet and pointed out all the shoes that they had in a size one. Dorothy, head down with shame had said, 'You pick mam.'

They arrived home and Dorothy took no joy in presenting her new red, double buckled shoes to Helen, in fact, her stomach had clenched with guilt and regret as Helen had just nodded as though she were pleased for her, and although she'd tried so hard to smile and be pleased for her sister with her new shoes, her sweet little face just unintentionally crumpled up with repressed tears.

A huge burst of coloured sparkles erupted into the air as the scene evaporated in a shower of harmonising Lumai. The tiny notes fluttered like musical butterflies all around her and Calla. She swept some of them into her aura to feel their love and their music. 'Oh Calla, I would never tire of this happening. All the glorious things that I've seen and felt here so far and this one has topped the lot of them.' Her whole aura expanded with new shades of gleaming golds and reds. She was giddy with delight and excited about bestowing the last of her gifts.

LUMAI TEN

Tony Barker

Dorothy stopped suddenly over the man. Calla watched as her glow took on a new hue and she knew that her decision was made. 'God bless him, what a mess, look at that aura Calla, it's full of light and colour but it looks totally squashed.' She propelled herself into it to investigate.

Fifty-three-year-old Tony was sat at his kitchen table with his head in his hands. Grey, overgrown hair and a grey stubbled face and neck. He couldn't think straight to draft this next letter, he'd had coffee after coffee to try to make himself get his head around it, but it didn't appear to be working. His mind was flitting from thought to thought hurriedly and none of them were helping. His stomach felt queasy with upset. He must be doing something completely wrong, but it was beyond him what it was. When he'd first been made redundant, he hadn't fretted at all, in fact he'd been excited for the new possibilities, he was confident in himself and his abilities and held high hopes for himself in securing something great, now though, all these months on, any hope had faded into a jaded disillusionment. And now, all he felt was a suffused and depressing disappointment in himself.

He decided to fetch the paper he'd heard the paperboy post through an hour ago. If he could read that, it would take his mind off writing these darned applications and then he might be able to read them a little more objectively.

He'd kept a rigorous log of all the companies he'd written to, all eighty-eight of them, each one crafted carefully and aimed at the individual company. Now he wondered if it would have been better to just write a basic one and send out more. Only ten had written back, only two of those had offered an interview and both of those had said he was great but that unfortunately, he'd been pipped at the post but that they'd definitely keep him in mind should any other vacancies arise. And now we were seven months down the line and desperation was the only emotion left in him.

He pulled the paper out from the letter box and sat himself down heavily on the couch. He could hear Karen getting ready for work upstairs. He'd never once believed that he'd be envious of someone getting ready for work, but he certainly was. His stomach was knotted. He was supposed to be the breadwinner and poor Karen had now been forced to increase her hours to full time since he'd been made redundant. 'I'm fine with it Tony honestly,' she'd said, 'I can always drop back down when you find a job so it won't be for long. Opportunities open up in life, yours will come along soon.' He'd loved her for that. She had such faith in him, even now when all this time had passed and still no sign of work, she kept encouraging him to carry on applying and not to give up. 'You're a good man Tony, it only takes one company to see the promise in you and this nightmare will be history.'

He couldn't concentrate on the paper. He went back into the kitchen to make Karen her morning brew. The tea caddy was empty, so he reached under and into the cupboard where she stored them. He felt something fall forward as he pulled out the box. 'Damn it,' he said aloud, he didn't want to have to start clearing up a spill. He crouched down on all fours to retrieve the fallen stuff, so that he didn't make more of a mess. It was just envelopes, letters. He pulled them out. He put them on the unit and opened the first one. He was instantly gripped by horror. His heart started to beat faster, and a nausea overcame him. A pile of credit card bills, debts and demands. Suddenly, his already desperate life unravelled into further chaos. Why on earth where they hidden in the cupboard? Why would she do this? He slammed them on the unit and paced about the kitchen. He needed to have this out with her quickly because he could feel a rising panic taking over his gut. He heard her steps on the stairs and quickly decided to shove them back into their hiding place. He'd have a good look at them later when she had gone to work, he couldn't bear to confront her yet. He would never want to cause her to feel anguished and worried all day. She didn't deserve that whatever she had done.

'Morning love,' she looked at him with such tenderness. 'Morning Karen, did you sleep okay?' She raised her eyebrows at him and smiled, 'Better than you I think, ah thanks love, you're a treasure,' she said as she accepted her mug of tea. 'Tony you're shaking, are you feeling alright, or have you been necking coffee again?' she reached out and gently touched his hand. He faked a hearty laugh, 'Too much coffee I think, should I make you a slice of toast?' She watched him as he buttered their toast, 'Our one little luxury, eh? Marks and Spencer's butter.' She nodded along, never planning to admit that she had been decanting a cheap supermarket brand into the same old tub for the last six months. Let him have his little imagined luxury, he was suffering enough.

Karen left for work, and he waved her off with a kiss and a hug at the doorstep 'Today's a new day Tony, keep heart.'

He went back into the kitchen and pulled out the stack of letters. He shifted the toast crumbs with the flat of his hand onto the floor and began to read the first one. A numbness began to descend upon him, the feeling of being very alone. A rawness that just wouldn't abate and kept attacking him the further he read. It was his fault all of this. Self-recriminatory thoughts swam around unchecked in his head. He was pathetic. No wonder poor Karen had got them into debt. He picked at his hopelessness as though it were a scab, fractious and moody with himself. Within an hour, he had put his business head on and set to work sorting it out. At least by the time Karen got home from work he'd be able to ease her worrying mind a little.

By the time she had arrived home from work he'd been to the bank to get a full statement, then he'd written a list of income and outgoings, then finally he'd written a budget plan which would see the debt get paid off slowly. They'd definitely be living hand to mouth, but it was better than living with the debt noose slowly throttling them. He'd put them in a neat pile on the kitchen table ready to ease her mind the instant she walked through the door.

Instead, he'd just nipped to the toilet, and she walked in to see her discovered letters just waiting for her. Repressed floods of anguished howls of pain escaped from her. 'Karen it's okay, it's okay love, I'm not mad at you,' he was shouting as he ran downstairs. 'I didn't know what to do Tony, I was at my absolute wits end,' she was sobbing loudly, 'I couldn't stress you out any more than you already were but then the washing machine and fridge freezer broke within a week of each other. What was I to do? Then the repayments just spiralled out of control.' Tony had hurried to her, he was holding her tightly to him, shushing her gently as she cried and talked into his shoulder. 'I cut out all superfluous items and made sacrifices in every possible way. The savings were drained already with trying to make ends meet. I know I've made everything worse. I'm so sorry.' He held her away from him holding onto her shoulders and looking into her eyes, 'Karen, I love you. You have absolutely nothing to be sorry for, you were trying your best. It's my fault, I've got us into this awful predicament, the guilt is eating away at my insides, but I have a plan. And I've also decided to stop aiming too high and just apply for any job that comes along. Every penny counts.'

She hugged him tightly, 'I'm so sorry, I just couldn't bring myself to tell you. I didn't want to light the touchpaper Tony, you were already destroying yourself.'

Dorothy felt in awe watching this couple as they wholeheartedly supported each other during this horrendous period of stress. She pulled her fluttering, singing Lumai into her. 'I gift them to you Tony,' she said gently as she dispatched them into this much needed soul. 'Look at them go Calla, they're a lively bunch,' she was laughing and twirling, itching to see what they did. Tony's lights billowed up high. 'He feels hope now but he's no idea why.'

The postman delivered the mail at 10am. Karen hated it when it was her day off on Tuesday's and she had to see his little face drop as the postman walked straight passed the house or when he delivered letters for her and not him. Tony heard it drop onto the mat. 'You know Karen, I don't know how or why, but I'm really confident that something's changing for me today. I feel so positive. That nausea in my belly has suddenly eased off and I feel all light inside, like I could reel off a perfect application form.' Karen laughed, 'Well I hope so for your sake, but if you do have any interviews coming up, they'll turn you away looking like that, you favour a right scruff bag.'

Karen hoped he wouldn't get that heavy depressed look that he did when the postman brought no luck with him.

'See, I'm still grinning and there's nothing for me.' He passed her the letter. 'You can keep that one Tony, it's a dental appointment for me,' she laughed but felt gutted that there was nothing for him.

The telephone rang, 'I'll get it love, you sit down, you work hard enough.' He picked up the phone. 'Hello and good morning, could I speak to Mr Anthony Barker please?' He shrugged his shoulders at Karen as she quietly asked who it was. 'Yes, Anthony speaking, how can I help?' The voice on the other side of telephone cleared his throat, 'Hello Anthony, it's Jason Jones from the finance team at Northern Electricals calling, you came for an interview six weeks ago and weren't successful.' Tony raised his eyebrows at Karen and put his thumb up. 'Yes, I remember you Jason, how can I help?'

'Well, I said I'd keep you in mind if another vacancy came up. I'd be extremely grateful if you would consider coming to work for us.'

Dorothy and Calla danced and swirled and whooped with joy, their lights and colours swishing in and out of each other, cheering and whooping with elation. 'Well Dorothy, unless you fancy living another life, that was your last bequest. I know you always thoroughly delight in gifting your Lumai, and I adore watching you do it. But now, the real fun begins, lets travel the depths of heaven together and reveal its true exquisiteness.'

CHAPTER THREE

The Portals

'Dorothy, stop peeping in and out of them all and just actually go into one of them for goodness sakes,' laughed Calla. 'They all look so fantastic though, I can't decide which one to go into first.' Dorothy was with Calla at the library. She was in awe of the thousands upon thousands of huge glowing doors levitating effortlessly and each one beckoning her with its undisclosed theme.

She looked at the faces and the lights of the souls coming and going into their chosen portal. Faces of absolute elation and joy, souls glowing with stunning, multicoloured radiance. Roars of laughter filled the air and her interest suddenly piqued when she overheard someone say, 'This is absolutely scrumptious.' She looked at Calla, 'A restaurant?' Really? But we don't need to eat?' She was amazed. 'We don't need to eat you're quite correct. However, you Dorothy, you, like to eat.' She was chuckling now, 'Take a look you won't be disappointed, you never are. And I have no clue how it happens, but you always seem to arrive at this portal first.'

Dorothy looked at Calla in awe and chattered excitedly. 'You know what this feels like to me Calla? Well, just imagine how you used to feel when you were ravenously hungry in life when all you could think about was food.' Calla laughed loudly at Dorothy's burgeoning lights as she continued, 'You'd start to picture what you wanted to eat, then you'd start to salivate as your imagination skipped ahead and finally, you would visualise that very first bite. Well, I feel exactly like that now, I'm in that visualising my first bite stage and I want to tuck right in.' Calla laughed, 'Well, this is the most perfect restaurant. Everything is free, delicious and prepared just for your palate. The food looks different to every soul here. Best of all, is that your most favourite souls are here to enjoy it with you. You do know that it's not real though, don't you?' Dorothy didn't care, it still felt absolutely real, every delicious aroma smelled exactly as she remembered from life. She shot from table to table delighted. 'Oh my word, just look at all these tables overflowing with every single one of my favourite foods. Now this is what I dreamt heaven would be like.' She was spinning and twirling between tables making Calla giggle. She saw a huge wooden table straight down the centre of the room. On each of the seats around it were her friends and family. She shrieked with pleasure, 'Hello everyone, oh gosh I'm so thrilled I chose this portal now that I've found you lot here.' They all burst out laughing, 'Dorothy, we're in all the portals with you, it takes a bit of getting your head around it at first that you can be everywhere, but you'll get there soon,' shouted her friend Jack from another life she'd lived.

At the beginning of the room and exploding in glorious technicolour was the salad section. 'As though I'm heading to the salads,' she laughed as she headed there drawn in by the scents of the crisp fresh vegetables. She could feel their colours, they tingled within her as she touched them. She could feel the textures and was absorbing the scents, their coolness. Huge hunks of fragrant juicy tomatoes, jostling for space with thick slices of magnificently charred, roasted deep green peppers. She flitted from table to table, 'It all looks so good Calla, I don't know what to choose,' Calla was amused once more, 'It's all a very carefully curated image Dorothy, so simply eat anything you fancy, taste everything, touch and absorb everything. You won't get full. After your last life, you stayed in here for the equivalent of four earth years.' They both laughed, 'Hmm, I can imagine. I might do that now.'

She stopped at the charcuterie board. Prosciutto wrapped grissini, garnished with tender leaves of fresh basil, its pungent aromas seeping blissfully through her lights. Chorizo and jambon de bayonne carefully sliced and crafted next to the sumptuous piles of plump and pert kalamata olives. 'All my absolute favourite foods,' she yelled out to her friends, much to their amusement, popping one juicy delight after another into her mouth. Calla watched her precious charge with love as an explosion of light and colour filled Dorothy's glow as she flitted from table to table tasting, relishing, absorbing and admiring. She posted a plump skewered mussel into her mouth, each bite filled with a garlicky allure. She savoured a thick slice of seared rib-eye steak, sumptuously buttered and with a serious depth of colour and flavour. 'Ohh, mmm, delicious,' she mumbled already looking for her next delight.

She found the seafood section with its tender cooked king of the sea turbot smothered in a rich hollandaise sauce and almost as soon as she'd relished a fork full of that, she was drawn by the most piquant aroma of creamy korma curry placed next to a bed of rice, stained perfectly with turmeric. She lifted a spoon of prawn masala, bracingly spicy with a robust kick, 'Phew, a hot one, just exactly as I like it.' She chatted to friends and family, everyone was so happy and loving. 'No wonder a life is hard to live after we've been here wrapped in this love,' she said to her dad. 'I know, but we certainly loved each other during our lives, didn't we?' And then, much to his amusement, she was off for food again.

She found a section which simply had potatoes in various forms, each variation delectable. There were crispy perfectly cooked chips and baked potatoes in their crunchy burnished shells, absolutely begging for a huge knob of salted creamed butter.

'This portal is the absolute pinnacle of perfection Calla, it's the stuff of dreams,' she said as she posted a succulent fermented pickle in.' Calla laughed, 'Dorothy, you say exactly the same thing in all of the portals, you never want to leave any of them and soon you'll learn that you never have to.'

A beautifully crafted wooden cheese board caught Dorothy's attention. It was heavily laden with all her favourite cheeses and pickles, olde Sussex, Brighton blue, Stilton, crumbly Lancashire. Next was a sea of vibrantly coloured dips, taramasalata, hummus, garlic mayonnaise, tzatziki with an array of vegetable crudites scattered with flavourful caper berries. 'I think I'm going to live my eternal life in here thanks Calla.' She headed to the sweets section. Chocolate fondue poured generously from a fountain, filling her with a heady sweetness that pervaded her soul. Luscious fresh fruit sat next to it for dipping, and huge, fat juicy strawberries just lay glistening with the promise of a sweet and juicy bite.

The millefeulles with a rich crème chantilly were

lusciously posted into her mouth and she could feel her lights blazing. Glossy chocolates with praline centres delicious enough to blow your mind were placed with a heaving array of utterly delectable desserts. Ladles of thick dairy cream adorned the tables offering a cool creamy finish. All this carefully orchestrated food, 'I'm like a kid at Christmas time. I hope you're anticipating a long lunch because I aint leaving here in a hurry.' Her dad who was watching and enjoying the scene with Calla, was laughing like a drain.

Finally, many moons later and Dorothy decided it may be time to move on.

'I'm going to look in another portal Calla, I fancy a change of heavenly scenery,' she was floating off happily towards a breathtaking door that had wisps of silver and a rich blue dashing in and out of its lights. Dorothy stepped in and absorbed the portal immediately. 'Wow,' she exclaimed out loud. She could sense the feelings of all the other souls in there.

'I can't resist going in here Calla. I already feel really drawn to its beauty and I've barely glanced in.' She could see a white sandy beach that stretched infinitely topped by a vast blue ocean in the distance.

There was birdsong in the air and the sun shone brightly down warming the soft white sand as if just for her. She glided towards the ocean, sensing the absolute power and vastness of it. She stood still and watched, relishing in the beauty of the way the echo of the wave hung in the air long after the wave had receded. Its sounds were heavenly. She was full to the brim with love.

The soft white sand indented softly as she moved over it. She immersed herself within it and felt the lights and lives of all who had lived within the shells. This was the most wonderfully intoxicating feeling which filled her with ebullient joy and appreciation for the sensations of the inestimable power of love that she was experiencing. She headed to the ocean, its blue hues and wave echoes splashing and calling out its welcome. She waded in. The water flowed through her, and she dissipated in its midst, just a vast consciousness left with which to savour its delights.

Dorothy dived deeper and deeper. The ocean had seeped into her, and she had seeped into the ocean. They were as one. She was the power of the water and the power of the wave. She swam over to the coral reef and began to navigate its system. Its colours were so bright and dazzling, she looked with intrigue at a tiny but absolutely magnificent plant. It was bright with a pulsing light, its colour the most stunning shimmering red, unlike any red on the earthly realm. She reached out to absorb it within her soul, its aroma was sweet and delicate, she became the plant like she had become the ocean and the reef. She felt lost in the ecstasy of it all, the sense of connection to everything overwhelmed her.

She spotted a little octopus and followed it. She observed it as it kept squeezing itself into impossible nooks and crannies and hiding itself away in tiny coral crevices. She swept herself into it. Magnificent. She could feel its intelligence, she could feel how it lived its life.

She watched as little creatures, absolute masters of disguise, changed their skin colours and altered the texture of their skin to blend in effortlessly with their surroundings.

She flowed herself in and out of the abundance of sea grasses becoming one with their lights. She knew this place well, it was as though she'd always been homesick for it and had known of it somehow on an unconscious level.

She glided through the ocean, weightless, a part of it. She was amazed by its dramatic physical features, its huge mountains, deep canyons and steep cliffs. She swam up and over them all. She saw that the ocean was alive, teeming with life, hundreds of thousands of life forms all alight with the same pulsing glows that every living thing carried, she swept herself through them and into them. She was mesmerised watching how the blue ocean colour was shot through with sunlight, causing penetrating light to glance upon the sea cucumbers and the pristine sponges.

She bobbed to the surface, allowing the sun to filter through her and fill her with its love and warmth. 'I'm ready for a new portal Calla.' And together they went back into the library excited for the next adventure.

'I'm desperate to go into this one,' Dorothy told Calla as she watched the ripples of illuminating colours cascade around the doorway from within it. 'I know I still have earthly lessons to complete, but being here would educate me so much in helping to prepare me to becoming a life guide.'

Calla agreed, 'Well, you've watched quite a few of the guides in action now, haven't you? It's the most wonderful role you could ever do, and you'd grow so much by guiding someone. The lessons in here are very difficult but I think you are ready now,' she was thrilled that Dorothy had grown so much during her last life. 'You'll learn exactly how to guide a life and you'll learn how to manage the difficulties when the living choose the wrong path. The role of the guide is to help the living, who already feel stranded, suppressed and oppressed, because they are, to seek guidance. They feel estranged and aren't able to comprehend their earthly surroundings with their true selves, because their true selves are buried somewhere within that muted body.'

Dorothy stepped inside to begin her journey of lessons.

Here, she learned the intricacies of the human emotions and that as a guide, you are an energy being capable and powerful way beyond your wildest dreams. You bridge the gap in the cosmic divide of earth and heaven. She learned that the learning centre sends spiritual awakening clues to humanity to offer them hope. Near death experiences by their thousands are gifted to people to spread the word. It all seemed so simple and made so much sense to Dorothy. Death is a familiar companion to those living a life, they lose people, and they know that death will come for them in time. She remembered that from all of her lives. She understood that their visual spectrum is poor and that they are completely oblivious to life on any other frequency, so unbeknownst to them, the heavenly realm resides right with them, hiding in plain sight.

Dorothy knew that becoming a life guide would be the most wonderful adventure of them all. 'You'll see, when you begin to shepherd your first soul, it's as though you are part of a graceful duet melded together as one. It is the richest tapestry, the richest habitat to be in unison with another soul, it's absolutely beautiful,' her tutor advised her.

Dorothy began to develop a new understanding of who she was, an acceptance. She knew that if she decided to live another life, that this part of her soul would pass down into her human form. She had learned a new tolerance of others that she had struggled with in all her other lives and though it was her deepest desire to be entrusted as a guide, she realised that she'd probably need to live a couple more lifetimes before she was able to offer the best of herself and complete the role with the justice that it deserved.

As she left the learning room, Dorothy decided to have a little fun in the portals, then she'd make the decision to go and live another life before establishing herself as a guide.

'I'm ready for another portal Calla,' she felt a brand-new excitement open up within her, I fancy going back to visit earth for a while.' She soared out from the learning room and hovered around a new portal door that was shooting out a rainbow of colours with bright sparks of light firing within its midst. She peeped in and found that she was observing the earth from space. 'This is beyond magical Calla, its miraculous. It makes me laugh to think that when you're a human, you don't want to die.'

She dove down through the stars and found her consciousness had taken on a different shape, she was so very vast. She was flying over the living earth, dipping in and out of the aura's of the living. She was a bright entity of enlightened consciousness. She watched as people busied about their days, feeling a deep sense of love for them all, she was aware of a thread that tied them all together. They were all one. We are all one. All connected.

She found Harold and the girls. She could go back and forth in their lives at will. She stayed with them and comforted them through their grief. She laughed with them as they developed a grudging acceptance of her death and learned to laugh again. She spent time with her beloved mam as she wept her death and whispered at her grave that children shouldn't die before a parent. She would listen to her heartfelt prayers as she asked her dad to look over her. 'He does mam, he does,' then she'd sprinkle a few lights upon her aura to make her day a little brighter.

She dipped in and out of people's glows, distributing sprinkles of her lights to ease small burdens as she had been taught to do in her lessons. She laughed with Calla as she stopped a set of keys falling down a drain and turning a piece of toast butter side up before it hit the ground. She shouted warnings to people who listened and to some who dismissed her. She watched tiny immature Lumai as they learned their craft in preparation for heaven, flutter from the churches and synagogues and mosques as they were released by prayer. Then she watched with joy as they landed in an aura that required them to ease their pains.

She flew over the hot, parched plains of Kenya watching the packs of dogs on the trail of an impala. She felt the thrill of the chase and the terror of the chased. She sunk into the aura of a huge thirsty elephant drinking water from a shrinking river, feeling the love he had for his herd. She watched as a young bull in must held aloft his huge trunk trying to attract a mate.

She watched as the drought tightened its grip with only a memory of rain now, on the great swathe of sand which had once flowed with the elixir of life. And she absorbed the feelings of a leopard mother on her high alert and constant vigil as she protected her remaining three cubs, and her deep grief when one had been hunted down.

She travelled the length and breadth of the earth, connecting with everyone and every thing, developing her own soul as she collided with every possible emotion.

She stepped out from the portal, her glow expanded and enhanced. 'Well, that was a beautiful experience, I could have stayed there for eternity, but then I remembered the thousands of other portals that I will adore, so come on,' she was laughing and pushing ahead, 'Come on Calla.'

Dorothy peeped into the portal having been attracted to its black sparkling billowing mass which clouded around the entrance. 'Gosh, I hadn't realised this was an actual room when I was in it Calla. I thought it was just some sort of transition place when you first pass over.'

She stepped inside. Again, an infinite room without walls. There were thousands of shining cocoons, their surfaces swirling with cloudy streams of colours and bright lights. There were sounds of a harmonious and relaxing choir gently permeating the air. 'It's the hospital

Dorothy,' said Calla, 'It's where souls come when they first pass over, so you're correct. I call it my soul spa,' she chuckled, 'But I still come here all the time to relish in the sensation as others do.' There were guides and spirits flitting in and out of the cocoons.

'The hospital helps people who have had a traumatic or a sudden passing. It also cleanses the souls who believe that an illness from their life is still afflicting them and then some souls take a lot of convincing that they aren't who they thought they were.' Calla's glow subdued with empathetic emotions. 'Here, souls will be cleansed of all their earthly traumas.'

'Can I look in one?' Dorothy asked. 'Of course you can, come on, we'll go together.' Dorothy was filled with awe. There, in a robe of lights, levitating in a thick black lightless tunnel was a soul whose aura was thin and dull. His guide Amaziah, whirled around and around him, speaking to him, loving him and assisting him back into his spirit life. He'd led a good life but had taken on too many lessons for such a young soul and he'd become wretched with them and had found his own way out. Dorothy pressed herself into his lights. She watched his life flash before her. 'No wonder he needs the hospital Calla, he's had an awful time down there.' She pulled herself out, 'At least he's mending now, he's surrounded in that delicious, loving, tender blackness that I remember so well.'

Calla smiled, 'It really is bliss, isn't it? Especially when you first pass over and realise that you are not who you'd thought and that you're connected to a universal consciousness, loved and cherished and not alone at all.' Dorothy smiled, 'I think I was there for earth decades,' it was unbelievable, divine, and I thought I never wanted to leave. Best find another portal now though and quickly, otherwise I'm likely to climb back in one of the cocoons for a while.'

Dorothy stepped into the portal that was radiating warmth and love and acceptance next. Its doorway had sounds of birdsong and rustling leaves. It gave off the aroma of nature and harmony and was welcoming. She looked around. The area was vast. Bright loving lights shone down onto an infinite flower heavy, grassy meadow. Just one single majestic oak tree stood at the centre. It was beyond massive. Thousands of years old. She wrapped herself within it, absorbing its power, its ancient knowledge and its connection to her. Its towering, knotted trunk sprouted thick gnarled branches which in turn supported vibrant light pulsing leaves. She travelled the journey of its root system that reached down for miles and anchored it well into the earth that surrounded it. She found that it was connected and aware of every other tree on this realm. She felt the deep hum of joy coursing within it and realised that it was more spiritually aware than she was and that all earthly trees were spiritually aware. She languished here in this state of harmony until her curiosity of the joy of other portals got the better of her. 'Calla, I'm going to dip in and out of hundreds of them now, all at once. I'm finally realising that I can.' And she allowed her consciousness and her lights to unfold as she expanded herself infinitely and joyfully.

DOROTHY

The Source

Dorothy and Calla were spending time reminiscing and learning over old lives lived. They were on the gated pathway enjoying its beauty. 'I feel as though I know I'm in heaven Calla. I feel utterly surrounded and entrenched in God's love, and yet, I can't see Him no matter where I look. 'Is God here, actually here?' Calla giggled, 'Of course He is Dorothy, right here now, in you, in me. You can feel His beauty. He's in that river, in the grass and the trees all the lights you see? Well, that's Him. I'm thinking you mean you actually want to see His physical form hmm? You just haven't asked yet, come on,' she beckoned towards the library.

Dorothy marvelled again at the vastness of the library, she found herself in awe again at the magnificence of it and saw more details of the intricacies that had gone unnoticed previously. 'How could I have missed those?' she asked Calla. 'Because everything is so magical here Dorothy, you can come back a hundred times to the exact same spot and you'd see some new beautiful feature to enjoy.'

'There, you see it?' motioned Calla once she had been able to drag Dorothy away from examining the glass in detail, 'above all the doors, there, on its own.' Dorothy looked beyond the hovering light doors and all the hundreds of spirits travelling in and out of them. She fixed her gaze on structure she hadn't noted previously. It appeared solid, though fluid at the same time. A whirling kaleidoscopic mass of warmth and colour. It's energy flowing out freely as though it were never to end. 'Just go to it, we're all welcome,' Calla gently propelled Dorothy forward.

She found herself at the very entrance to the billowing mass. Intoxicated with love was how she would explain it to Calla later, she felt wonderful. She turned to convey her joy to Calla, who smiled back with delight.

As she began to enter, the swirling mass dissipated and gave way to another endless room. A white, pearly bright, beautiful light glowed infinitely in every possible direction. Dorothy felt herself being gently pulled along, deeper and deeper into the room. She knew she was travelling faster than the speed of light, though there was no pull or friction that she could sense, no gravity at all. She could sense no turbulence and was not buffeted around. She felt that she was travelling on a higher frequency of energy. She knew that she was travelling millions and millions of miles, yet still in this sempiternal room. Suddenly, though without any sense of force or pressure, she was still.

And then there, right in front of her, He was. She was transfixed by the power emanating through Him and from Him. The divine. The creator. This monumental, loving, luminescent God. The source. And he loved her. He cradled her. He swaddled her like his precious newborn child. He loved her with all his heart and soul. He loved her for all eternity. Perpetually. A complete and absolute, unconditional love. It poured from Him because he overflowed with it. And Dorothy drank it all in. She knew that He loved each and every one of us in this exact same way, with this exact same depth of feeling. He knew every soul just as well as He knew himself. So tangibly full of power. She could feel His light flooding through her, pouring into her very being, exuding His depth of love for her, like nothing ever felt in the earthly realm. True, pure, unreserved love. They were one. She was Him and He was her. He knew her and she knew Him. He wanted her there, she could feel it emanating from Him and through her.

She recognised that all the lights she had seen since arriving here, the grass, the trees, the other spirits, herself, everything, were all from Him. God. He was the creator. The Father. The supreme being. He blazed with glory. His all-embracing love filled the air like a scent, its invisible preciousness an entity in itself.

We were all His creation, His children.

Dorothy was in awe. She gazed into His eyes. 'I'm sorry I forgot you,' was the only sentence she could formulate. In response He chuckled gently. 'Dorothy, you needed to forget me. You needed to forget all of this, then you would be free to live unfettered. Free to learn. Free to choose. Free to make mistakes. If you lived a life with all this knowledge, it would completely alter the way you behaved. I forgive you Dorothy. Absolutely and entirely. I'm so very proud of you.'

Dorothy sank down to His feet. 'Oh Father, I'll do better next time, I promise.' She gazed into His familiar face. His eyes, blue as the ocean, were mesmerising, alive with compassion and love. His hair was pure white, white as freshly fallen snow. His every feature exuded warmth. His every feature loved her. She wanted to remain here for eternity, wrapped completely in His love, wholly intoxicated. He nodded as He absorbed her thoughts, 'You are with me forever Dorothy, you are here already. You're everywhere Dorothy, a fractured consciousness. You're living lives, guiding others, shepherding them in to their first life experience. And all of it is fuelling your spiritual growth. You're assisting the living as we speak. You're doing it all now. All in this very moment,' His words amazed her, as He continued, 'There is only now. There isn't a before or after. No past, present or future. All events happen simultaneously, all moulded together as one. You can project yourself into any given moment.' He allowed her to muse on this before He continued, 'Our energy has substance Dorothy, it exists everywhere and anywhere and forever. It occupies all time and space. Like a wave returning to its ocean, we will all return to this state and merge right back into the universe. You'll remember soon, let Calla guide you.'

Dorothy struggled to comprehend the words that He spoke, but she trusted in Him that she would understand soon. 'Come with me,' he said, his eyes smiling. She reached out to Him and He gathered her into Him. 'Love is in abundance here. Nothing that's required or wanted is scarce. The only things to do here are to grow and to learn. Let me show you our true world.' And He swept her across the universe, taking her through organised, methodical energies. Her hugest questions answered with complexity, yet simplicity. He carried her through the earth and the living. He showed her the threads of connections that bound us all as one, as His creation. He showed her that planet earth is all but non-existent in terms of the vastness of the world of the afterlife. He guided her through galaxies and showed her so dense a field of stars that she became overwhelmed with emotion and love.

They surfed on a wave of light together and

He released them into a world of glistening stars. They collided gently with bouncing orbs and together they absorbed the sparking, loving energy from them. They watched as tendrils of resplendent lights, slipped into and through everything, emanating love. 'Love endures throughout eternity itself Dorothy, it brightens and kindles all the lights to a brighter hue. All the light you can see, its created from good.'

He carried her within Him as they travelled through cosmic rays with their clusters of tiny particles, their colours conveying unimaginable love. They listened and felt the joy of the sonorous clanking heavenly bells which joyfully heralded the delights of this perfect heavenly realm.

They travelled through superclusters of galaxies and laughed with giddiness as they glided together throughout the solar system. They watched the stunning auroras as their vivid colours shimmered like softly blowing curtains.

Wrapped in His love in this total ecstasy, Dorothy wondered how she could possibly have forgotten all this? She recalled it all now, she had been here for thousands and thousands of years, and she would be here for infinity.

She looked up into His divine face. 'Thank you, thank you for showing me all this again. I'll always love you and I'll always do my best to serve you.' He looked down at her with love, 'And I'll do exactly the same for you. Now go and have some fun.'

DOROTHY

Choosing Emily

'What would you like to learn Dorothy? How can you grow?' Calla began the discussion regarding Dorothy's next life as she always did. What did she need to happen?

Dorothy looked at Calla, 'There's so much I want to learn Calla, but living a life is so very hard, isn't it?' Dorothy knew now, that as her higher self, her spirit self, she couldn't ever make herself feel pain, or guilt, or regret or feel any of that negative emotion. She'd learned so much at the university, but her spirit couldn't expand any further without more earthly lessons and she so desperately wanted to be a life guide like Calla.

'Yes, life is tough Dorothy, as you are aware, but as you know, earth is the only place where you can make your mistakes and learn from them. These experiences need to be sought on a physical plane, where you aren't aware of the watchers. It's the only way to grow, the only place to grow. It's the school for souls. But yes, I completely agree. It's tough.'

They were in the new life gallery room in the library, flitting through thousands and thousands of potential new parents.

'Why don't you choose a life where there are plentiful, peaceful breaks Dorothy. Better to live ten liveable lives than one that you must get out of because it's too traumatic.' Dorothy was listening intently to Calla's advice. 'I'd like to have an easy ride again this life Calla, I'm a bit scared of a tough one.' She'd had a few of those when she hadn't listened to Calla and had chosen to take too many lessons in one go. She'd been a much younger soul then. She knew now that it wasn't worth doing that if she wanted to learn thorough lessons and actually complete the life. She'd had to bail out of a couple of them and the consequences for those around her had been dire and painful.

'I like the look of this family here,' said Dorothy as she hovered over, and in and out of Lauren and John England's auras, flitting between the both of them. 'They're nurturing and warm, and I've worked with them both before in other lives. And they're due a new soul soon, a baby girl.'

Calla gently shifted herself in and out of their auras. 'They're lovely Dorothy, and both old souls themselves. Okay then, if you're certain, let's get started then. Lesson plans?' Dorothy laughed at Calla's official tone. 'Well, we have a lot to plan.' said Calla in response joining in with the laughter. 'Well then, have you thought about which lessons are you choosing this time? Concentrate on the ones you didn't do so well in as Dorothy. Choose what gifts you'd like her to pass on to others.

'Well, I promised God I'd do better this time around, so I'd like some lessons on patience and acceptance of others, you know, not making judgements about folk. Definitely a bit of compassion wouldn't go amiss either.' She knew that Calla was already aware of what she was feeling, so tentatively spoke, 'Calla, I'd like her to tell the story of heaven, of love, of God, I know you said good luck with trying it. And I know it's been tried countless times before, but at least if I try, I'll know I've tried. All those near-death experiences people have been gifted with, and they've gone back and are too scared to tell their stories in case people judge them and say they're weird.' She could feel some sort of calling within her but couldn't explain it properly. 'What about all those people who remember their reincarnation and are still it's not believed or are doubted?'

They were still hovering over John and Lauren who were chatting animatedly, oblivious to what was happening around them. 'What I would like from it, is for people to understand that love, care and compassion are the absolute. All that's required. And to simply believe that there's life after death. All those people in the depths of grief because their loved one has gone forever, could dare to hope a little if they believed.' Calla listened intently. 'I'd like her to write it all down. In a book.' She was becoming more determined as she spoke. 'Then, when she writes her book, people will get a chance to read it, a chance to believe. They may give an extra smile that day or help someone out. Imagine the glorious Lumai Calla?' Dorothy beamed with hope.

'Well, I'm here to guide and advise you Dorothy, it'll be an extremely difficult beginning for you' said Calla uncertain if it was attainable. 'You'll only be able to put the tiniest of details into her head about what our life truly is here. Then you'll need to keep all these memories alive and potent, long enough for it to still be of interest to her by the time she's matured.' Calla wasn't convinced it could be done. 'If you're allowed to speak of it as she grows, as you grow, it'll become old news, and you'll lose all interest in it and lose any desire to write it down. And of course, it'll need putting into perspective for you to somehow make it understandable. It'll be like squashing a whole ocean full of knowledge onto a teaspoon trying to fit it into a human brain, or like giving a child a thick book before it's learned how to read.' The more Calla thought about it, the more doubtful she was becoming. 'You just won't have the foundations to work with Dorothy. You won't be able to understand it or comprehend it. There isn't the vocabulary there to the frequencies and densities. It won't be possible.'

Dorothy listened attentively, determined to find a way to make this work. 'I can do it Calla, I know I can. I just need to envision just enough of it to be able to articulate it on paper.' Calla didn't want to prevent Dorothy's wishes, but she could envisage this new life being a train wreck if a child wasn't allowed to express what they knew. She changed tack, 'but if you're not able to understand it and your brain can't fathom it, then you'll just struggle mentally. That won't allow you to have a good life journey, will it? It'll already be a tough ride you're giving yourself until you've managed to write it all down.' She couldn't bear for Dorothy to give herself a tough life.

'Look at all the joy and Lumai that you brought back with you after your last life, I think you're setting yourself up to fail. You, she I should say, won't be able to develop properly, you may just send her mad Dorothy. Please reconsider.' She implored Dorothy. 'I'm sorry Calla but I'm quite determined. I know I can do it. But just in case you're right, we'll make it a short one. I'll come back here when she's lived 24 years and written the book.'

EMILY

Time to go home

It's absolutely freezing cold outside. I've had the central heating on since I woke at 6am after I had no choice but to get up as I had to take an insistently whining Hettie downstairs and out in the grounds for a wee. I switched it on and shot straight back into bed and under the duvet. I can feel the air warming around me, but my fingers are still red and cold as I tap away my words. I turned 24 years old yesterday and I'm on the cusp of finalising this novel. I've completed what I set out to do when I was Dorothy, but I don't think that she and Calla had thought this through properly.

I feel like I've been given a life sentence suddenly. Dead at 24. I'm certainly not afraid to die, because I know I won't die but I'm scared of how I will die though. Wouldn't anyone be? 'Will it be today Calla? Will it hurt?' She isn't listening as usual.

I can't believe that I only recalled this little nugget of information as I'm writing my final pages. It's almost like I've been stitched up, by myself, my own soul. Bloody hell what a mess. I most certainly wouldn't have bought Hettie. What would become of my poor hound now? She's not even one yet.

I don't think that they anticipated that my life would actually be a good one. They thought I'd be messed up with all this knowledge. Presumably they thought I'd want to die, or at least wouldn't be too keen on living. But it's the polar opposite. I've never felt better, especially since I was getting free of all this malarkey. I actually love my life. I love my mum and dad, Grace, Jess and Beth, Hettie and I even love Barry a bit. I really want to live. 'I hope you're reading this over my shoulder Calla,' I say aloud, just in case she isn't tuned in somehow.

When I'm certain that it's warm enough to leave my bed, I climb out and kneel beside it. I've never been a person to pray but I really need Him now. 'Hi God, I'm begging you to let me live a while longer. Before I came back to be Emily, Dorothy and Calla, well me I suppose it was, decided to only grace me with twenty-four years. It's not enough Father and I really need more time. I promise I'll do so many good deeds that you'll barely recognise me when I come home, I'll be lit up like a bonfire. Anyway, that's all, I know you'll understand how I'm feeling. Amen.'

I've secretly said my goodbyes to everyone. They didn't know of course, but they'll remember that our last conversation was decent. 'Are you cracking up a bit cock?' asked Barry when I told him to knock on if Hettie was whining and I didn't seem to be reacting to her.

I've made a will. I don't have a thing of value of course, but I'm hoping that if this book sells a copy or two, then the dogs trust will enjoy any proceeds. The solicitor was looking at me kindly and I had to tell him that I had no intention of dying soon. I think more than anything, he was confused that I wanted to write a will when I had nothing to leave. I could see him smirk a little when I told him I'd written a book that I thought might sell. I imagined his aura to be mouldy and that gave me a nice sense of satisfaction.

I'm struggling trying to second guess my death scenario, so I'm looking at everyone and everything with suspicion, though I'm pretty sure that it's going to be from a fall as Calla had warned me through the medium. But why would I fall? I'll stay off my bike, I won't climb anything either. Or was that just a general warning? Maybe I'll get the whole year and die the day before I'm 25? Oh well, what can I do? I'll just have to live for today.

I determine that instead of constantly contemplating what horrible death may fall upon me, I'll try to cherish every day, every moment if I can, despite the fact that I feel coated and shot through with angst.

I'll have a walk up to mum and dads. Our Grace

is home and I promised her I'd see her over the weekend. Maybe I'll persuade her to come for a walk with me.

I munch on a slice of buttered toast and enjoy a brew before wrapping up warm and setting off. 'Freezing but gorgeous,' I say to Barry as we meet each other at the bottom of the stairwell as he's off to the shop for his liquid breakfast. 'Just freezing cock, nowt gorgeous about it,' he replies laughing.

We set off, turning right down the lane towards the woods and as we near, I unclip Hettie to let her run free. The roads are icy, and I wonder if I'll slip and hit my head. A quick death I suppose. We reach the woods and its tree lined pathways and my feet feel to have a better purchase on the rougher ground, but Hettie slips and slides as she runs at speed over iced puddles, shocked when the surfaces crack loudly. 'Slow down you mad hound,' I'm laughing out loud at her antics. The fading yellows of autumn have long since gone and now in its place is the icy white of winter.

My fingertips are already frozen despite woolly gloves, and I push them deep down into my pockets seeking shelter for them. I blow steam clouds with my breath, and I can feel the frozen air nipping my cheeks and ears. The sun sends generous shards of crisp yellow light through the trees pretending to warm the earth and the grass is white with frost, reminding me of the light filled grasses in the visions of heaven. I love it. I love these crispy, bright, cold days.

After a couple of miles, we head left towards the main road where we'll cross the road and complete the rest of the journey down the canal. 'Come here Hettie,' I call her to heel and clip her lead on way before the busy road. 'Are we going to see Henry?' I put on my high-pitched excited voice for her, and she wags her tail so hard that her hind legs wag too.

Once over the road, we head over the bridge and down on to the canal towpath. Years ago, the footpaths had been made of cinders and mud, but they have all been renovated and are now quite lovely to walk on. The canal itself is frozen solid. There are bricks and stones all over its surface where kids have been trying and failing to smash it. I unclip Hettie to let her run free again.

We only had around a mile or so to walk so I pulled my phone from my back pocket to tell mum to get the kettle on. I could see Hettie a good fifty yards in front, sniffing around in a shrivelled blackberry bush. Suddenly, a cat leapt out from it and dashed straight over the frozen canal, followed immediately by Hettie. 'Hettie no,' I screamed, but she was already in hot pursuit, she shot over the frozen mass and was on the other side. I could feel myself filling with adrenaline. How will I get her back safely? I ran my panicked head through some possibilities quickly. I shouted over, 'Hettie, stay there,' she understood and stood still. My plan was to either wait until someone on the other side could grab her for me, or both her and me continue to walk either side until we came to the next bridge where we would join up again. There wasn't a soul around though. I was really panicking now. I started to walk slowly. 'Good girl, stay there,' I shouted, but she didn't understand. She started to tentatively step down onto the ice. 'No girl no, stay there, stay there,' I was pushing my hands through the air to show her where to stay. 'No Hettie, stay there.' But, despite being wary, she seemed oblivious to any real sense of danger, and she started to cross. My heart leapt into my mouth, and I held my breath as she stealthily walked over. A loud foreboding crack. I saw the panic on her face as she realised what was happening, then, scared by the event, she attempted to make a run for it. I saw her dig down her hind legs as she prepared to bolt, and I heard a loud snap. 'Oh my God no, Hettie, help me please someone help me,' I was still screaming as the ice completely broke, and she went straight through the gap and completely disappeared from sight. Oh, dear God no, I could see her fur under the ice and her head bumping the surface as she struggled to find the hole she had fallen through. I tentatively but hurriedly stepped down onto the ice. It felt solid enough. I hurried to the hole and knelt down. 'Hettie, Hettie,' I was crying and shouting now as I pushed my whole arm into the opening swishing it around to let her know where to come. 'Here Hettie, here girl,' I knocked on the ice with my knuckles. I couldn't see her. I stood up to walk around. She was gone. I started to stamp and bang my feet to attract her. 'Hettie. Hettie. Hettie,' I was screaming my head off now.

Then, without warning, another huge crack and I felt the whole world open up beneath my feet. I plunged straight down and the freezing water causing me to inadvertently take a breath. The panic, the wild panic as I coughed then immediately inhaled again. Oh God I'm drowning. I looked up for the hole. It was just there, a foot or so above me, I tried to push myself off the floor but sank into its murky, muddy depths instead. I desperately needed a breath, I coughed and inhaled again, nasty murky canal water. I kicked my legs and reached up towards the light above the hole, my lungs burned like they were on fire. I was right near the surface, just hang on for one second longer.

As my hand broke through the surface of the water, reflex caused me to take another breath. My final one.

A beautiful, familiar, humming, rhythmic vibration filled my very core. Ah this feels so good. A sudden popping noise and I was sucked clean out of my body. So, here I am, warm and content in the blackness. Back in the bliss, back in the deliciousness of home. I don't have the same confusion as I usually do when I first arrive here. I know exactly where I am and exactly who I am. 'Calla,' I call out because I know she'll be nearby, 'I'm not ready yet. I want to be back at the canal, I want to be living that life, not here. I don't want to be here yet.'

I instantly found myself back and watching the scene below me and presumed my prayer had been successful. Hettie, drenched wet through was stood on the ice barking and barking. She was repetitively bouncing up on her hind legs and slamming her front paws down heavily onto the ice. A man had thrown his pushbike down on the path and was looking into the canal to see why the dog was so distressed. He had started to tentatively make his way over the ice towards Hettie, when he saw my blonde head bobbing about face down. He instantly started to shout. 'Help, help, help me someone. I need help, someone is under the ice,' He grabbed the back of my hair and yanked my head out of the water, still yelling and yelling. Hettie continued to bark and bark. And all the while, I was the observer again.

I could see a young couple with a buggy running over the bridge towards us. I watch as the man grabs my shoulders and heaves me out of the hole, like a dead weight, pulling and pulling at me until I lay flat on my face on the ice. I feel no emotion for that cold, wet lump. No attachment whatsoever. I watch as he drags my limp, dead weight over to the canal edge. I watch as the other guy begins to assist in pulling me up and onto the safety of the bank. I watch as Hettie sits by my body her little body shivering violently, as they start trying to breathe life back into me as they begin resuscitation. I watch as the woman shouts that the ambulance was on its way.

I watch as her small baby, all snuggled up and warm with her winter blankets tucked neatly around her, slowly gives in to sleep. She has as much interest in the goings on as I do.

I find myself back in the blackness. It's perfect. Nothing to think about here. I simply feel intense love and complete fulfilment, everything is exactly as it should be. I look around to enjoy its velvety wonder. I know I'm in the hospital and I know Calla will be here soon. A small speck of light in the distance starts to grow. Soon, the wondrous light bathes me totally. It fills me with joy.

'Calla?' I knew she'd be close. She sweeps into me with her massive expanse of warmth. Whirling and spinning into me joyfully. A cosmic collision of love. 'Well done Emily, look at your lights, you've grown monumentally, I'm beyond proud.' I pull her in to welcome her, gathering her within me and mingling our bright and airy auras. 'I honestly thought you'd forgotten me Calla, I begged you for help so many times and you completely ignored me.' Calla tinkled with laughter causing pretty sparks to shoot around in her glow. 'You'll see in your life review that I never once left your side Emily.'

'I'm not staying Calla. This Emily life has so much more to give, and I want to go back,' I spoke with expectation. 'But you completed the life Emily. You did the whole plan. People are really excited to see you back. You did a fantastic job. You're unsettled and a bit confused because you've just arrived and you're still feeling attached to her. Go back and spend some more time at the hospital to recuperate, you'll soon settle.' Calla is trying to help me, but I'm determined.

'I'm not still attached Calla, I've just seen her and she looks like a lump of cold meat. I know I'm not her, but her life has been so taken over with Dorothy's life and this side, that there was barely any room for her, she never really lived, I'm going back.' I scoot in and out of her to make my message loud and clear.

'You can live another life if that's how you feel Emily, but hers is spent now. She's lived what she's supposed to, what we decided upon.'

I just can't accept it, I can't. I really want Emily to get her life. 'She's been short changed Calla.'

I know my way around unlike Dorothy did because it's all still so fresh in my head. I've never been allowed to forget it. So, I visualise the library and I'm right in front of it. I go inside and completely ignore all the levitating glowing portal doors that are beckoning me in with their fun and their promise of warmth and welcome.

I locate the source with its swirling mass of colours and lights, and I enter the room to find my God. 'Father, Father, help me please,' I'm calling out to Him before I've even travelled the vortex and arrived in His divine presence. I feel the all too familiar sensation of being pulled without friction, then I find myself suddenly back in the midst of the love of my Lord, my Father. I'm completely taken aback. The love that exudes from Him and soaks into my very soul shocks me. I'd forgotten how He adored me. How I feel to be beside Him.

He looks resplendent. I'm mesmerised all over again by His love for me and mine for Him. I mustn't get lost here in this euphoric rapture and forget about Emily. 'Come here,' He says and pats the seat beside Him. I move towards Him and am swamped by unmitigated bliss. I can feel that I'm losing Emily, but I just can't pull myself away from this. It's intoxicating. I belong here, I'm home, I'm loved, and I'm cherished.

I start to babble, 'Father, I've barely lived Emily's life because she's been so consumed with Dorothy's life and the afterlife. I had to write it all down because that was the plan we made.' I could see Him smiling at me, loving me, as though I was His young toddler child, and He was kindly allowing me to express myself. He spoke tenderly, 'Last time you came to me, you said you'd try to live a good life and you did

Emily. You completed your whole life plan. Look at your aura, you've grown immensely. Your lights are almost as bright as Calla's now.' He allowed my lights to mingle with His. 'Your greatest desire is to be a guide yourself and you're accomplished enough to do that now. This was your graduation. I'm so very proud of you.'

I basked in His pride for me, but it still felt unjust to let Emily go. 'Please let me go back Father. I don't need any plans. I'll just take whatever lessons life throws at me.' I caressed his beautiful face as I spoke. 'I'd just like to let Emily actually be Emily, without any of this knowledge skewing her decisions and behaviours. No wonder I was good knowing that everything I was doing was being scrutinised.' He laughed and tenderly held me, and I continued, 'My life may have had its flaws and its frailties, but the zest for life I had, the humour I enjoyed, the absolute magnificence of life, well, it's a gift, a thrill. I'm begging you to let me go back and just be her. I promise you I'll do some really good stuff and I'll be super kind.' I was pleading now. 'Honestly Father, I feel that I've been trodding through this last life in Dorothy's shoes and I've been so busy watching her journey, that there was no room for my own journey with its skanky trainers.' He pulled me forward in a loving embrace.

I woke to a kiss. A handsome guy indeed. Something is so wrong though. I'm frozen solid, I'm so very cold. I'm coughing and choking. I can barely breathe. My lungs are burning badly, and they just won't let enough air in. 'She's breathing, she's breathing. Put her in the recovery position.' I hear lots of voices. 'Put these over her, she's frozen,' I feel blankets being gently placed over me, but they don't help. I'll never get warm again. I can taste a putrid taste in my mouth. I cough and cough, but it's an effort to drag any air in and I'm panicking that I can't breathe. 'Help me,' I implore the man leaning over me with panic in his eyes. 'The ambulance is here now,' someone shouts, 'It's on the bridge.' I pass out.

When I awake again, I'm still frozen. I'm in the back of the ambulance strapped onto a stretcher with its blues and twos blaring out and I sense the speed is fast as I jolt into the seatbelts with my hips and shoulders on every slight bend that we take. I have an oxygen mask on and though my lungs burn badly, I can breathe better.

I start to remember what happened and I begin to panic that Hettie has drowned. I remember falling in after her and I'm not sure how I know this, but I remember seeing her on the ice bouncing her paws frantically trying to reach me under the water. I'm a little confused by this because it couldn't have happened like that could it? I must have seen her when I'd been pulled out of the water and now, I'm getting it a bit mixed up.

I try to sit up to see if she's in the ambulance. 'Lie down love, try to relax, you're in safe hands now. What's your name love?' The ambulance lady tries to be kind and holds my hand. 'Hettie?' I ask her. 'What's your surname Hettie?' I pass out again.

When I wake again, I'm as warm as toast. I'm wrapped in a delicious warming blanket, and I can feel the warm air being pushed around me. It's luxurious. I have an oxygen mask on my face and two bags of fluid dripping slowly into a cannula in my arm. I hear mum's shaky voice in the background.

'She's been brought in about an hour ago, Emily England, I'm her mum. She fell through the ice on the canal, the police said she's here.' I try to sit up to shout for her, but my voice is just a rasp, and it hurts too much to try again.

She comes rushing through the curtain, crying her eyes out. 'Dads on his way, oh Emily you bloody idiot. What would you do that for? Why would you risk your life for a bloody dog? You had to be resuscitated Emily. You were dead. Can you imagine what that would have done to us all?' Fresh tears coursed down her cheeks. 'Where's Hettie? Is she okay?' I manage to croak painfully.

'She's absolutely fine Emily. The guy who pulled you out of the canal took her home. He said she was traumatised enough without being shipped off to a vet. He's warmed her up in his bath,' she was still sniffling. 'A woman thought she recognised the dog but wasn't sure. She told the police that she thought it was our Henry, so when they came knocking and you hadn't turned up, we put two and two together,' a fresh wave of anguished tears escaped.

'I'm so sorry mum, please don't cry. I'm okay now.' The curtain opened again, 'Oh bugger Emily, you scared us all to death.' Dad looked pale and shaken. He came straight over and hugged me. 'Sorry dad.' I really was. I'd not expected the ice to give way.

Later that night as I drifted off to sleep, I began to remember bits and pieces. I sat up shocked. I had died. I had seen Calla and my God. They'd helped me. It wasn't the clear visions coming through like Dorothy's had been. In fact, I could already feel them fading and melting away. But for now, I knew that they'd allowed me to remain triumphantly and defiantly alive. 'Thanks Calla. Thanks God,' I whisper.

I was finally allowed home a few days later and I went to recuperate at mum and dads for a couple of days. They'd been looking after Hettie for me. 'Hettieeeeeeeee,' I croaked, as I stepped through the door. She bounded up and span in excited circles at my feet, squealing and squealing her welcome, licking my face until I made her get off. I rubbed her neck and her ears. God, I loved this dog. I'd do the exact same thing again for her, but of course I wouldn't tell mum and dad that.

There was a pink envelope propped up between the salt and pepper pots on the kitchen table. I picked it up to take a nosey.

To Emily. I sat down and opened it. A get well soon card, signed Dan with a telephone number. 'I have a card off a Dan mum,' I called out, but I don't know anyone called Dan. Mum shouted out from the living room where she was busy unpacking my patient belongings bag. 'It's the guy who pulled you out of the canal love, the one who took Hettie home with him, he needs a thank you from you I should say. I've got his address from when we went to pick Hettie up.'

How sweet of him, it should be me sending him a card not the other way round. I'll sort something out when I'm feeling up to it.

'Emily,' Grace welcomes me with a hug, carrying in with her the odour of cold air that's pervaded her woolly coat. I breathe it in as she hugs me, and it makes me want to go for a walk. 'Mum says you're staying for a few weeks, that will be so lovely.' I laugh, 'I'm definitely not Grace, a few days is more like it, until I'm feeling better, and my chest clears up. I'm still a bit tender when I cough.' She looks at me with a worried expression, 'God Emily, you scared the living daylights out of us. People were saying that a body had been pulled out. Even the police couldn't confirm if you were alive or not, can you imagine how mum and dad were? Thank God for that guy.'

So, I texted Dan (on my miracle phone that had never ceased to work despite its drowning,) to convey my thanks and told him a card was en-route even though he was adamant that it wasn't necessary. He said just the fact that I'd survived was enough for him. He'd had to have a few days off work with the trauma of it all, he said, because he couldn't sleep for keep reliving it. He told me that mum and dad had dropped a couple of bottles of wine off and a JD voucher. Sweet of them that, I'd said, they hadn't mentioned it to me.

I finally came home a week later. A bit fatter, completely loved and desperate for some peace. And anyway, Dan is coming for a takeaway and wine later. We've barely had more than an hour pass without sending a text or speaking or FaceTiming each other. I'm pretty smitten. I think he is too because he said if we ever have kids, he'll tell them that daddy's first kiss, was to save mummy's life. I'm hoping for my second kiss later.

EMILY

Peace at Last

It's going to take me some time to adjust to my new life without all these memories fighting for my thoughts. The day after I'd finished my book, I printed it off, hole punched and treasure tagged it together, then left it in a drawer for a whole month. When I'd felt ready, I read it from start to finish in two days flat, and now I feel a complete easement within my soul. All my thoughts and memories laid out, released. I can finally relax and enjoy being Emily.

You would expect that I would want to live my Emily lifetime as a nun, that I would be always on my best behaviour, constantly aware that I will be accountable for all of my behaviours, words and actions. How I make others feel. Yet I'm not, I'm living my life.

I'll try not to get too caught up in the nine to five circus of life and I'll always consider myself very lucky that I was given some insight as to why we are here. Glad that I wasn't a muted, closed down, disconnected vessel. I am going to try my very best to live a very authentic life and be true to myself.

I know what I should and shouldn't be doing, like I also know that I shouldn't be eating that cake, and I shouldn't be having that last glass of wine, but hey, I'm trying to have the whole human experience here.

As humans, we are an incredibly odd species. Our emotions change like the tide, our definite plans and resolutions disintegrate when they prove to be hard work. And me, I'm the worst of all because I know better, I try not to, but I just can't seem to help myself judging the girl who vainly posts Facebook pictures showing you her newly painted nails so that her Rolex inadvertently shows. She isn't rich, she just thinks she is. She's the same girl posting the bikini shot to show off her lovely body but trying to hoodwink you that she's showing you the view. I can't help myself feeling nauseous about it.

I try my hardest not to judge the way the scruffy woman in the queue in front of me spends her money on alcohol and cigarettes while her child is refused the colouring book, and yet I know that both her and the child will learn from this eventually, they may have even chosen it.

I'm accidentally judging people because they aren't attractive (even though I'm not, and anyway, it's completely irrelevant what your face looks like). I'll be watching a film with Jess and say, 'Well, he isn't handsome, is he? Why did they choose him to lead? Yuck.' Then I'm joining in with the bitching session at the pub about Simon from work being a total pratt (he really is though). I just can't help myself. It's human. It doesn't mean I'm failing. I try my hardest to see any upsets from every person's viewpoint. I try not to refuse a new experience.

I also understand that if something problematic keeps on happening in my life, that I haven't dealt with it properly for my spirit and that it'll just keep popping up in this life and all my lives until I actually sit and sort it. I'm trying hard to live a relatively good life. I'm aware that every smile I give, every action I take, grows and multiplies. All of it, every teensy, miniscule thing you do comes back on you, whether it's in the life you're living at the moment or in the afterlife. It can be a wondrous thing or maybe a not so wondrous thing if it was a bad thing you did. It's like throwing a stone into a river and watching the ripples, each ripple is the karma, good or bad. Every action causes a ripple. So, try to do good stuff is what I'm telling you. You are here for a reason. Each and every one of us is here for a reason. Don't ever doubt it. Only you can do what needs to be done, no one else. Perhaps it's just one small gesture, a touch, a helping hand or a few kind words.

You can't always do things the best way, humans are humans and somewhere along the way, people will try to take advantage of your kind nature. So, you can try to acknowledge and honour the essence of who you know someone truly is deep inside, but you can also pay attention to who they are being. If they aren't being very nice then you can set boundaries. If they get hurt, you did no wrong and you tried your best. That's all you can ever hope to do.

Remember how you feel when you've helped someone? You feel good right? It's a two-way thing. Once you get to the other side, that good deed is no longer a two-way thing, its exponential, the love that it creates is phenomenal.

Life is chock full of tragedies and triumphs with its roughly hewn guidelines that you and your guide have agreed on before you arrive are etched out carefully for each of us. These are chopped and changed moment to moment as we make choices and decisions to take us on our own pathways. There's no such thing as fate. The choice is invariably yours. Always.

I try hard to live each day to its fullest and enjoy life, to love to feel the air on my face, hear the sodden earth squelching under my boots. I love to make someone smile, to be of service to others, to truly smell the flowers, close my eyes and feel life.

I try to take pleasure from simple things, the first crunch of an apple, the soft, luxurious bite of chocolate cake, the hilarity that ensues when I post a spoonful of peanut butter into Hettie's mouth, the amusement I feel when I listen to a naysayer naying.

Life is a real challenge, for all of us. You're saddled with all these emotions. It's a feelings driven ride. Just remember not to let your life be ruled by all those physical self-things that aren't really you at all. We all come from divinity, we all return to divinity.

I'm sorry I can't convey all the knowledge and wisdom that Dorothy learned, it's just too vast for my small human brain and its massive limitations. Our brains are confined to basic stuff. Filling it with what Dorothy saw, would be like dropping off an iPhone or a laptop with a group of cavemen, and expecting them to understand them, they simply wouldn't be able to comprehend what was in front of them.

So, all of those thoughts that keep you up at night, all the things you could have done differently, or said differently, go and sort them out. You'll sleep better. Don't go in pursuit of beauty, you are already the pinnacle of beauty.

Stop gazing over the gate at the lush, green grass that's just out of reach. It's probably just weeds. And try to remember, that not one person in this life is better than you. Not one.

To continue a life here is only ever a maybe, any one of us could die tonight, tomorrow really is ever only a maybe. The safe idyll of life seems untouchable, we all presume that we will see the morning and that our loved ones will too. We never really believe that we will die, and when we are faced with death, we beg and plead, chase our doctors down for better treatments, beseech and bargain with a God that we never speak with, just to let us live a little while longer. Each of us unaware that our death is actually a release into a world of resplendent glory.

Heaven is far greater, far more solid and permanent. It's where we live our true lives. Earth is the transient place, it's not our true home, it's just a school, and we keep on coming back until we graduate.

So, try to embrace your lessons, try to see that we are all connected. Be of service. Do a good deed. Be tolerant. Be kind. Smile. Forgive people, it's a gift to forgive, it frees you. Life is a journey, and you can choose to do with it whatever you determine. Give away what isn't needed, you'll find that life can be better with less.

I know that I chose my own lessons. Know that you did too.

EPILOGUE

I'd given mum, Grace, Grandma, Jess and Beth a rough copy of this book because they all like a good read and none of them are backward about coming forward if it needed putting in the bin or if there were spelling errors or whatever. I was hoping that it would help them to see what I'd experienced my whole life, that they'd see my life through my writing and realise that all the strange stuff that I'd always said actually had substance.

Jess said it was wonderful, thought inspiring and she was glad she was mentioned in it. Grace said I'm still weird but in a good way and that she thought it was good enough to try and get it published. Grandma said it was a really good piece of fiction and at last I'd found a way to channel my imaginations.

Mum said it's a bit bulky with all these sheets of paper but she's definitely going to make a start soon and she'd definitely read it if it was a proper book. Beth says I should have mentioned that she is becoming a successful stand-up comedienne, where she can now raise laughs by picking on people and they actually pay her for it and her sleep is much improved.

In the meantime, I decided to upload it onto a popular platform. It's sold a few copies and I think Calla had a hand in that. So now, as you can see, my 'fictional' novel is now in print.

I wish each and every one of you, an exquisite death.

THE END

ACKNOWLEDGEMENT

To my daughter Laura, who has always championed my writing. To my son Mike, who hasn't, but he'll watch it when it's on Netflix.

To each of my five wonderful grandchildren, they know they're my world.

To my dear pal Louise because she's always been there, and to Gill who's already flying with the angels. And finally to my wonderful sister Carol who always has my back.

ABOUT THE AUTHOR

Trish Farrington

Trish lives in the small village of Astley in Manchester England. She lives with her two dogs Betsy and Hattie. She is a retired nurse, (though she still works one shift a week). She spends her spare time helping to look after her elderly dad, or with her children and grandchildren.
It was the death of her mum that triggered the idea behind this novel, she found that she was suddenly questioning the idea of life after death after always being a staunch believer. She found that writing it had helped to heal a great swathe of her grief.
For any reader, her only hope is that you enjoy it.

Printed in Great Britain
by Amazon

43741425R00189